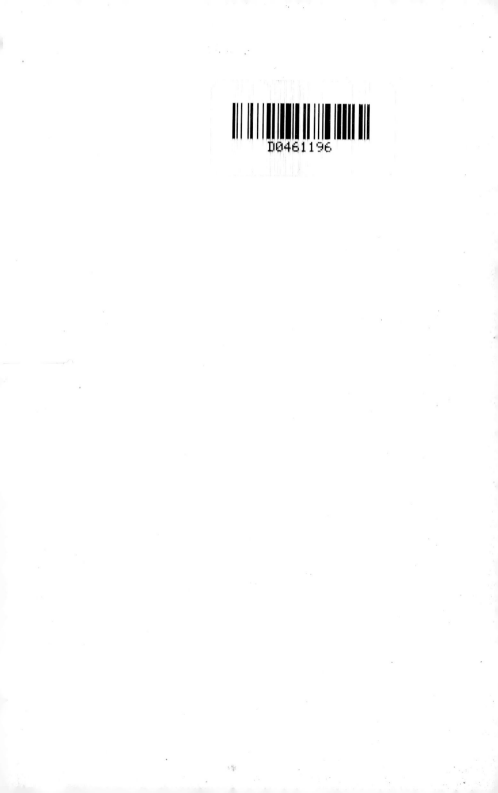

D0461196

THE CHICKEN ASYLUM

ALSO BY FRED HUNTER

The Ransom/Charters Series

Presence of Mind
Ransom for an Angel
Ransom for Our Sins
Ransom for a Holiday
Ransom for a Killing
Ransom Unpaid

The Alex Reynolds Series

Government Gay
Federal Fag
Capital Queers
National Nancys
CHICKEN ASYLUM.

THE CHICKEN ASYLUM

Fred Hunter

ST. MARTIN'S MINOTAUR
NEW YORK

THE CHICKEN ASYLUM. Copyright © 2001 by Fred Hunter. All rights reserved. Printed in the United States of America. No part of this book may be used or reproduced in any manner whatsoever without written permission except in the case of brief quotations embodied in critical articles or reviews. For information, address St. Martin's Press, 175 Fifth Avenue, New York, N.Y. 10010.

www.minotaurbooks.com

ISBN 0-312-27117-4

First Edition: October 2001

10 9 8 7 6 5 4 3 2 1

For Ellen Hart, who provided the catering

THE CHICKEN ASYLUM

Oh, no, no, no—the best dinner I ever had was at Chez Louis," said Jonathan Bradshaw, his face glowing reverently at the memory. "The appetizer alone!"

His partner, Brian Lemon, nodded eagerly in agreement as he chewed a bit of meat.

"What was it?" Nathan Breslow asked.

"*Ris de veau á la financiére*—one of the great classic fillings for bouchées."

"Ahhh . . ." the assembly responded.

All except me. I had spent the past two hours tensing the muscles behind my eyes to keep them from rolling to the back of my head. I was getting a headache.

"The braised sweetbreads garnished with truffles, mushrooms, and olives were absolutely beyond reproach," Jonathan continued. "Now, the soup . . ."

Brian nodded again, making little mewing noises.

"The soup was *velouté d'avocat frappé!*" He launched into a description of this dish in alarming detail.

The table was set with obviously expensive crystal and china, all of which looked like it had been in the family for years. I was afraid to cut all the way through my cornish game hen for fear of scraping the knife on the surface of the plate. The tablecloth was white lace, and glowing in the center of the table was a candelabra that must've come from an estate sale at Liberace's.

The dining room itself was uncomfortably close. A massive mahogany sideboard with ornate carvings apparently designed by the same artisan responsible for the furnishings at Hill House loomed on one wall. It was lined with grandmotherly blue-and-white china and a collection of Hummels. The other walls were covered with shelves and chockablock with tchotchkes, everything from glass animals to porcelain figurines.

Jonathan and Brian, the hosts of the party, had prepared a dinner fit for a coronation: canapés that I couldn't hope to describe, cold asparagus soup, salads, and the aforementioned hens, roasted until the skin was a light, crisp brown and the meat juicy and tender. Christ, I was beginning to think like them. I don't remember how Peter and I met Jonathan and Brian, but at that particular moment I was ready to buy back the introduction at a premium. They weren't trying to make us feel uncomfortable; they were being themselves. They just happened to be from Mars.

The other guests, none of whom we'd met before, seemed perfectly at ease in a conversation that sounded as if it had been cribbed from the menus of various four-star restaurants.

"What was the entree?" asked Nathan, who had been listening with rapt attention to the remembrance of our host's favorite dinner.

"Oh!" Jonathan replied with a satisfied purr. He turned to his partner. "Do you want to tell them?"

Brian nodded again. "*Darne de saumon au Champagne!*"

"Well, I understood one word," I muttered to Peter as the other couples exclaimed noisily.

He coughed.

"How was it?" Eli said breathlessly. He was Nathan's better half.

"Perfection," said Jonathan with a smack of his lips. "Absolute perfection. And the dessert was fresh strawberries wrapped in crepes and covered with a custard sauce flavored with Grand Marnier."

"Ahhh!" said the couples, leaning back in their chairs in unison. They were beginning to sound like a congregation: "Crepes be with you," said the priest. "And also with you," the congregation replied.

Amen.

I mean, I have nothing against food porn—that excessive epicurean elitism that some of our acquaintances enter into—except that it's like regular porn: I'd rather be engaged in the activity than watching it. Or listening to it.

"Well! The best dinner *we* ever had . . ." said Leonard Weise, turning to his partner, Sammie. "You remember, don't you?"

"Of course! At La Scala!"

"In Italy?" I blurted out, my mouth falling open.

Sammie blinked at me. "No, in Rogers Park." He turned back to the other gourmands. "The antipasto was tomato basil tart."

"I've never had that," said Nathan.

"It's a tart filled with sliced tomatoes, basil leaves, and grated parmesan. Olive oil is drizzled over it . . ."

And the congregation said Amen.

". . . it's baked, then cooled to room temperature before being served. After that was the wild mushroom soup."

"Porcini mushrooms," Leonard clarified.

The most frustrating part about this dinner was that Peter was seated to my right rather than across the table from me, so we couldn't exchange meaningful glances. I suppose I could've done it with his ear, but it doesn't have the same effect, and it's likely to be noticed by everyone except the person it's meant for.

"The pasta," Sammie continued, "was tagliolini with asparagus." He smacked his lips as if once again savoring the noodles.

"How about that?" I whispered to Peter. "I recognized another word."

"Much, much more delicate than spaghetti," Leonard explained.

"And the entree! Oh, God, the entree!" Sammie exclaimed.

Leonard nodded. *"Pollo arrosto in tegame."*

He proceeded to describe the roasted chicken, the garlic, the white wine, and the perfectly sautéed pancetta, with the assembly hanging on his every word with poised forks and watering mouths. His rhapsody on the tenderness of the early peas bordered on vegephilia. As he eloquently recounted the succulent morsels, the perfect wine, and the exquisite service, the congregation seemed to lift from their seats in exaltation, their breathing increasingly heavy.

"And then, for dessert . . ." Sammie said, pausing dramatically. He glanced around the table at the expectant faces that had been brought to the height of excitement. He took a deep breath and pronounced, *"Il diplomatico!"*

"Il diplomatico!" the rest exclaimed with ecstasy as they fell back into their chairs, chests heaving, completely spent.

"Il diplomatico," Nathan repeated in a soft whimper, his head lolling to one side.

"Cigarette?" I whispered to Peter.

"Shh!"

The guests began to rouse themselves from their exhaustion, remembering the feast that was before them. They straightened themselves in their chairs and resumed eating.

"More wine?" Brian asked as he rose with the cut-crystal carafe.

"Oh, yes!" Eli replied, pushing his delicate stemmed glass forward with two fingers.

As Brian continued around the table, Jonathan cleared his throat and turned to me. "So . . . Alex, Peter. You guys like to dine out, I'm sure."

I glanced at Peter. This was the moment I was dreading.

"Uh-huh."

"Well?" said Sammie. Having already performed, he was apparently anxious for the opportunity to lie back and allow one of the other guests to service him.

"Well . . ." I said weakly. "I had a really nice club sandwich at Kaplan's once."

*   *   *

"You know, we *have* eaten in some nice restaurants from time to time," Peter said as we drove home.

I was behind the wheel of the dark blue Saturn Mother bought to replace the Honda Civic that was blown up by a mad Democrat. Way back when she bought the Civic, she'd chosen robin's-egg blue because it set off her eyes. This time she'd chosen a dark blue Saturn because the color would be less conspicuous for surveillance, and nobody would believe they were being followed by a Saturn. That's how much our lives had changed in the past five years.

"I know we've been nice places," I said. "But not like those people. I like to have a good time when I go out to eat, not worry about whether or not I'm soiling the napkins."

Peter laughed. "They were a bit . . . much. But you couldn't think of anything better than a club sandwich?"

"Did you want me to tell them the truth? That a normal meal for us is tossing turkey legs over our shoulders while downing tankards of grog? Where did we meet these people, anyway?"

"Jonathan and Brian? We met them at the fund-raiser for Howard Brown, remember?"

"Oh, yeah. Well what the hell did we do to make them like us?"

Peter turned a slightly puzzled frown in my direction. "Those guys really bugged you, didn't they?"

"No," I replied with a sigh. "They just have different interests. Way different. They made me feel like the type of person who wipes his mouth on his sleeve."

"Well . . ."

"I mean, I'm sure everything they served tonight was a gourmet's delight, especially from all the ooohing and aaahing over it. But to my little unrefined eyes the appetizers looked like crickets on a shingle, and that asparagus soup looked like something Linda Blair spit up. Maybe I'm just uncultured, but—" I glanced at Peter and felt one of those unexpected pangs of sappiness.

"But what?"

"When you and I go out to dinner, I barely notice the food."

His smile was visible in the passing glow of the streetlights. He moved a bit closer and rested his left hand on my right leg, then slid it down to caress my inner thigh.

"If you don't stop that I may lose control," I said. "I mean of the car."

The internal surge shouldn't have been a surprise. It's my normal reaction to having been around people with whom I have nothing in common, a situation that reminds me of how lucky I am to have found Peter. I couldn't wait to get home, get naked, and show him how much he still meant to me.

After parking in our rickety garage, we went up the walk to the back porch. The diffused glow from the living-room lights through the window in the back door meant that Mother was still up, which wasn't surprising, since it was barely ten o'clock. But as much as I love her, I had hoped she'd already be in bed. When you're on your way to a tryst, nothing can drain the blood from certain parts of the body faster than having to stop and chitchat with your mother.

"Alex? Is that you?" Her lilting British accent floated from the living room as we came in through the back door. Mother moved to America before I was born, and although it's been over thirty-five years since she's lived in her native England, she's been able to maintain her accent through sheer perseverance and strength of character.

"Yes, Mother," I replied, imitating Dagwood Bumstead.

"We have company!"

"Oh, shit!" I whispered to Peter, who smiled and nibbled my ear.

"Stop that!" I said, pushing him away. "I don't have any books to hold in front of me!"

We went through the swinging door into the living room and Peter slammed into my back when I stopped dead. Mother was seated on the couch, tea service for two was on the oval coffee table in front of her, and Duffy the dog's errant tail was swishing back and forth under the table like a furry tongue licking wooden lips. The visitor rose to greet us. It was Agent Lawrence Nelson, our boss from the CIA.

Nelson was still as striking as ever, with skin that looked perpetually tanned and straight dark hair kept at a businesslike length. A tiny bit of gray had appeared at his temples, and I liked to think we had a hand in putting it there. Over the past year our connection with Nelson and the CIA had picked up somewhat. Nelson had been pleased enough with our performance on our last couple of official cases that he threw more work our way, although that work still mainly amounted to courier-type assignments that usually required only my participation: things like carrying an important package from one terminal to another at the airport, or meeting some VIP's plane and making sure he got to his hotel all right. Of course, I was never told what was in the packages, or who the VIPs actually were; but the pay was good, and I'd gotten to the point where I didn't mind being a secret carrier pigeon. I couldn't expect much more, since we live in Chicago, and most of the espionage here involves local government rather than national.

But I always hoped these little assignments would lead to bigger ones, and sometimes they did. I had a feeling this was one of those times, because none of the usual things we were asked to do required Nelson to leave his aerie in D.C. and honor our little hovel. His presence meant something important was in the works.

"Did you enjoy your dinner?" he said with his usual enigmatic elegance.

"How did you know we were out to dinner?" I asked suspiciously.

"Your mother told me."

"Oh." I could feel my face hotting up.

Mother gave me her most wicked smile. "It gave me quite a turn for Larry to show up while you were out. The moment I clapped eyes on him, I thought, Lor', what has Alex gotten us into now? But he assured me that this has nothing to do with you."

"Thank you?" I replied questioningly, not knowing how happy I should be about the way she'd put that.

"What's going on?" asked Peter, whose tone always remains rather firm when confronted with Nelson.

"I haven't the foggiest," Mother replied, motioning for all of us to sit. "Larry arrived just before you did."

Nelson resumed his seat and Peter and I pulled up chairs on the opposite side of the coffee table.

"We want to enlist your aid in something fairly important," he said. "And I wanted to wait until you returned before getting into it because it involves all three of you, to some extent, and it is likely to upset the routine of your household."

"Our household?" said Peter.

"A stakeout!" I exclaimed. "You mean you want to use our house for surveillance!"

"You'll have to excuse Alex," Mother said to Nelson. "He's a hopeless romantic."

Nelson was looking at me with his usual lack of emotion, but the pause indicated that any show of eagerness on my part was suspect. According to CIA protocol, you're supposed to want to help, but you're not supposed to look like you want to help. At least, not enthusiastically.

"No, it's not surveillance," he said, then turned back to Mother. "It's a bit more intrusive."

"Good heavens!" she exclaimed. "I don't like the sound of that!"

"Let me explain. As you probably know, if you pay any attention to the news at all, we've been keeping a close eye on Iraq—"

"You could hardly do that from our house," I said.

"Alex, please!" said Mother.

"We've been making periodic attempts to find their cache of chemical weapons. That is, the United Nations team has. Unsuccessfully. We've found signs that they have them, but never the weapons themselves. On one of their recent inspections, the team was approached by an Iraqi soldier, very much on the quiet, who has offered us help."

He stopped, and after a pause, Mother said, "Yes?"

"He told us that he can pinpoint not only the location where the weapons are usually kept, but the many places to which they're moved when we make our inspections. And he's willing to do this in exchange for sanctuary."

"Yes?" Mother said again, drawing the word out warily.

"And we have agreed to this."

"What makes you think he has the information?" I asked.

"We have enough reason to believe that he's in a position to know what he says he knows. We had to move quickly, because if anybody over there even suspected that he'd approached us, he'd be dead. To say nothing of what would've happened to him if they knew what he was planning to tell us."

"I don't understand," said Mother. "Why did he approach you in the first place? Why does he want to leave Iraq?"

"He has his own reasons."

"And they are?"

"His own."

"Larry," Mother said impatiently, "surely you don't—"

"We also believe that his reasons for needing to leave Iraq are valid," he said, cutting her off. "Valid enough that he would risk betraying his people, who would surely kill him if they found out about it."

"I see," said Mother meaningfully.

"I don't," Peter said. "All of this is very interesting, but what does it have to do with us?"

Nelson sat back comfortably against the back of the couch. The move was more casual than anything I'd ever seen him do. It couldn't be a good sign.

"He'll need to be debriefed."

"You mean questioned," Peter said flatly.

Nelson ignored him. "We'll need a few days to talk to him, get all the information he can give us, and hopefully check to see if any of it is true—although I doubt very much that he'd lie to us and run the risk of being sent back."

"So?"

"And we'll need a safe house in which to do that. Somewhere that he can stay for a few days while we debrief him. Someplace nobody would suspect."

From the silence that followed this statement I knew Mother and Peter were as stunned as I was.

"A safe house?" I said incredulously. "You mean *here*?"

"Yes."

"Our 'ouse 'as 'ardly been safe since we got involved with your lot!" said Mother.

There go her aitches, I thought. And so many of them! This had really thrown her.

"I don't think it's known to any—" Nelson broke off abruptly, catching himself. In all the time we'd known him, this was the closest I'd ever seen him come to making a slip. He resumed diplomatically. "It's not likely to be known to anyone who'd be interested."

"And who exactly would that be?" Mother asked.

"I have no idea."

"Come on, Larry," I said, using the familiar of his name. I always get the impression that Mother is the only one who could call him Larry with impunity, but I've tried to nettle him with it so many times without success that I was beginning to think this was just a little game I played with myself. "I've always thought of you as honest. Now who would be after this soldier of yours?"

"I really don't know that anyone would follow him to this country," he replied. It didn't escape me that what he'd just said meant nothing.

"Why don't you put him up in a hotel or something?" Peter asked.

"Because we want him to be as comfortable as possible, and in the friendliest atmosphere possible. Somewhere that he can be looked after."

"You mean watched."

"I mean exactly what I said. Granted, in a hotel it would be more difficult to be sure of him without keeping someone there in his room. Your family would be a much more natural setting."

You could cut through the skepticism permeating the room with a knife. It didn't go unnoticed by Nelson. The silence was broken only by the gentle thumping of Duffy's tail against my loafer.

"I realize the arrangement might seem a bit unusual to you, but we actually use private homes for this kind of thing more often than you'd think."

"Well," said Mother, "wouldn't it be better to use someone who's had more experience, then?"

Nelson shook his head. "No. In this case your inexperience is an asset."

"Gee, thanks," I said.

"Someone more experienced in this type of affair might make him feel like he's being watched, and that's the last thing we want."

"You're being uncommonly accommodating to him," said Peter.

"It's in our best interest, and I think it's best for him. You have to remember how this man has spent his life. Living in Iraq is bad enough, living in the Iraqi army, especially for someone who never wanted to be there, is hell. We don't want to bring him to this country and make him feel like a prisoner. So yes, we do want an eye kept on him, but as discreetly as possible, and in the friendliest manner possible. I thought you would be the best people for that."

I could feel Mother's heart melting from across the room. If only we could believe Nelson. I'd never known him to lie outright, but past experience had shown that he had turned the sin of omission into an art form.

"How long would it be for?" Mother asked.

"No more than three days. During the day I would be here with another agent doing the debriefing. The evening is the only time you'd have him alone."

"What happens to him after that?" I asked.

"He goes on to his new life as an American citizen."

Nelson didn't bother giving this any particular inflection, choosing to let the words to carry their own weight. Mother, Peter, and I looked at each other, then rose in unison.

"Well," said Mother, "I think this calls for a family meeting. If you'll give us a minute, Larry, we'll repair to the office."

"The office?" I said.

"The kitchen," she replied with a purposeful nod. Then she added to Nelson, "Excuse us."

She led Peter and me into the kitchen and closed the swinging door, which provided the illusion of privacy. We huddled close together in the center of the room.

"Well, what do you think?" said Mother.

Peter and I exchanged glances, then I slowly said, "Gee, I don't know . . ."

Both of them raised their eyebrows at me.

"You don't?" said Peter.

"Why are you so surprised?"

"Because you're the one that always wants to rush into this CIA nonsense."

Mother added, "I expected you be jumping for joy at the thought of doing your spy bit again!"

"This isn't exactly a spy bit!"

"If you mean we probably won't get shot at for doing it, then most likely you're right," Peter said with an impish smile.

"What do you mean by that?"

"I'm beginning to worry about you. You seize every opportunity to put us in danger, but you don't want to do something relatively safe."

"I didn't say I don't want to do it." My tone was coming awfully close to a whine. "I just . . . don't know that I want to have an Iraqi soldier around the house. Is that so wrong?"

"Why wouldn't you?"

"Why *would* you?" I countered. "You never want to get involved in this CIA business."

He put his hands on his hips. "There's a difference between trying to save someone from a burning building and throwing yourself into a fire."

"That sounds profound," I snapped. "What's it supposed to mean?"

"You know exactly what I mean! You rush into things without thinking. Just because I try to get you to consider the dangers is no reason to accuse me of not wanting to get involved!"

"Boys, boys!" said Mother. "We're getting a bit afield. Could we please stick to the matter at hand?"

It was a good thing she'd interrupted, because Peter and I were on our way to the worst argument we'd had in years. It didn't matter that I was in an untenable position: I knew he was right. In the past I'd been far too eager to run ahead, and Peter had been the one to remain rational in the face of situations that could most charitably be called bizarre. But I was still angry. I didn't care that my position didn't make sense. Your husband is supposed to support you in your inconsistencies, not point out the facts.

"Now," Mother continued, "Alex, exactly how much do you object to having this soldier here?"

"Well . . . what would we do with him?"

"He's not a piece of furniture, darling. We don't need to fit him in with the decor. We would just treat him the way we would treat any other guest."

"How many guests have we had who've spent their lives killing people?"

She looked at me quizzically. "This man was conscripted—or whatever they call it over there—into his situation. And he's trying to get out, if we can believe Larry."

"That's an awfully big if."

"And if it's true," she concluded, "then I think we should help him."

"I agree with you," said Peter. Then he turned to me and asked quietly, "Alex, are you afraid to have this man in the house?"

I started to protest but could feel the blood rising to my face again. "The only thing I know of these people is what I've seen on the news."

"And that can't exactly be the whole story," said Mother.

"That's just the thing! I don't think we're getting the whole story from Nelson—as if we ever would. Is it just me, or does it sound like there are people after this guy? I mean, despite what some people may think—" here I shot a pointed glance at my husband—"I do know better than to throw myself in front of a firing squad!"

"You do?" He looked like he was trying very hard not to laugh.

I sighed, then laughed myself. "I can see I'll forever be haunted by my past record."

"Maybe there *are* people after him," said Mother, "but he'll only be here for a few days, and I think Larry is perfectly right when he says that nobody would suspect that a soldier is being kept here."

"Well," said Peter, looking as if he was going to take a baby step over to my side, "we never can be too sure of who knows what when it comes to Nelson and his cronies."

"And there's another thing," I said. "Even though he'd probably be safe here, I still think Nelson has some other reason for wanting us to take this guy in. It can't just be because he considers us the Perle Mestas to the Iraqi army. It would be much easier to keep him in Washington, wouldn't it?"

"It would be the first place anybody would look for him," said Peter.

"Exactly. I have to think this is much more dangerous than Nelson is letting on."

"Come on! Despite some of our exploits, Nelson wouldn't ask us to do it if it was that dangerous."

"Are you talking about the Nelson out there in our living room?"

From the look on his face, Peter was doing a quick survey of the past. "You're right."

Mother raised her hands to forestall further argument. "So are you both saying that you don't want to do this?"

We turned to her in unified disbelief. "No!"

"You mean you *want* to do it?"

"I think we should," said Peter.

"I don't want to," I added, "but I think you're right. We should do it."

There was a beat, then Mother threw her hands up in the air.

"Why do I bother with these meetings?" With that she marched out through the swinging door, propping it open as she passed. We followed close behind.

"It's settled, Larry," she announced. "We'll do it."

"Good," he said, getting up from the couch. "He's on his way."

"*Now?* You were pretty sure of us, weren't you?"

Nelson headed for the door. "As I said, we had to act quickly. He's not in the country yet, but he's on his way. We should have him here by late tomorrow afternoon." He paused with his hand on the knob. "And yes, I was pretty sure of you."

He pulled open the door and started to make his exit, but I stopped him.

"Nelson! You haven't even told us his name!"

He glanced at me over his shoulder. "We haven't chosen it yet."

He passed through the door, and Mother closed it behind him.

"Well, this is a short 'op from the average," she said. "How exactly does one prepare for a soldier, I wonder?"

"We could dig a trench in the living room and erect a bivouac," I said.

She narrowed her eyes at me. "I hope you're not going to be tiresome in front of company."

After a lengthy discussion of how we would spend the next morning, Peter and I went to bed. It was now after midnight, and I was both exhausted and keyed up. Any thought of making love had long since flown from my head, but it was nice to lie there in his arms and feel the warmth of his skin against mine. He dropped off almost right away. Peter has such a clear conscience that he could successfully sleep through a nuclear attack. I rested my head against his chest, the dark brown hair tickling my ear, and listened to his heartbeat. It eventually had the same effect that one of those electronic teddy bears has on a baby: I drifted off.

But I slept only fitfully. I kept dreaming that we were lying in bed together and the door opened and Saddam Hussein, clad in camouflage gear and a dirty beret, crawled in across the hardwood floor like Renfield creeping up on the unconscious maid in *Dracula*—only Saddam had this big, ugly knife between his teeth. I tried to cry out but couldn't, and Peter kept sleeping soundly, his nose emitting a rhythmic hiss.

When Saddam reached the bed, he took the knife from his mouth and raised himself up into view. He leered at me, muttered something in his native tongue, then drew his arm back and with one swift swing sliced my throat.

"What is it?" Peter exclaimed anxiously, scrambling up to a sitting position.

It took me a moment to realize I had cried out in my sleep. I found myself sitting up in bed and clutching my throat, my whole body damp with sweat.

"It's nothing," I panted.

"Are you all right?"

"I'm fine. I just had a nightmare, that's all."

"Are you sure you're all right?"

"Yes. Really. I'm fine," I said, sliding myself back down under the covers. "It was just a bad dream."

I hope.

TWO

The next morning Mother set about cleaning the house even though she always keeps it spotless. I think it was more an effort to keep herself busy and quiet her nerves than anything else. Cleaning has a kava-like effect on her. Duffy followed her around, looking up at her with that anxious attentiveness that only a Westie can truly achieve. Peter and I were relegated to transforming my home office into a proper bedroom.

Temporarily losing my office wasn't a big sacrifice, since I'd all but completely let my business go after getting tangled up with the CIA. I had been a freelance graphic artist, but let my work dwindle down to one old and valued client. I guess hanging on allowed me believe that if my part-time position as homo-in-residence for the government ever fell through, I'd have something to fall back on.

Peter, on the other hand, has managed to hold onto his own job at Farrahut's, the chic men's clothing store, despite taking an extraordinary amount of time off to spy. He likes to think the freedom he's given is because he's a very good salesman, but personally I believe Arthur Dingle, his boss, has kept him on because Dingle is a lonely older man who hopes someday our marriage might dissolve and Peter will turn to him for solace. Dreams of "comforting the widow" have kept many a man going in old age.

The second-floor room I use as an office was equipped with a daybed with a cover patterned with large maple leaves, and matching curtains that Mother made in one of her frequent flights of domesticity. And there was a collapsible drafting table and a desk that held my PC. We wanted to make the room as homey as we could, so I closed the table and put it in the hall closet, then we moved my computer equipment to the floor of the closet in our bedroom. We then pushed the desk against the far wall and positioned the bed under the window.

"You think we should bring that little dresser up from the basement?" Peter asked.

"I think there's enough room in the closet for his fatigues."

"Alex . . ."

"I'm sorry, I'm sorry. I didn't sleep well last night, okay?"

"I know. I was there. You're really worried about this, aren't you?"

I sighed heavily. "If you can go by my dreams, I'm actually only worried that Saddam Hussein will get me."

"You're kidding!"

"No. He broke into our house and came slithering into our room in every way humanly possible, and some that weren't. The last time he crawled in through an air duct, like Bruce Willis."

Peter came over and gave me a kiss on the forehead. "You don't have to worry, honey. I don't think anyone could fit in the air vents in this house."

I pushed him away playfully. "You're a big help."

When we went downstairs we found Mother vacuuming while whistling "I Whistle a Happy Tune." When she goes Deborah Kerr on me I know she's not as confident as she would like us to believe.

"Do you think we should get some flowers for his room?" she said over the noise of the machine.

"I think he'll be satisfied with indoor plumbing," I replied. "What do you want us to do next?"

She reached into her pocket and pulled out a small sheet of

paper. "Here's a list of the groceries we need to lay in. I do hope he'll like the food. I have no idea what's he's used to."

I looked up from the sheet. She raised a warning finger at me. "Whatever it is, don't say it!"

Peter and I spent about an hour at the grocery store, then returned with a trunkload of bags that we toted to the kitchen and placed on the table. Mother had stowed the vacuum and was polishing the dining chairs when our arrival interrupted her. She stored the rag and the lemon-scented polish and set about putting the groceries away. It's not that we were unwilling to do it, but Mother rules the kitchen and is never quite satisfied with the way we arrange things, even though we've always put them exactly where she does.

By the time we'd gotten the guest room in order, finished the shopping, disposed of the bags, and polished the house to a blinding shine, it was still not quite noon. All we had left to do was have lunch—something Mother was loath to do for fear our soon-to-be-resident soldier might see a latent crumb on the table—and then spend the rest of the day waiting for the arrival of our guest and his escorts.

There is something both anticlimactic and anxiety producing about being ready too early, particularly when you don't know when an event is going to take place. Peter and I sat on the couch alternately crossing and uncrossing our legs, and smoothing out the cushions, while watching a string of Charlie Chan videos, a slight regression to my childhood, during which a local television station showed the films every Sunday. There's something comforting about Charlie Chan: he's soft-spoken in a way that will cure even my worst bouts of insomnia. Mother sat at the dining table, leaning forward so as not to dull the chair's newly polished back, and pretending to read the latest edition of *Condé Nast Traveler*.

It was four o'clock when the doorbell finally rang. We all froze in place for a moment, then got up and headed for the door.

"It doesn't want three of us," Mother said somewhat sharply, effectively stopping Peter and me in our tracks.

She opened the door and said, "Good afternoon, Larry."

"Jean," he replied before coming into view.

She took a step back and Nelson walked into the doorway, where he stopped and turned sideways. He extended his arm inward, signaling the visitor to enter.

My mouth dropped open when I saw him. I'd been expecting the soldier to be a big, burly, hairy-backed, unshaven monster in camouflage gear, with ammo belts criss-crossing his chest and unpleasant smells wafting off of him. The last thing I expected was what had just come through the door. He had short, neatly combed black hair, dark skin, and even darker brown eyes. His lashes were long and black, and his eyebrows, which I'd imagined would look like unkempt hedgerows, were so neat and straight I suspected he'd had them trimmed.

And he looked to be about fourteen years old.

He wore a pair of tan Dockers, a white shirt unbuttoned at the collar, and had a dark green duffel bag slung over his shoulder. He was followed in by Nelson and another man who seemed to be the same general make as Nelson but nowhere near as suave. Mother closed the door after them.

"Let me introduce Jean Reynolds," Nelson said. "Jean, this is James Paschal."

"Nice name," I intoned.

"How d'you do?" Mother said, offering her hand and stopping just short of a curtsy.

He spoke with an odd combination of fluidity and haltingness, like a river of lite syrup hitting an occasional rock. He gave her hand one brisk shake. "Very nice to have me."

Nelson continued. "And this is Alex Reynolds."

He grabbed my hand and gave it one strong yank. "Nice to have me." Looking into those big, brown eyes that were clearly striving for sincerity, I realized what he was really trying for was "Nice of you to have me."

Peter received the same abrupt shake and greeting; then the

four of us turned back to Nelson. He inclined his head toward his companion and said, "And this is Agent George Dunning, who'll be helping with the debriefing."

Dunning had a square head and small eyes that made him look as if he were squinting. His nose was a bit too large to be in proportion to his face, and his lips were thin and flat. We all muttered greetings at him simultaneously, and he grunted in reply.

"Jean," said Nelson, "James has had a long trip and is very tired. If it's all right, we thought we'd leave him with you for the rest of the day and begin the debriefing tomorrow."

"Of course," Mother said, casting a sympathetic eye over the boy. "Why don't I show you to your room?" She put her arm over his shoulder and he flinched like someone who's been abused and mistrusts any unexpected contact. If Mother noticed, she didn't show it. She also didn't relent. She guided him to the stairs and they started up.

Dunning slued his eyes to Nelson and said, "I'll check it out," and followed them up the stairs.

The muscle in Nelson's cheek flexed slightly. I had a feeling he'd just prevented himself from smiling.

"What's this all about, Nelson?" I demanded once Peter and I were alone with him.

"What do you mean?"

"That kid's in the Iraqi army? He looks like he's barely out of puberty! What are you trying to pull?"

He allowed a significant pause before responding. "He's not from Chicago, Alex. He's eighteen years old and he's been in the army for four years. I assure you that he is in a position to have the information we want."

"Oh. Sorry." I felt put in my place, but not enough to lose the feeling that Nelson hadn't told us everything. "Did he come off the plane looking like that, or did you guys fix him up?"

"We provided him with new clothing, of course."

"He looks like he's been to Supercuts."

"They get the occasional haircut in Iraq."

I sighed. "All right, all right."

"What's bothering you, Alex?"

"Well, when you said you were bringing an Iraqi soldier here, I pictured a middle-aged man with a spittoon. Don't ask me why. But this is just a kid! You've brought him to a strange country and you're going to keep him in our house for a few days, then what? Tag him and release him into the wild?"

"No. Of course we'll set him up in life, and he'll have an agent assigned to him for a while to help him make the transition and teach him about life here." Once again, he almost smiled. "Will that be satisfactory?"

I stared at him for several seconds. It was anything but satisfactory, but there was no point in arguing with Nelson. If he had something up his sleeve, he wasn't about to give it up.

"I guess it'll have to be."

He didn't get the chance to respond. Mother chose that moment to come back down the stairs, followed closely by Dunning.

"He's going to lie down for a while, the poor darling," said Mother. "The moment he saw the bed, he fair fell into it!" She turned an accusing eye at Nelson, who she seemed to hold personally responsible for the boy's exhaustion.

"I'll bet he looks like an angel when he's asleep," I said.

Peter leaned close to my ear. "Honey, would you please stop it?"

"Well, we'll leave him in your hands for now," said Nelson. "He shouldn't be any trouble. We'll be back at nine in the morning to get started. We're staying at the Imperial Inn Lake Shore if you need to contact us. Jean." He gave a slight nod to her, then to us. He and Dunning then left, the latter without saying a word.

"If I didn't know better, I'd say you cowed our Nelson," I said to Mother.

She knit her brow. "Whatever do you mean?"

"You looked at him like he'd personally been torturing the boy."

"I did not!" she said firmly. Then she added, "But it wouldn't surprise me if your CIA has been worrying that young man with questions ever since they got him on the plane."

"*My* CIA? Mother, you sometimes forget you're an American citizen."

She folded her arms and curled one corner of her lips. "I believe you know what I mean."

"Oh, of course." She meant the CIA I'd foolishly gotten us involved with. It didn't matter that she enjoyed that involvement as much as I did—a fact that I knew far better than to point out at that moment.

"You should've seen the way he looked at the bed. The poor dear probably hasn't slept in days."

"He's safe now," said Peter. "He'll be able to get some rest."

The three of us fell silent. Mother's eyes were narrowed and she appeared to be mentally castigating whoever had ill treated the boy, and Peter was looking at the floor, his brow furrowed. We were all at a loss: we'd been expecting the house to be a flurry of activity once our guest had arrived. The last thing we expected him to do was fall asleep the minute he crossed the threshold.

"So what do we do now?" I asked.

Mother shrugged. " 'Ave some tea!"

It was well that we had a snack, because at seven o'clock our soldier was still fast asleep. I looked in on him once and found him lying on top of the covers fully dressed with his knees drawn up to his chest and his arms wrapped around them, like he was ducking and rolling from a SCUD missile in his dreams.

I had only meant to peek in and see if he was all right, but I stayed and watched him for a while, overcome by sadness. This kid was about half my age, but he'd probably already seen more atrocities than most Americans will personally witness in a lifetime. The thought of it made me feel that I really hadn't experienced much of life, despite my status as occasional agent.

It was then that I noticed something unnerving: in the dim light I could just barely see small crescents of white. His eyes, which I could've sworn had been completely closed, were open to slits. He was watching me.

I quietly backed out of the room and closed the door. When I went downstairs, Peter was staring at yet another Charlie Chan movie with glazed eyes—he didn't grow up in Chicago. Mother was waiting at the foot of the stairs.

"How's he doing?"

"He's still asleep."

She studied my face. "Is something the matter?"

"Uh, no. I was just thinking he must've had a very hard life."

She smiled and gently touched her fingers to my cheek. "It'll be better for him from now on." Apparently she was happy to hear something other than fear-motivated bilge coming out of me. "Right! Now, I'm going to get dinner started. It should be ready by eight. We'll get our young man up then—he has to have a proper meal—and then he can go right back to bed if he likes."

She clapped her hands together as if to punctuate her plan, then breezed off to the kitchen.

Within the hour Mother had whipped up three huge shepherd's pies, roughly enough for twelve people. Shepherd's pie is considered simple fare by British standards, but it's one of our favorites. Since we hadn't known when our guest would arrive, it would've been impractical to attempt anything more elaborate for his first dinner with us. Earlier in the day Mother had thrown together a raspberry trifle for dessert that wanted only the finishing touch of whipped cream.

At eight o'clock everything was ready; Peter and I had set the table and the food was laid out. Mother stood at the head of the table for a moment, surveying her work with satisfaction, then needlessly straightened the twin blue candlesticks before lighting them. Our guest was still in bed.

"Will you go and wake him?" Mother said to me.

"Okay."

I went up the stairs and down the hall to the door of my office. This time I knocked before entering. When there was no reply, I opened the door quietly and looked in. He was no longer curled up in a ball, but had stretched out with his hands at his sides. He still looked awfully rigid.

"James?" I said softly.

He didn't respond, so I repeated his name a bit more loudly. This time his nose twitched, then after a pause his entire body kicked into motion sluggishly, like a drugged machine.

"James?"

He rolled his head sideways and looked at me.

"James?" he repeated questioningly, his voice heavy with sleep. Then he remembered that this was his new name. "Oh, yes. Hello."

"Dinner is ready. Why don't you come down and eat? You can come back to bed right after that, if you want."

"Yes." He sat up and was still for a moment, disoriented and trying to get his bearings. Then he rose and came over to me. "I am so sorry. I have been very tired."

"That doesn't surprise me."

We stepped out into the hallway and he squinted as his eyes adjusted to the light.

"Do you have someplace to wash?"

I had to think about that one for a second. "Oh, yeah! The bathroom. Right over here."

I led him to the doorway. "The blue towels are for you to use. Do you know how to . . . do you need any help?"

He looked faintly scandalized. "I do not need help, thank you."

He went in and closed the door but didn't lock it. I didn't want to wait by the door, because if someone did that to me it would defeat my purpose. So I went down the hall and stood by the head of the stairs. After a couple of minutes I heard the toilet flush, then the door opened and he joined me. We went down the stairs together.

"Ah, James!" said Mother, giving him her warmest hostess smile, "I hope you enjoyed your little nap."

"Yes."

"Well, have a seat here and we'll have something to eat." She motioned to the chair at the foot of the table.

His big brown eyes goggled at the sight of the spread. I don't know if it was because he was amazed at the amount of food that Mother had prepared for four people, or if he was just mystified by his first glimpse of a shepherd's pie. As usual, Mother had made decorative tracks across the top of the mashed potatoes with a fork before browning them. I wouldn't have been surprised if this was the first time James had ever seen food given any sort of presentation. Mother sat at the head of the table, and Peter and I took our places on either side. As always, Duffy sat quietly at her feet.

There was an uncomfortable pause, then Mother said, "Peter, why don't you pass me James's plate and I'll serve out?"

He complied, and I inwardly winced when I saw distress flash across our guest's face, as if he thought he was being robbed of his dinner. But it quickly disappeared when Mother snatched up the serving spoon and began to heap food onto his plate.

"Would you like some bread?" she asked as she replaced the spoon.

"Yes. Please." His eyes were riveted on his plate.

She folded back the cloth that covered the basket of bread and added two dinner rolls to his plate, then passed it back to him. Without waiting, James grabbed up his spoon and started shoveling the food into his mouth with an unbridled abandon that was absolutely mesmerizing. He ate as if he were afraid that at any moment someone might snatch the food from him. For all I know, they might have done that to him in the army.

Mother quickly filled our plates and her own, apparently not wanting to embarrass our guest with eating alone, and we dug in. Next to James, who grasped his spoon like a spade and barely took a breath between mouthfuls, the three of us with our "properly" held forks and irregular pauses looked positively dainty. But I was fascinated by James, whose obvious enjoyment of the meal bordered on bacchanalian. It was an awfully stark contrast to the quasi-formal dinner we'd attended to night before. I had one of those moments when I wondered what the hell our lives had become.

We ate in awkward silence. Until we'd actually sat down with him, I hadn't realized exactly how hard it would be to make small talk with an Iraqi soldier. Actually, the soldier part probably didn't matter that much. It would've been hard to do it with anybody who'd been dropped into our dining room from a foreign country. I tried to think of things to say, but failed. I mean, "How 'bout those Kurds, huh?" hardly seemed appropriate. Peter, Mother, and I exchanged glances here and there, silently prodding each to start the conversation. It was Mother who finally took a stab at it.

"So, James, how do you like America?"

"I do not," he replied with his mouth full.

Her eyes widened. "I beg your pardon?"

"I say that wrong. I mean I do not know. I only have seen plane and room and plane and room. The rooms have been nice."

She broke into a smile. "I see."

The ensuing silence was broken only by the sounds of James's spoon scraping against his plate. Clearly this was going to be harder than we'd imagined. We were naturally curious about his home country, and why he'd wanted to leave it, particularly since Nelson had implied that James had a secret reason for defecting. But I was afraid that asking him about it might be misinterpreted as an interrogation, and he'd doubtlessly already had enough of that, or would soon. And what was there left to talk about? His future plans? So far as we knew, he didn't know them.

I made the next attempt. "So, James, what do you hope to do now that you're here?"

He paused in mid-shovel, his eyes wide and those long, thick lashes making him look like a big, dark doll. "I will answer questions."

"No, I don't mean now that you're here in this house, I mean now that you're in this country."

"Ah. I will settle . . ." A cloud crossed his face. "Somewhere." He resumed eating.

"You don't know where yet?" Peter asked.

"I do not know America so well. I do not hear much about it, except that everyone has much money."

"Uh, not everyone," I said.

"I don't hear talk of many American places in my country, except maybe for California and New York. They say there are many people there."

"There are. Especially in New York."

"I am used to many people. But I worry. Now I'm here, I worry about fitting in."

"Well, you speak English well enough to live in New York. Where did you learn it?" He paused in his eating again, eyeing me suspiciously. I added quickly, "I only wondered. I mean, I didn't realize that they taught English in your country at all."

He gave me a half-smile. "I understand that . . . America . . . in America people learn only one language. But English is very confusing."

I was certainly finding it confusing at that moment.

He picked up one of his dinner rolls and started to mop the surface of his plate with it.

"He's right, you know," Mother chimed in, trying to ease any embarrassment over the slight—intended or otherwise—to her adoptive country. "Even in England we learn French as a second language. But over here they tend to only learn English."

"Well, that takes up most of our time," I said.

James popped the damp roll into his mouth and chewed it noisily while cleaning his plate with the second one.

"There's plenty more, if you like," said Mother.

He looked up with delight, as if the thought of seconds were beyond his comprehension. He handed his plate back to her. She refilled it, and we spent the rest of the meal watching in amazement as he quickly polished it off with unflagging gusto.

When he'd finished that and had some dessert, he sat back in his chair and sighed deeply. "This is good." His eyelids suddenly drooped, and I realized how exhausted he really was.

"You want to go back to bed, don't you?" Mother said sympathetically.

"I am very tired."

He made no move, apparently not feeling he had the freedom of the house. We once again found ourselves in an awkward position. It seemed as if none of us could think of a way to tell him he could go on up without sounding as if we were sending him to his room. After a moment, Mother looked at me significantly and cocked her head toward the staircase.

"Oh," I said stupidly. "Well, I'll show you back up."

He smiled gratefully. The two of us rose and I led him upstairs.

"You know, while you're staying with us, you really can do what you want," I explained when we reached his doorway. "I mean, if you want to go to bed, you can just do it. You don't need our permission or anything."

His forehead was lowered, and he looked up at me from under his eyebrows as if concentrating hard to understand what I was saying. The meaning seemed to catch up with him a few seconds after I finished speaking.

"Thank you," he said simply.

"Now, if you need anything during the night, just come and get us. Peter and I are in that room." I pointed to the door at the front of the hall.

"I took your room?"

"No, no," I said easily, trying to allay his evident concern. "That's just my office. I don't use it much."

"Office?" He looked very confused. "I think you work for government?"

"I do. Sometimes." I pulled out my wallet and withdrew one of my old business cards, which mostly serve as scratch paper now. "See? I used to have a design business."

He took it. "So I do not take your room?"

"No, that's our room. We share it."

His smooth young brow furrowed. "In house with so many rooms, you stay in same room?"

"Yes," I replied after a beat.

"You are brothers, no?"

Oh boy, I thought. It had been over twenty years since I'd been in the closet, and I never shrink from being open about myself, but with all James had had to digest already—no pun intended—I didn't think it was the time or place to further tax his understanding by trying to explain my relationship with Peter. Hell, I didn't even know if he'd gotten far enough in his English lessons for me to attempt it, anyway.

"No, we're not brothers," I stammered. "We're just . . . it's just always been our room."

"Oh?" He looked even more confused.

"Yes." I quickly added, "Good night." I retreated.

THREE

Despite our many years together, I still love to watch Peter get ready for work in the morning, if only out of the corner of my eye while I'm getting dressed. He's precise about it while not appearing to pay any particular attention to what he's doing, which is completely in character for a man who gives no indication of realizing how beautiful he really is. He's managed to stay in shape despite not having a lot of time for the gym: his chest is firm and his stomach flat. In all the time we've been together there hasn't been a lot of change, except for a slight deepening of the lines around his eyes, and a couple of gray hairs in the center of the dusting of brown on his chest. And I love him so much that just the thought of growing old with him gets me excited.

He slipped his arms into the sleeves of a tan shirt that made his skin look a shade darker, tucked it into his light brown pants, and buttoned everything up. He then knotted a coordinating tie around his neck, pulling the knot to his Adam's apple and getting the back end just a hint shorter than the front. Perfect on the first try. I don't remember ever seeing him have to tie a tie twice.

As he ran a brush through his dark brown hair, I stood next to him and looked at our reflections. We couldn't be more different:

our basic build is the same (although I'm not as firm as he is), but I'm light-skinned, with blue eyes and hair that was once unkindly referred to as dishwater blond. Next to me, Peter looks downright Mediterranean.

After a moment, he noticed the puckered look on my face.

"What?" he asked my reflection.

"After you've been married for a long time, aren't you supposed to start looking like each other?"

He laughed and laid the brush on top of the dresser. "Only on television. Real life doesn't have a casting director. What brought that up?"

I squinted at my reflection, then at his. "I don't see it! There's no way anyone would take us for brothers."

He rolled his eyes. "Jeez, Alex, are you still on that? James was just trying to make sense out of something he didn't understand."

"I didn't help any."

Peter turned from my image to the original. "What's really the matter?"

"I've never done that before," I replied after pursing my lips.

"What?"

"I'm usually perfectly honest about our relationship. It made me feel . . . just . . . creepy to hedge like that. I half expected a cock to crow."

He smiled at me lovingly. "You didn't lie. You just didn't tell him everything."

I snorted. "I've been working with Nelson too long. It's rubbing off."

"This isn't anything like Nelson. You just didn't want to confuse James more than he has been. You were thinking of him." He gave me a peck on the forehead. "Besides, it's none of his business, anyway."

"I guess," I replied, somewhat mollified. "But if he asks me about our relationship again, I'm going to tell him straight out, confusion or no confusion."

"That's my little activist," he said, giving my cheek a pinch in a perfectly accurate imitation of Mother.

*   *   *

Mother had decided to serve breakfast in the kitchen rather than the dining room, reasoning that if we were supposed to provide a friendly atmosphere for the first phase of James's transition to American life, we should treat him like one of the family rather than a guest. I couldn't help but think the poor kid was going to get a warped picture of the American family from a British expatriate, her son, and his husband. But then, no more warped than he would get from television or the religious wrong.

When Peter and I came into the kitchen, Mother was busily stirring a skillet full of scrambled eggs while another pan sizzled with browning sausages. She paused in her stirring just long enough to snatch the toast that had just popped up from the toaster and whisk another pair of slices into it. She reminded me of one of the robots in those "home of the future" cartoons Warner Bros. used to put out. The air was full of the heavy, alluring smell of grease.

"Oh!" Mother said over her shoulder when she noticed us. "Would you butter those, darling?" She jutted the egg-caked spoon at a plate of toast sitting on the counter.

"Sure," I replied.

"I'm afraid I got started a bit late. Wouldn't you know it? The first morning James is here and I have to oversleep!"

"Well, he's not down yet," said Peter as he poured orange juice into the glasses that had already been laid out.

"And I hardly think he'll be starving this morning after the way he packed dinner away," I added.

"He didn't really eat all that much," Mother said, shooting a chastising glance at me as she turned the sausages. "Although he did do it rather quickly." She laid the spatula on the counter and picked up the oversized spoon she'd been using on the eggs. She then tilted the skillet just a touch and gave the mass another healthy stir. "These look done. Would you go and tell James it's time for breakfast?"

"Okay."

I put down the butter knife and brushed the crumbs from my hands, then started to go. But the minute I turned around, I let out a startled cry. James was standing in the doorway. There was something a bit too creeping-through-the-underbrush-with-a-bolo-between-the-teeth about the way he'd silently appeared behind us—just like in my nightmares.

"I'm sorry!" I gasped out, putting a hand to my racing heart. "You startled me."

He looked befuddled. "I am sorry."

"Nonsense," said Mother, waving me off. "I'm glad you came down on your own. It shows you're feeling a bit more at home."

"Or that he smelled the food," I whispered to Peter. I let out another yelp at the sharp poke to my ribs.

"Boys, stop playing," said Mother. Then she turned back to James. "Have a seat, luv."

"Thank you."

He crossed to the foot of the table and sat down. This morning he was dressed in a white shirt and navy blue chinos with a black belt, along with white socks and black shoes. He looked exotically preppy.

"How did you sleep?" Mother asked.

"Good. Much good."

Mother began scooping the eggs into a serving bowl. "Poor thing. You were absolutely dead last night."

His forehead creased. "Dead?"

"It's just an expression. It means you were very tired."

"Yes, I was."

As soon as we sat down to eat it became apparent that Mother wasn't going to allow any of the awkwardness or embarrassment of last night's meal. She kept up a steady flow of prattle so effortlessly that you would've thought she was in running for Hostess of the Year.

She did a wonderful job of it for the most part. However, I almost choked when she said in the most natural way possible, "You know, I've never been to Iraq. How's the weather there?" I didn't hear his reply, because I was busy coughing into my paper napkin. This really was taking the British obsession with the weather a bit far.

Amazingly enough, she managed to draw James out a bit. In his halting English he told us a little about his country. He said nothing about the army, and none of us asked. Still, the bulk of the conversation fell to Mother, with Peter and I adding an occasional "uh-huh" when prompted by her, or an interested "hmm" whenever James chose to speak.

James kept his head lowered as if passionately interested in the contents of his plate, although he was eating considerably more slowly than the night before. One thing I found a little unnerving was that several times I noticed him shifting his eyes back and forth between Peter and me. I didn't know if he was still trying to put two and two together or if he'd figured it out and was having trouble dealing with it. Either way, it reaffirmed my resolve to be completely up-front with him should he broach the topic again.

When we'd finished eating, Peter got up and said, "Well, I'd better get to work."

"And I'll get this lot cleaned up," Mother chimed in, rising with a plate in each hand.

"I help," said James.

"No, you don't need to do that, you're—" She broke off, then added. "You can if you'd like. I'd certainly appreciate it."

He picked up the other two plates and followed her to the sink while I walked Peter to the front door.

"You should go out today," he said as he slipped into his jacket.

"Why?"

"It'll keep you from sitting around the house wondering what they're saying in the debriefing."

I laughed. "You're probably right."

He put his arms around my neck and touched his lips to mine, holding them there for several seconds before releasing me.

"See you later, honey," he said as he opened the door. I closed it after him.

When I turned around, James was standing in the kitchen doorway, staring at me with saucer eyes. I smiled at him and went up the stairs.

Nelson arrived so promptly at nine o'clock that I suspected he'd been waiting on the front stoop with a stopwatch. He was accompanied by Dunning and another man he introduced as Lester Bagnold, whose job it was to serve as interpreter in case James's English should fail him in fulfillment of his part of the bargain. Bagnold was a weedy young man, all knees and elbows, and had thick, nearly black hair that looked as if he combed it with a garden rake. He wore a sweater-vest that was too big for him (possibly because they don't knit them that long and thin), gray corduroy slacks, and a pair of brown plastic-framed glasses that were in a perpetual state of sliding down his nose. Each time he pushed them back up automatically without seeming to notice he was doing it, like a man with an elaborate tic.

Although Mother had made some inroads in getting James to open up over breakfast, at the sight of the agents he immediately reverted to the sheepish, cautious animal he was when he arrived.

"So, Jean, where can we set up?" Nelson asked.

"You can use the dining table, if that's not too public."

"That will be fine. Gentlemen?"

He led the three of them to the table. As they started to take seats, James nudged Dunning away from the chair at the foot of the table, then quickly sat down. He glanced over at me and smiled.

"Let's get started," Nelson said. He laid his briefcase flat on the table, opened it, and brought out a tape recorder and a set of maps that looked almost like blueprints—only they were musty white instead of blue—and unrolled them.

"Could I get you some coffee or anything?" Mother asked, hovering in the kitchen doorway.

"Yes, thank you. That would be nice," Nelson replied. Mother went into the kitchen. Nelson flattened out one of the maps and was about to speak when suddenly he stopped. He raised his eye to mine. "We'll be a while, Alex."

"Oh! Yes, of course," I stammered, my cheeks reddening. I joined Mother in the kitchen, closing the swinging door behind me. She was filling the filter of our coffeemaker.

"Well! I've been summarily dismissed," I said.

"What, luv?"

"I was ordered out of the room in the nicest possible terms."

"Were you planning to stay in there?"

"I thought it might be interesting."

"Really?" she said with surprise. "I should think it would be deadly dull, watching them map out Iraq."

I stared at her for a second. "Have you ever noticed how bizarre our normal conversations have become?"

"You know what I mean!" she said with a backward flip of her hand. "I can't imagine you being interested in what they're doing."

"All right, I thought maybe James could use a friendly face."

She looked even more surprised. "Really?"

"Yeah. Did you notice the way he tensed up when they got here?"

She sucked in her lips for a moment, glanced in the direction of the dining room, then leaned close to me, keeping her voice very low as she answered. "Yes, I did notice. But I think there's other reasons for that, don't you?"

"What?"

"Well, after all, however you look at it he's betraying his country, isn't he?"

"That's putting it a bit strongly!"

"Oh, I don't mean anything by it. In his case, all it proves is that he's got a conscience. And I'm glad he's doing it—we don't want anyone having those weapons, do we? But you have to remember that he's still going against the way he was brought up, and that can't be easy for him."

"I never thought of it that way. Poor kid."

She smiled at me lovingly. "You know, sometimes I think you're softer than I am."

"There's no need to get insulting," I replied.

The interrogation—or, I should say, the debriefing—went on for a full eight hours with barely a pause for lunch. As the day wore on Mother became increasingly solicitous about James's welfare, and interrupted them with growing frequency to see if he wanted anything. Several times over the course of the day I passed through the dining area on the way to the kitchen, each time trying to maintain the I'm-alone-here-and-there's-nothing-going-on-around-me attitude of a daily commuter, so that our friendly neighborhood spies wouldn't think I was spying on them. Every time I passed, James looked up and watched me, as if drowning for want of a friend, however foreign, while Bagnold babbled at him in Arabic.

By the time they'd finished for the day and Nelson and company had departed, poor James looked like he'd had a slow pass through an old-fashioned wringer. He slumped on the couch with his hands on his stomach, fingers intertwined. There were small crescent-shaped stains under his arms, and bags under his eyes. He had trouble keeping his eyes open as we watched the early-evening news, and he nodded off before Mother came out to set the table for dinner.

"Poor little thing," she said. I joined her as she quietly placed the silverware by the plates. "He looks all in."

"Nelson and his pals are so eager to get what they want they seem to forget he's a human being," I said indignantly. "Hell, he hardly even got a break for lunch."

"I think I may have to have a word with Larry tomorrow." She laid the last knife down with a loud thunk.

James was still dozing in front of the TV when Peter got home from work. He greeted me with a kiss and asked me how the day had gone.

"Shh!" I replied, motioning toward our sleeping soldier. "I'll tell you later."

We didn't wake James until Mother was about to put dinner on the table. He roused groggily as I gently shook his shoulder.

"I'm sorry." His voice was dry and cracked with overuse. "I was tired."

"There's no need to apologize. Dinner's about ready. You want to eat, right?"

His eyes lit up at the mention of food. "Yes. Thank you. I wash first."

He rose from the couch and bounded up the stairs is if he was afraid all the food would be gone if he took too long.

Dinner that evening was a bit fancier than the night before. Mother had made a large beef roast with carrots, onions, and enough boiled potatoes to feed an army, let alone one little soldier. Once again James greedily cleaned his plate two or three times. After the rigors he'd been put through that day, and after what Mother had said about how he was essentially betraying his country, I could've cried just watching him. It was as if he'd had to sell his soul to get a decent meal. I wondered if there would come a time when he'd think that was poor compensation for destroying his life as he knew it, even if that life had left a lot to be desired.

Mother didn't attempt to force a conversation, figuring that James had had his fill for the day. But he was much more talkative on his own.

"I am tired," he said, stabbing his second helping of beef with his fork and sawing at it with his knife. "Questions, questions, questions . . ."

"Surely you expected that," said Mother.

He speared the slice of beef with his knife and popped it in his mouth. "Yes, but so many! They want to empty my head in one day!"

"Yes, well, I thought they went a bit over the top myself."

"And there are more days of it!"

"Don't you worry, luv. You'll get through it and you'll be the better for it."

He stared down at his plate, toying with one of the potatoes with his fork. His eyes teared up. "I feel I cannot think anymore."

"Nelson has that effect on people," I said.

Mother eyed him with compassion. "You're doing very well."

From her expression, I wouldn't have wanted to be Nelson when she had her "little word" with him.

"I feel like I am in . . ." His voice trailed off and his breathing quickened as he searched for the right word.

"Purgatory?" I offered.

His face fell open. "What is this?"

Peter looked at me across the table with a single raised eyebrow, challenging me to explain.

"Um . . . purgatory. I mean, you feel like you're stuck between one world and another."

James brightened. "Yes! This is it!" He paused, and the brightness drained away from him. He looked as if he were deflating. "Only I don't know what this new world is. I feel I am in a cage."

"But you mustn't," said Mother. "It's only a couple of more days now. Then you'll be off to a new life, and you'll settle in very quickly."

There was a beat; then James grunted and dove back into his food.

We spent the rest of the evening in front of the television set, Peter and I close together at one end of the couch and James at the other. He alternated between being fascinated by American TV and being fascinated by us. Although he tried to keep his eyes riveted to the various programs, several times I caught him shooting sidelong glances in our direction. The attention made me so nervous that at one point, when Peter laid his hand casually on my leg, I quickly crossed my legs to knock it off. He looked at me questioningly, and I gave a slight nod in the direction of our guest. Peter sighed heavily and folded his hands in his lap.

By nine o'clock James was nodding off again, but even though he was clearly exhausted he made no move to retire for the night until Peter and I announced that we were going to bed. I was beginning to wonder if it was considered bad manners in Iraq to go to bed before your hosts.

We said good night to Mother, who'd spent the evening poring over more magazines at the dining table, and led James upstairs.

"Good night," I said as he went toward his room.

"Yes. Good night."

I could feel his eyes on us as we went down the hall. He didn't go into his room until we closed our door.

"Have you noticed the way he watches us?" I asked as we got undressed.

"The only thing I've noticed lately is you acting like a nut," Peter replied without rancor.

"I'm serious!"

"So am I. What was that business of pushing my hand away?"

I was going to try claiming it was an accident, but that sounded lame, even to me. I tossed my jeans over the back of the chair by our bathroom door.

"It just . . . made me uncomfortable with James there. Did you really not notice him watching us?"

"Maybe a little," Peter relented as he draped his trousers over mine. "He's probably just curious. Why should you care?"

"I don't!"

He tilted his head and pursed his lips into a little smile. I backed down.

"I don't know," I said as I stripped off my shorts. "It's just he's gone through so much already, and you should've seen how Nelson's boys treated him. I don't want to do anything to freak him out even more. What would he think if he knew about us? I mean, they shoot gay people over there, don't they?"

"Alex, they shoot gay people over here, too." He dropped his khaki boxers to the floor, lifted them up with his foot and grabbed them, then tossed them on the chair.

"I know," I said with a sigh, hoping to derail him before he'd fully climbed up on his soapbox.

He came to me and wrapped his arms around my shoulders,

pressing our flesh together. He gave me a slow kiss during which my already stirring nether regions came to full attention.

"Honey," he said as our lips parted, "I'm not going to pretend to be something I'm not, even for the sake of détente. Are you?"

I took a step back, looked down, then raised my eyes to his. "Well, not right now."

I woke in the middle of the night in a sort of postcoital dreaminess. I was lying halfway on my stomach with one leg straight and the other crooked up between Peter's legs. I was disoriented for a moment, then realized I'd been woken by the sound of a soft click. I glanced over Peter's shoulder at the clock on the nightstand, which read 12:57.

I gently extricated my leg from his and rolled over on my back, wondering what the noise had been. Suddenly I felt my heart constrict: I could sense movement somewhere. I tried to scan the room without moving my head, not wanting to show any sign of being awake. Through the darkness I finally made out that the door was opening. For a moment I thought I was having my Saddam Hussein nightmare again, but my racing pulse and rapid breathing soon convinced me otherwise.

"Peter!" I anxiously whispered into his ear. "Peter! Wake up!"

"Nuh?" he said so loudly I almost jumped out of my skin.

"Shh! There's someone in here."

"What?"

"Alex?" James's voice said quietly in the dark.

"James?" I reached over and switched on the lamp on my side of the bed. The three of us recoiled from the sudden flood of light. When my eyes had adjusted, I found our young soldier standing at the foot of the bed clad only in a pair of tattered briefs. Apparently his makeover hadn't extended beneath the surface.

"Is something wrong?"

"I have question."

"You have question now?" I said, my eyes widening. Then I quickly corrected myself. "I mean, you have a question now?"

"Yes." He came around the side of the bed and sat on the corner.

I glanced at Peter, who I suddenly felt was very conspicuous. "What is it?"

James stared at me with those big Bambi eyes, marshaling his courage, then said, "You are homosex?"

I blinked. "Personified."

His forehead wrinkled.

Peter sighed in my direction. "Yes, we are."

James turned back to me. "Your mother, she knows this?"

"Well, you could hardly expect us to be sleeping in the same bed under the same roof as my own mother without her knowing about it!" I didn't mean to sound snippy, but I was so flabbergasted by the direct questioning and the late hour that I couldn't help it.

"This is yes?" he asked blankly.

"Yes."

He looked even more distressed. He raised his hands, holding his palms a few inches apart. "You need to use much more little words."

It was my turn to look perplexed. "Smaller words?"

"I think he means fewer," Peter said in a tone for which I would be getting him back later. "Honestly, Alex, English is his second language."

"She does not mind this, your mother?" James asked.

"Of course not. She loves me. Us!"

He was silent for several seconds during which his breathing quickened. At last he said, "You see . . . Alex . . . Peter . . . you see . . ." There was mounting urgency in his voice. "I am homosex, too!"

I almost said "Oh dear God!" but the look on James's face kept me from exclaiming. His eyes were wide and searching both of our faces, as if he feared a very elaborate trap had been set for him, the object of which had been to trick him into this confession. For the second time that day, I felt like crying just looking at him. He had the panic-stricken look of someone who has just made his first bold step out of the closet and is prepared to retreat at the slightest sign of rejection. But his fear went beyond that. Although I really didn't have any concrete information on how gays were treated in his country, I didn't doubt that he could've been killed for admitting it there.

But then in a rush something else dawned on me: this wasn't the first time he'd admitted to his sexuality.

"That's wonderful," said Peter with heartfelt sincerity.

James's tension began to drain so quickly that he almost giggled with relief. "Yes?"

Peter nodded.

"This is why you needed to come to this country, isn't it?" I asked.

"Yes. In my country it is dangerous to be such. If anyone knew . . ." His voice trailed off. From the worried expression on his face, the outcome must've been vividly playing through his mind. "But for many years I hear about America, and I think maybe I come. It is better here. They say that sex is very free."

"Well, you can still buy it."

Peter heaved a world-weary sigh. "Alex . . ."

"Sorry."

"I don't mean this," James explained. "I mean you can be here."

Both Peter and I were momentarily stumped by this one. Then suddenly it came to me. "Oh! You mean that you can be gay here. Homosexual. Yes. Well, for the most part."

Peter muttered, "Alex . . . fewer, fewer, fewer . . ."

James sat staring soberly at his own knee for almost a minute. Then he said very quietly, "This is good." He rose from the bed. "I think I can sleep now."

He started for the door but paused when Peter spoke. "James. I think you're very brave."

"Thank you," he replied with a rueful smile that showed he didn't share the same opinion of himself. But for the first time there was some warmth in his tone. It was as if he finally felt like part of a family. He turned and left the room.

"Jesus!" said Peter, putting his right hand behind his head and lying back against his pillow. "What do you think of that?"

"I think he's a bastard!" I exclaimed.

Peter looked absolutely shocked. "James?"

"No, Nelson!"

"Why?"

"Because now it all makes sense!"

"What are you talking about?"

"Do you remember what Nelson said when we asked him why James needed to leave Iraq? He said, 'He has his reasons.' "

"So?"

"So! James must've told him what his reason was. Nelson knew all along!"

"Of course he did. So what?"

"Don't you see? James is gay! That's why Nelson wanted him to stay with us!"

There was a beat, then Peter said, "You're probably right. But so what?"

"So why didn't Nelson tell us that to begin with?"

He shrugged. "I don't know. Probably more of his need-to-know crap."

"Well, tomorrow I'm going to tell him we needed to know. I mean, what was the point in setting James up with us if he wasn't going to tell us he was gay?"

"I don't know, honey." He yawned and turned over on his side. "Worry about it in the morning, will you? Let's get some sleep."

I lowered my head back onto my pillow. "Huh. A gay Iraqi soldier. What will they think of next?"

FOUR

Peter and I overslept the next morning. We found Mother and James already eating when we came down. James was much less sullen over breakfast and ate with less determination than before. Apparently he was beginning to trust that we wouldn't snatch the food from his mouth. Maybe it was because he knew we were sisters under the skin: soldiers might take your food, but fellow faggots wouldn't.

He was also a bit more effusive, telling us a little about his family and what meals had been like back home. "Nothing like here," he assured us, spearing a sausage with his fork. He held it up in front of his eyes and gazed at it with wonder. He talked at great length in his halting English about the lack of food in his country. I was beginning to think that Iraqis were as interested in food as the British are in the weather, although the latter couldn't claim their interest sprang from scarcity.

Mother seemed to find the new openness surprising, but I hadn't yet had a chance to get her alone and tell her what had happened during the night.

Along with his new measure of ease, James had developed a noticeable restlessness. While he talked he continually kept his foot tapping, not making any noise but causing the table to vibrate. And he shifted in his seat more often than not. The semiconfinement he'd suffered since leaving his homeland was obviously wearing on him.

Peter was running late, so he hurried through breakfast and raced out the door before I reached it. I stood there like Donna Reed, complete with the confused pout, and right on cue my faithful husband popped back in the door and gave me a peck on the cheek.

Nelson and the boys arrived at nine o'clock on the dot. They made straight for the dining table, ready to launch back into questioning poor James without so much as a by-your-leave (as Mother would say), but she caught Nelson by the arm just before he sat down. With the formality of a duchess in a West End comedy, she said, "Might I have a word with you, Larry? In the kitchen?"

"And me too," I chimed in.

"Of course."

We went into the kitchen and I closed the door.

"Is there a problem?" he asked.

"The problem," Mother said in a measured voice, "is that boy."

"Has he given you any trouble?"

"Quite the contrary. You're the ones giving me trouble. You practically worried that boy to death with your questions yesterday. You had him so frazzled that from the moment you left he could barely keep his eyes open."

"It's what he's here for," Nelson said.

"I know that, and so does he."

"And so do I," I added, sounding exactly like one of the Cratchit children.

Mother continued. "But for gawd's sake! He's almost a child! And he's a human being—who's trying to help you, I might add. I don't like this business of you grilling him like he's a bit of beef!"

"What do you suggest we do?"

Mother tilted her aquiline nose upward. "These aren't suggestions, Larry, they are house rules. I want you to give him breaks at regular intervals. You have to let him get up and stretch himself now and then."

"We don't have him chained to the table," Nelson said without emotion.

"Not physically," I said. "But Nelson, you're 'the authorities.' He probably feels he can't move without your permission. Hell, he practically feels he can't move without our permission!"

Nelson eyed me for a moment. In a rare spirit of concession, he said, "I don't think I'd really considered that."

"Quite right, you didn't!" said Mother. "And another thing. I want him to have a proper lunch."

If Nelson ever displayed any emotion, he would've registered his surprise. "We fed him yesterday."

"Yes you did. Exactly as if he were in a zoo. And made him work straight through it, at that! I intend to give him a proper lunch. In here. With us. Away from your people!"

After a beat, Nelson said, "Understood." There was a long pause. "Anything else?"

"Yes," I said. "Why didn't you tell us he was gay?"

"What?!" Mother exclaimed.

"James told us last night," I said to her. Then I turned back to Nelson. "Well?"

"I didn't think it was your concern."

"Oh, right! Are you going to tell me that that's not why you wanted him here with us?"

"I told you exactly why I wanted him here. I thought he'd be more comfortable."

There was that maddening honesty again. That was exactly what he'd said. He'd just left out the most important part.

"You thought he'd be more comfortable with us because he's gay, right? So why didn't you tell us?"

A smile formed behind his eyes. "You surprise me, Alex."

"*I* surprise *you*??"

"Yes. I would think that you'd believe it is up to an individual to reveal his own sexual identity."

The hinges that hold the top of my head on started to snap. There's nothing I like less than having my own ethics thrown up at me. I wasn't going to let him get away with it.

"Tell me something: Were you really concerned about his comfort, or did you think that throwing him in with a couple of gay guys would make him feel safe enough that you might get more information out of him?"

"There was never any question of that," he replied easily. "He's been more than willing to give us information." He was silent for a moment. "Now, if I may?"

"Wait," I said, stopping him as he headed for the door. "One more thing. Just how much of an eye are we supposed to keep on him?"

"What do you mean?"

"You said you don't want him to feel like he's in prison. Exactly how free is he?"

"As free as he can be under the circumstances."

I could feel my teeth beginning to gnash. It hardly seemed possible, but sometimes Nelson could be even more opaque than others. "I mean, can he come and go as he pleases? Can he go out?"

"He shouldn't go out unaccompanied."

"I see," I said suspiciously.

"He doesn't know the area. He would get lost. You can take him out with you if you like. As long as you're careful."

"I don't like the sound of that," said Mother.

Nelson shrugged. "Just common sense. We're as certain as we can be that nobody has any idea where he is, and the chances of someone recognizing him are practically nonexistent. But if you do take him out, I would like you to stay alert to anything unusual."

"Like what?"

"Anything. I don't foresee any problems, but if you notice something, let me know."

I folded my arms across my chest. "Nelson, why do I get the feeling there's more going on here than we know about?"

He shrugged again. "I've told you all you need to know." With that he went through the swinging door.

Mother looked at me. "Not exactly a comfort, is he?"

The debriefing continued throughout the day with Mother popping into the room every now and then and announcing in her best Lady Bracknell, "I think it's time for a break now, don't you?" The agents (except for Nelson) were visibly annoyed by her interruptions, but didn't protest, which was just as well, because it saved Mother the bother of knocking their heads together. And at noon the three of us—four, if you count the dog under the table— had a quiet lunch together in the kitchen while the agents enjoyed a silent sandwich in the dining room.

Mother's plan did work. When the agents left for the day, James was far less wrung out than he had been the night before. In fact, he was so grateful to her that, like so many men before him, he started to fall under her spell. He followed her around as she tidied up the dining room—much to the consternation of Duffy, who looked as if he felt his position was being usurped—then stayed with her in the kitchen while she prepared dinner. I was grateful for that, because it meant that when Peter got home I was able to greet him with a very affectionate kiss.

"Wow!" he said, leading me upstairs. "What was that for?"

"It was just nice to get to greet you without the scrutiny of our homo-in-waiting."

He laughed. "What?"

"All this time I thought he was trying to figure us out. Now I'm not so sure. Maybe he was looking for pointers."

"Well, if he was, he didn't get very many from us."

We reached the bedroom and Peter started to change from his suit to a pair of jeans and a light-green Polo shirt. I love that color on him because it intensifies the color of his eyes.

"Did you talk to Nelson?" he asked.

"Yeah," I replied with an ironic laugh. "And he claims he didn't tell us about James because he thought it was up to James to tell us."

He raised his eyebrows. "Hmm."

"You sound impressed!"

"I am. I didn't think he had that kind of scruples."

"You're kidding! You think he was right not to tell us?"

"Well, Alex, you'd usually be the first one—"

"Wait, wait!" I cut him off with an upraised palm. "I'm going to like it a lot less coming from you than I did from Nelson. Am I the only one who thinks it's different in this case?"

"Why?" he asked as he hung his suit in the closet.

"Well, because . . . because . . . I don't know, it just is!"

"I don't see it, honey," He produced a sly smile. "Unless you think we should be told the sexuality of anyone we give asylum to."

"You make it sound like that happens once a week."

"Alex . . ."

I threw up my hands. "All right! All right! I give up! I guess I was just . . . surprised by this turn of events. Now I know how Stephen Rea felt in *The Crying Game*."

Peter laughed and wrapped his arms around my waist. "You really are a nut!"

"I love you." I ran my fingers through his hair, pulled his head toward me, and kissed him gently. "Now, how about after dinner we take James out?"

"Out? Where?"

"I don't know. Anywhere. He feels all pent up. It'll do him good to go out and have some fun!"

He pulled away from me. "Can we actually do that?" From his tone I got the feeling he wasn't warming to the idea.

"I asked Nelson. He said it was all right."

"He did, huh?" he replied skeptically.

"Yeah."

His lips spread into a loving smile. "You really feel sorry for him, don't you?"

"Yeah, and a little guilty for thinking he might crawl in here and slit out throats."

After giving it some thought, he shrugged. "It's all right with me, but where do you want to go?"

I thought for a minute. "Why don't we take him to Charlene's?"

"Charlene's?" Peter echoed in disbelief. "You want to take an Iraqi soldier to a gay bar? Hasn't he suffered enough?"

"He might enjoy it."

"I thought you were the one who was worried about giving him culture shock."

I sighed. "Look, he's only going to be with us for another day. Sure, the CIA will have somebody helping him, but they're not going to introduce him to the gay community, wherever they end up settling him. Come on, Peter, he might not get another chance for a long time. We're the only gay people he knows in America."

"Alex, we're the only *people* he knows in America!"

I spread my palms. "All the more reason."

He folded his arms across his chest. "You know, you get more and more like your mother every day."

"Didn't somebody say that if you want to know what a gay boy will be like in thirty years, you should look at his mother?"

He laughed. "Will you tell me one thing? How exactly are we going to explain him at Charlene's?"

"Explain what?"

"The fact that you and I have an Iraqi soldier in tow."

"Oh, that. Do you think anybody will care?"

He nodded. "We're bound to run into someone we know. And they'll think it's a bit peculiar."

We fell silent. Then it came to me. "I know! We can just say he's a foreign exchange student."

Peter curled his lips. "Of course."

We left for the bar at about eight. Mother waved after us from the back door as if she were watching her child go off to his first prom.

James had been excited when we told him our plan. He told us in his broken English that he was anxious to see the sights. Peter replied with, "You'll see sights, all right," and for the first time in months I got to poke *him* in the ribs.

But now that we were on our way, James seemed more apprehensive. Of course, that might've been my imagination. It's more likely he was experiencing some sensory overload now that he was out. He stared bug-eyed through the windows as we drove down Halsted, his head turning to follow a passing building or pedestrian, then swinging back when he could turn it no farther. He was also probably bewildered, if not scared: He'd had two days to become familiar with our house, and now that he was outside of its safe confines, I'm sure he felt less secure.

I turned on North Avenue, drove over to Wells and hung a right. Parking wasn't terrible, since it was the middle of the week and the middle of the evening, but we still had to park four blocks away from the bar.

I hadn't been to Charlene's for a couple of years and expected it to look the same. Gay bars in Chicago have a tendency to remain unchanged until they disappear. So I was surprised when we walked through the door and found that the once black walls of the dimly lit bar had been painted dark red, and the huge neon lips that once adorned the north wall were gone. In their place were art deco sconces. The tables were the same, but were covered with plastic lace cloths, and atop each one was a candle burning in a glass bowl surrounded by plastic mesh, and a bud vase with a pink rose. A long, discreet fixture had been mounted overhead and sent diffused light across the fluffy clouds that had been painted across the ceiling.

"Good grief!" I exclaimed quietly to Peter. "Charlene's hormone treatments must've finally kicked in!"

We'd managed to arrive after the happy-hour mob had dissipated, and just when the late-evening crowd was starting to show up, so there were plenty of people but still enough room to maneuver. One thing that hadn't changed was the noise level. The same huge speakers were mounted in the corners of the ceiling, and Blondie was blaring out "One Way or Another." Everyone was talking very loudly to be heard over it.

We found two empty stools at the far end of the bar. Peter chose to stand, so I sat beside James, who faced outward and watched the men dancing together with a look of absolute wonder on his face.

It was several minutes before the bartender came down to us.

"Alex," he said. "Long time, no see!"

"Hi," I replied vacantly. I had no idea who he was.

"It's me, Ernie!"

"Ernie!" I exclaimed, dumbfounded. "I don't believe it!"

"Yep. There's been some changes around here!"

There certainly had been. When last we'd seen Ernie he was sporting a crew cut and one large gold hoop in his left ear, so that along with his girth he'd looked like a cross between Mr. Clean and Curly. Since then he'd added a few more pounds and let his hair, which was greasy gray streaked with light gray, grow down to his shoulders. Both of his lobes were now pierced and held a pair of earrings of dangling metal strips augmented with tiny feathers. He wore a pair of slashed jeans and an ultra-tight black leather vest that made him look like a stuffed sausage. He'd gone from a gay Stooge to a gay biker.

I waved a hand up and down him. "I like it!"

"Thanks. Hi, Peter."

Peter reached between James and me and shook Ernie's hand. "Nice to see you again."

James turned around when he realized we were talking to someone. When Ernie saw that beautiful face his eyes practically leaped out of his head.

"Hellllo," he said. "Who do we have here?"

"He's a foreign exchange student who's staying with us for a few days," I blurted out in one breath.

I could actually feel Peter's eyes rolling behind me. Ernie's eyebrows snaked toward the bridge of his nose.

"Ernie, this is James," said Peter.

The bartender snatched one of James's hands up into his ham-like paw and shook it. "Glad to know you!"

"Your first time here?"

"Yes."

"You got an ID?"

"An ID?" James said blankly.

"Oh Christ, I hadn't thought of that," Peter said under his breath.

"No, he doesn't," I said quickly. "He just got here. But it's okay. We can vouch for him. He's twenty-one."

"Yeah?" Ernie replied skeptically.

"Come on, Ernie," Peter said nonchalantly.

He shrugged. "Oh, okay. What'll you have?"

I don't know that he would've conceded so quickly had James not been quite so good-looking. I turned to James. "Do you like beer?"

"Beer, yes," James replied.

"Your first drink your first time here is on me," said Ernie.

James looked Ernie up and down, then turned his puzzled eyes to me.

"He means it's free," I explained.

"Oh. Thank you."

Ernie hurried to the center of the bar and snatched a bottle of Bud from the cooler, then came back and slapped a white napkin in front of James. He then twisted the cap off and placed the bottle on the napkin.

"Sorry about the foam," he leered.

"This is okay." James picked up the bottle, put it to his lips, threw back his head, and drank like a soldier. At least I guess it was like a soldier. When he put the bottle down, half of its contents were gone. He wiped his mouth with his sleeve.

Ernie's eyes never left him. I'd forgotten his predilection for the barely legal. I leaned over toward him and said pointedly, "We'll have the same."

"What? Oh! Right!"

I looked over my shoulder at Peter. "It's nice to see not everything has changed."

As Ernie got our drinks Blondie was replaced by Pat Benatar demanding to be treated right. James swiveled around on his stool and leaned his elbows back on the bar as he returned to watching the dancing. Ernie brought two more beers to us, placed them in front of me, and I paid him.

"I never see anything like this," James said over the music, his eyes shining like a kid in a candy store.

I gestured toward the throng gyrating through a swirl of colored lights. "Well, this is America!"

"I do not think I could do this."

"Why not? It's perfectly all right. There's nothing wrong with two men dancing together."

He stared at me with puzzlement. "No. I mean I do not know how."

Over the din I heard Peter snort into his beer bottle. I blushed. "Oh. Of course. Sorry."

We didn't say anything for a couple of minutes. James was too awestruck to speak, and Peter and I were too old to try to hold a conversation over bone-rattling music. Despite the decibel level, the lights, and the movement, I noticed that James had drawn the attention of a new arrival, who had stopped about halfway across the room. He was tall and slim, and his hair was *Village of the Damned* blond. He was dressed in a nondescript way and seemed a bit unsure of himself. He came over to us and carefully wedged himself in between James and the man sitting on his other side. He ordered a beer and after being served spent some time alternately stealing glances at James and looking down at his drink, trying to work up the nerve to say something. James remained perfectly oblivious to the attention.

Finally, the young man cleared his throat, straightened his spine and, looking exactly as if he were about to climb Mount Everest, said, "Hi!"

It was a second before James realized the guy was speaking to him. In fact, the guy had to repeat himself first.

James reluctantly drew his eyes from the dance floor. "Hi."

The young man smiled. "This your first time here?"

"Yes."

"I'm Bob." He offered his hand, and James shook it.

"I am James."

"Hello, James!"

There was a long pause during which my heart went out to Bob. James stared at him in that direct way of his that seemed to be waiting for the next question.

Then it came. "You're not from around here, are you?"

Peter placed a cautionary hand on my arm. After eight years of marriage he can read my mind: I had been about to blurt out our cover story again.

To my surprise, James answered, "I am student."

Bob blinked. "Oh! You mean a foreign exchange student?"

"Yes."

They fell silent. With his limited English James wasn't much help in keeping a conversation going, and Bob appeared to be trying to think of how to proceed. Finally, he said, "Do you want to dance?"

James looked at the dance floor and his face practically collapsed with distress. "I not know how."

With unbelievably good timing, the music shifted from Benatar back to Blondie, this time the slow and sensual "In the Flesh." The crowd fell into each other's arms.

"Come on," said Bob, taking James's hand. "You don't have to know anything to do this."

"Is good?" James said to me.

"Is all right," I replied.

James almost catapulted off his stool and Bob led him onto the dance floor. They stood on the periphery of the other couples, and James faced his partner uncertainly. Bob finally took James's arms and wrapped them around his own waist, then put his arms around James's neck. If James had been unsure of what to do at first, once he was in close proximity to another man, he sure as hell found out fast. He plastered himself against Bob like a full-body version of the *Alien* face-hugger. Bob didn't exactly look like he minded. If anything, he looked delighted.

"That's our boy," I said to Peter in my best imitation of June Cleaver.

Peter wasn't amused. He took a long drink, his eyes never leaving our little charge.

"What's the matter?"

He pursed his lips. "You remember what happened to some concentration camp survivors when they ate too quickly after being freed?"

I glanced over at James. "He'll be all right."

"I hope so."

Blondie soon gave way to Diana Ross and "Upside Down." James continued to cling to Bob, unmoved by the change in tempo. Bob finally took hold of his arms and physically pushed him back a bit, then leaned close to his ear and said something. James looked at the other dancers and shook his head. The two of them came back to their stools.

"Thank you," James said warmly. "Thank you . . . so . . . much."

"No, thank you," Bob said with a wide grin. He raised his beer bottle to James, then took a long drink.

James turned to us, his face fairly beaming. "This is . . . I don't know how to say!"

"Wonderful," I said.

"Hmm?"

"I think you mean, 'This is wonderful!' "

"Yes," he said uncertainly. "It makes me very happy."

We listened to the music and watched the dancers. Bob hovered anxiously on the side of our threesome, trying to will us into a quartet. He made occasional forays into conversation with James, something that was difficult even under less noisy circumstances, and seemed undaunted by the monosyllabic answers. I had to give Bob credit: it's hard to hold up both ends of a conversation.

After a while, James leaned over to me and said, "You know where is toilet?"

"Yeah." I pointed toward the back of the room. "You see that doorway? At the end of the hall, that's where the bathrooms are."

"Thank you."

He made his way past the end of the dance floor and threaded through the close tables where people sat in huddled conversations, then went through the doorway.

"You think one of us should go with him?" asked Peter.

"He made it clear to me his first night here that he knows how to do it himself."

He sighed heavily. "You know what I mean."

"He'll be all right."

"Well, hello boys!" a familiar voice announced behind us. We turned to find Stevie Sullivan, one of our oldest friends. Actually, one of Peter's oldest friends, who I'd inherited through marriage.

"Hi, Stevie," I said, echoed by my husband. "I'm surprised to see you here."

"Not half as surprised as I am to see me here! La-di-da, as the saying goes." He sounded uncharacteristically dejected.

"Is something wrong?"

"Ernie, sweetie, beer!" he called down the bar. He turned to me as he took a seat on James's stool. "I'm here to drown my sorrows."

"What's wrong?" Over his shoulder I saw Bob slide off his stool and head in the direction of the bathroom.

Stevie sighed dramatically. "I have been dumped again, of course!"

"I'm sorry. Was this . . . the redhead? I can't remember his name."

"The redhead?" he replied, squinting at me. "You mean Jerry? Oh dear God, no! I haven't been with him for two years. He decided to go into the seminary." Ernie put the beer in front of him, and he snatched it up. "With his superior oral skills, Jerry will be a welcome presence in the Archdiocese of Chicago! Cheers!" He took a healthy drink.

"Who was this, then?" Peter asked.

"My most recent debacle? Willy. He was a sweet young man, about the size and shape of the Pillsbury Doughboy: not much to look at, but guaranteed to rise. No, no, I shouldn't be bitter. But we were planning to move in together! I mean, I thought he was finally it! We were actually shopping for furniture!"

"What happened?"

Stevie frowned. "He fell in love with a cashier at Ikea."

"I'm sorry," I said, fighting not to laugh. Peter took a bit of my arm in between his thumb and forefinger and twisted it to help me.

"I guess he wanted the discount more than he wanted me. Cheap bastard." He paused for another gulp of beer. "So here I sit.

The only meaningful relationship I'm having at the moment is with reruns of *Magnum, P.I.* I mean, where are all the devoted husbands I keep hearing about?" He glanced at Peter, then back at me. "Oh. I forgot. You took him."

"There's a lot of other guys out there," I said, though it couldn't help sounding trite. Anything said in response to that would have.

"Not for the plucking. Especially when you've got more than one!"

"What?"

"I saw that beautiful piece of chicken that was with you."

"Chicken?" I said, my voice rising.

He flapped his wrist at me. "Oh, Alex, don't go all Mama Rose on me. Who is he, anyway?"

"Just a friend. A student. He's only in town for a couple of days."

"Just my luck! All the good ones are either married or straight." He took another drink. "Or leaving. If you'll excuse me, I'm going to go mingle. I'm sure Mr. Right is just waiting for me in this sweaty mess of alcoholics."

Peter and I laughed, not without concern, as Stevie slid off his stool and made his way into the crowd.

"Poor Stevie," I said when he was out of earshot.

"He doesn't have a lot of luck in love, does he?" said Peter ruefully.

"He's not going to get lucky here."

Peter laughed. "Yes he is."

"You know what I mean!" I took a drink. "So Stevie's alone again and we're giving asylum to chickens. Do you ever wonder what happened to us?"

"No. I always knew we'd end up in some kind of asylum."

We laughed and then stood finishing our beers in companionable silence through the next couple of songs. Then Peter glanced over toward the doorway. "Hasn't he been gone a long time?"

"Huh? Oh, you mean James. I guess."

"Maybe you should go check on him."

"In the bathroom?" I said after a beat.

"Yeah."

"Here?"

"Yeah."

"I'm not going back there to see what's he's doing!" I jerked my thumb at Bob's empty stool. "Dennis the Menace here followed him in."

Peter shrugged. "Just another reason to make sure he's all right."

"Why don't you go?"

The corner of his mouth crooked into a wicked smile. "Coming here was your idea."

"I thought we'd just sit and have a couple of drinks, I didn't think he'd do things like dance and go to the bathroom!"

Peter shook his head and sighed with exasperation.

"All right, all right! I'm going!" I said, starting across the floor. Before I reached the doorway I was relieved to see Bob emerging. He looked decidedly dissatisfied. I thought perhaps he'd tried to hit on James and found the language barrier unscalable, and smiled inwardly at the puzzled expression that would've been on James's face when confronted with terms that couldn't possibly have been in a course in English as a second language, even in the most progressive Iraqi schools. At least Bob looked physically intact, which meant he hadn't gotten heavy-handed about it. I've had passes made at me in bars (before I was married, of course) that consisted of an injudicious hand applied to my crotch. I had a feeling that that wouldn't be too wise an approach to use on someone trained in mortal combat.

I reached the doorway and stopped in my tracks. At the end of the short hall, between the twin doors for the men's and ladies' rooms, was a pay phone. And James was on it. He had the index finger of his free hand stuck in his ear in an effort to hear whoever he was talking to, and his back was turned to the doorway, so he didn't see me. Even at that distance and with the noise I could hear him babbling in his own language into the receiver.

I was so startled that for a moment I froze in place. Then I quickly turned and went back to Peter.

"What's wrong?" he asked when he saw the look on my face.

"Nothing."

"Come on, Alex, what is it? Did you walk in on something?"

I took a drink. "You could say that."

I was silent as we drove home, but James didn't notice. After the secretive phone call, he'd danced a couple more times with Bob— apparently the language barrier doesn't matter much when you're virtually being Rolfed on the dance floor. I swear James held him so tight I fully expected his face to be printed on Bob's shirt when they parted, like the Shroud of Turin. When he was back with us, he continued to behave like the perfect little Iraqi homo who didn't know nothin' about nothin', sitting on his stool and lapping up atmosphere and beer in equal measure. On the way home he bubbled with excitement, though he was hard pressed to express it. Since he had learned "This is wonderful," he repeated that over and over again with varying degrees of enthusiasm. The way his face shone was completely at odds with the furtive way he'd looked when making his surreptitious phone call.

Mother greeted us with a broad smile when we got home and asked James if he'd enjoyed himself. Predictably, he answered, "Yes. This is wonderful!"

"I'm so glad," she replied, giving him a hug from which he didn't recoil.

"I'm going to bed." I was too preoccupied to realize how abrupt this sounded.

"What?" said Mother.

"I'm going to bed."

"Are you all right?" Peter asked.

"Yeah. I'm just tired."

Without further discussion, I left them standing in the kitchen looking fittingly surprised.

I heard James say, "Something is wrong?"

"Not at all," Mother replied, her tone doubtful.

Ordinarily I would've told my loved ones straight out what was bothering me, but I couldn't do that in front of James; and having become sympathetic toward him, I was so disturbed by this sudden new wrinkle that I didn't much feel like bouncing it off of Mother and Peter until I could come up with some sort of plausible explanation on my own.

I undressed and got into bed, but of course couldn't sleep. Try as I might, I couldn't think of a single legitimate reason James would have for phoning somebody. If he'd needed to get in touch with Nelson or Dunning he could've easily (and more logically) done that from our house. He didn't have to do it furtively at the bar.

About an hour after I went to bed Peter came into the room. I pretended to be asleep, still not feeling like talking, and listened as he removed his clothes and climbed in beside me. I was lying on my side with my back to him, but I could feel him looking at me. Finally he spoke my name softly to see if I was awake, then after a brief wait leaned over and kissed me lightly on the cheek. He then lay back and went to sleep.

I tossed and turned for hours, trying to explain away what I'd seen, but continually came up against a blank wall. When I looked at the clock and found it was almost two, I gave up. I got out of bed as quietly as I could, slipped into my powder-blue terry-cloth robe, and went downstairs to make some tea. I thought maybe that would relax me.

I filled the kettle with water, switched on one of the front burners on the stove, and placed the kettle on it. When I turned to sit down I cried out. Peter was standing in the doorway, his hair attractively tousled and his eyelids at half-mast. He was wearing his dark green silk robe.

"Jesus!" I exclaimed quietly. "I didn't hear you!"

"What's going on?"

"I couldn't sleep."

"I know," he said, coming into the room. "I heard you get up. When are you going to tell me what's wrong? What happened when you went to check on James? Did he make a pass at you or something?"

"Oh, I wish!" I said as I dropped into a chair at the kitchen table.

This fully opened his eyes. "What?"

"I mean, I wish it was as simple as that."

"Well, what happened?"

I sighed. "When I went back to the hallway, I found him on the phone."

Peter sat down across from me. "What?"

"Exactly! I can't think of any good reason he would've been making a call."

"Did he see you?"

"No, his back was to me."

"So he doesn't know you saw him."

"Right."

He sat back in his chair, looking as flummoxed as I felt. Only it looked better on him.

I said, "I mean, I know I was a little scared about having him here at first, but you know, over the past couple of days I've started to feel sorry for him. Now I don't know what to think."

"About what?" said Mother, who'd silently appeared at the door.

I started so suddenly I slammed my knee into the leg of the table. "Jesus Christ!" I exclaimed, cradling my knee with my hands.

"Shh! You'll wake James," she said as she came over to me.

"If you two don't want me to cry out, then you should stop creeping up on me like that! What are you doing up?"

She curled her lips at me and replied nasally, "I'm British, darling. I could feel tea being made." There was a beat, then she added, "I could hear you moving about down here. I wanted to know what was up with you."

I told her. When I finished, she said, "My, that certainly is a puzzle!" The kettle had begun to boil. She lifted it off the stove and switched off the burner. "I wonder what it means."

"He's not supposed to know anyone in America, is he?" said Peter.

"I can't remember if Nelson actually said that, or if we just assumed it because they wanted James to stay with us," I said.

"Then who was he calling?"

I thought for a moment and finally had an idea. "Maybe . . . maybe he was calling someone in Iraq."

"From a pay phone in a gay bar? Why would he do that?"

"Obviously," said Mother as she poured the hot water into her favorite ceramic teapot, "because he didn't want anyone to know he was doing it."

"It doesn't make any sense," I said. "He wouldn't want anyone in Iraq to know where he is, would he?"

"He could've been calling his family there," Peter offered.

"I suppose. But wanting to talk to his family, that would be perfectly natural. Why hide it? Why not just ask if he could do it from here?"

"Oh, I can understand that," said Mother. "It's quite possible Nelson told him he didn't want him to do it, lest someone trace his whereabouts."

She dropped a couple of tea bags into the pot and set it on a trivet in the center of the table, then set out mugs for each of us.

"The question is, what do we do about it?" I asked.

"Well, that's easy. We have to tell Larry," said Mother.

"Tell Nelson? I don't know. I'd feel like I was tattling."

"No, darling," she said as she took her place at the table. "Telling him that James broke a window would be tattling. Telling him that James may be planning the overthrow of the American government would be prudent."

"Oh, come on!"

"Look, honey," said Peter, sitting up as straight as his tired body would allow, "we're always getting into scrapes because we don't tell Nelson when something happens. For once, why don't we do the sensible thing and let him know, and see what happens."

At least he'd had the good grace not to point out that I was the one always getting us into scrapes.

"But it could just be something innocent," I said at last. "He's

65

watched a lot of TV. Maybe he was calling one of those nine-hundred numbers."

"There's one way to find out," said Mother as she reached for the pot. "Ask James who he was calling."

She started to tilt the spout toward my mug, but I covered it with my palm. "No thanks. I don't want any."

"What?"

"It'll keep me awake. And I don't need any help doing that."

James was full of innocent smiles at breakfast the next morning as he whipped through his bacon and eggs. He looked so happy and angelic it was hard to believe he was an evil insurgent bent on taking over our country.

Mother, Peter, and I spent the meal exchanging glances and giving discreet nods in his direction. They seemed to have decided by tacit agreement that it was up to me to broach the subject of the phone call, since I was the one who'd seen him making it. Even as focused as James was on his food, he eventually noticed what was going on. He stopped eating abruptly and stared at us.

"Something is wrong?"

Mother and Peter looked at me. I cleared my throat. "No. No, of course not. We were just . . . I was just wondering if you knew anyone in America."

There was a beat; then he said, "Why do you ask this?"

"Well, at the bar, when you went to the bathroom, I happened to see you . . . on the phone."

"You watch me?" he said, clearly distressed at the idea.

"No! No, it's just you were gone a long time, and we were worried about you. So I went to see if you were all right."

He seemed to accept this. It was several seconds before he realized that we were all still waiting for him to answer the question. He tapped his fork against the table a few times, looking down at the cloth. I wished I didn't feel like he was trying to come up with something. Finally, he looked at me.

"I have . . . I have . . ." He bit his lower lip. "I don't know the word in English."

"The word for what?"

Mother crooked her eye at me. "Darling, if he knew that he wouldn't be searching for the word."

"Maybe that interpreter—Bagnold—can help," Peter said.

"No!" James said loudly. "No! Please! I have . . . father . . . brother . . . son . . ."

"Your whole family is here?" I exclaimed.

"No," he replied with frustration. Then he drew an invisible line in the air with his index finger as he repeated, "Father . . . brother . . . son . . ."

For a moment we were at a loss, then Mother brightened. "Of course! You have a cousin here in the States?"

"Cousin! Yes!" He smiled with relief at identifying the proper term, but the smile was short-lived. "Not here . . . in Chicago. But here!" He waved his arms to encompass the entire United States. "I call him, tell him I am good."

"But you could have done that from here," I said.

The distress returned. "You are . . . very nice. But you are with Mr. Nelson."

"You mean we're with the CIA? Well, yes, but not entirely."

He once again appeared to be confused, for which I couldn't blame him.

"Never mind," said Mother, "Yes, we're with them."

"So what?" I said.

"Mr. Nelson must not know I do this."

"Why?" said Peter.

James struggled to put it into our language. "Mr. Nelson say no person must know where I am, for me to . . . to be safe. But I want my cousin to know I am good."

"Did you tell him where you are?" Peter asked.

"No, no, just that I am good."

"Ah," said Mother, "well, that explains that, doesn't it?"

She casually resumed eating, and after an uncomfortable pause, the rest of us did, too. I was surprised that Mother seemed so satisfied, because I certainly wasn't. James's explanation was plausible, but my feelings about him kept getting thrown into reverse, and it was going to take a little while for me to shift gears again. For his part, James hadn't exactly dived back into his meal with his usual gusto. He pushed the eggs around his plate with his fork before finally scooping up a bit of them and putting them in his mouth. In my present frame of mind it seemed to me that he was eating guiltily. Then again, he could've just been worried that we would tell Nelson what he'd done.

I watched Mother as she ate her eggs, raising her fork to her mouth with the steady rhythm of a well-trafficked automatic door. I got the feeling she wasn't quite as satisfied as I first thought.

I sighed inwardly. Nelson had been right: James's presence had severely disrupted our home life, if for no other reason than that we couldn't readily discuss our problems with each other while he was there. Especially since *he* was our problem. I suppose that would teach us to bring our work home.

Mother suddenly dropped her fork on her plate and said, "That was lovely, though I say it myself! I'll just start clearing up."

She rose from her chair with her plate in hand.

"I help," said James, starting to get up.

"Don't be silly!" Mother said pleasantly. "You haven't finished yet. Alex will help me."

"I will?" I said with surprise, a forkful of eggs poised at my lips.

She eyed me significantly. "You're done, aren't you?"

"I guess I am." I put down my fork and got up. I glanced at James and added, "Watching my figure, you know."

His big brown eyes blinked at me. "Huh?"

"I'll explain," said Peter with a smirk as I followed Mother across the room to the sink. She turned on the tap and started rinsing off her plate. Peter kept James talking while Mother and I had a conversation covered by the rushing water and whispered at such a low level that I could barely hear her myself.

"Bloody awkward with 'im always underfoot," she said.

"What do you think?"

"I don't know what to think."

"I don't either. I'd like to believe him, but . . ."

"But you were in a two-and-six over that phone call."

"Yeah. What should we do?"

She took my plate from me and I watched sadly as she scraped the remaining half of my breakfast into the garbage disposal. "I think . . . when Peter is leaving for work you should tell him to call home when he gets there."

"What?"

"Shh!" she said with a glance over her shoulder. "Just a little diversion." She switched off the tap and went back to the table.

Like any dutiful son, I obeyed my mother and gave my husband a big, wet kiss at the door, then whispered in his ear, "Call us the minute you get to work."

He drew back and looked me in the eye. "What? Why?"

"Uh . . . I don't know."

"Huh?"

"Just do it!" I whined softly.

He shrugged resignedly. "All right."

Soon after Peter left, Nelson, Dunning, and Bagnold arrived. They immediately went to work at the dining table with James, whose spirits dulled at the very sight of them. It was beginning to look like a board meeting that had gone on too long. Mother announced that she and I would be busy cleaning the second floor, which elicited a disinterested nod from the agents.

She led me upstairs to her room.

"You never said anything about cleaning today," I said as I sat on the cedar chest at the foot of her bed.

"We're not, darling. It's part of the diversion. I wanted to be up here when Peter calls so we can talk to him privately without arousing suspicion."

"To Peter?" I asked, totally baffled.

"No, you nit! To Larry!"

"You wanted Peter to call so you could talk to Nelson?"

"Yes!" she said happily, as if that explained it all. When she noticed my expression, she added, "Well, I couldn't very well ask him for a private chat in front of everyone. It would be noticed."

"Of course you could. You've already hauled him into the kitchen to give him a dressing down."

"Yes, in the kitchen. But this talk has to be somewhere where there's no possibility of our being overheard. And I can't very well say 'Larry, darling, could you pop up to the bedroom for a chat.' And we do need to talk to him."

"About what?"

"About what?" she repeated, giving it the 'wot' pronunciation of an incredulous Englishman. "About that phone call! Honestly, darling, sometimes you're dreadfully slow!"

"You mean you still think we should tell him about it?"

She folded her arms, and I had the feeling we were on the verge of an argument, even though I didn't really know how I felt about telling Nelson. "Of course. Why wouldn't we?"

"Didn't you believe James? About his cousin, I mean?"

She heaved a frustrated sigh. "It's hard to tell. The explanation wasn't exactly quick to his lips, but then nothing in English would be, would it?"

"If you don't know, then why bother Nelson with it? It'll only cause trouble for James."

"Larry said that if you took him out you should report anything unusual. I think his making a casual phone call from a gay bar falls into that category, don't you?"

"Yes, but . . ."

"But what?"

"Well," I said slowly, "it's just that I think James trusts us. If we do this we're bound to ruin that."

She pursed her lips. "He didn't trust us enough to tell us he wanted to make a call, did he?"

"There's trust and there's trust. I don't think he's in a position to put his full trust in anybody. And what he said is probably true—I mean, if he was really just calling his cousin—that he's afraid of getting in trouble with Nelson."

"I know," she said, sitting beside me and giving my leg a pat. "And it does go against the grain, the idea of telling Larry the truth. I mean . . . well, you know what I mean. But I do think we should do it. This could be very serious, and if it is, we should do something about it before we're in over our heads."

I shook my head sadly. "I just don't like the idea of betraying his trust."

Mother tilted her head to one side and displayed a sly smile. "Then we'll just have to be careful with Larry, won't we?"

I didn't have time to ask her what she meant by that, because we were interrupted by the ringing of the phone. Mother went to the Princess phone on her nightstand and picked up the receiver.

"Hello? . . . Oh, hello, darling. Thank you very much for calling." She started to hang up, then put the receiver back to her ear at the sound of Peter's voice. "What? No, I just needed the phone to ring. Bye, luv!" She replaced the receiver and turned to me. "Now, go down and tell Larry he has a phone call."

"Oh. Okay."

As I went down the hallway I mentally kicked myself for only just realizing why Mother had wanted Peter to call. I then mentally kicked her for allowing the government's penchant for needlessly sneaky tactics to rub off on her. I went halfway down the stairs and leaned over the banister. The four of them were huddled over a map, and James had his index finger firmly fixed on a spot in its center while he said something to Bagnold in Arabic.

"Nelson, there's someone on the phone for you," I said.

"Thank you," he replied after a pause. "I'll take it in the kitchen."

"No!" I exclaimed, causing the other three to look up. "I mean, you might want to take it up here. There's more privacy."

"Very well."

He followed me up the stairs and down the hall to Mother's room. She closed the door, giving it a little tap as if that would strengthen its seal.

"There isn't really anyone on the phone," she explained. "We just needed a word with you in private."

"Yes, I realized that when Alex told me I had a call," he said without inflection.

"What?" I said. "How did you know?"

"First, because no one knows I'm here, and second, because I carry a cell phone, and anyone who would be calling me has the number."

"Then why did you say you'd take it in—" My mouth fell open and I slowly dropped onto the cedar chest. "Oh, my God! You were putting me on."

"Why are you so shocked?"

"Because I didn't know you had a sense of humor!" I replied accusingly, as if he'd willfully been hiding it from me all these years.

He turned back to Mother. "You had something you wanted to discuss?"

"Well, I'm afraid it's rather delicate," she said, joining her hands together and touching them to her lips. "Do you think we can confide in you without you getting all shirty about it?"

"That depends on what it is."

"No, really, Nelson," I said. "We need to know if we can tell you something that you'll feel like doing something about without you doing something about it!"

"Um-hmm," he said, looking at me with a slightly puzzled frown. "Once again, that depends on what it is."

"You really never will give us an inch, will you?" I said disgustedly.

"Alex, please," said Mother. Then she looked at Nelson. "I suppose we're being unfair, but you know I feel a bit protective about that boy. He trusts us, and I don't want to hurt him."

"I see." He turned to me. "Does this have anything to do with your trip to the bar last night?"

"You followed us?" I said, rising from my seat.

He gave me a half-smile. "Someone did. Only to make sure you were all right."

"Oh, honestly!" said Mother. "There's nothing for it! You might as well tell him!"

Of course, at that point giving Nelson any information was the last thing I wanted to do, but I was in a bit of a quagmire, since basically that was what we were being paid to do. It went through my mind that I enjoyed being an unofficial pain in the ass to the CIA much more than I did being an official one.

"All right," I said. "While we were at the bar James made a phone call under the guise of going to the bathroom."

This confession was met by an anticlimactic silence.

"That's all?" Nelson said.

"Isn't that enough?" I replied, surprised by his nonreaction.

"Does he know that you saw him?"

"Yes, because I asked him who he was calling."

"You did?" Nelson said, in a hesitant way that betrayed some displeasure.

"It was Mother's idea!"

She wrinkled her nose at me. "Gallantry is completely foreign to you, isn't it?" She turned to Nelson. "It was worrying Alex, so I said the easiest way to find out who he was calling was to ask him."

"And what did he say?"

"Just that he was calling a cousin in America to let him know he was all right."

"Hmm."

"Does he have a cousin here?" Mother asked. She looked as perplexed by the way Nelson was acting as I did.

"It's possible."

"Does he know *anyone* in America?"

"Again, it's possible."

Mother's eyes narrowed. "I must say, Larry, I know you like to be a blank wall, but I am baffled that you don't seem more . . ."

"Interested," I offered.

"Thank you. Interested in this."

"Oh, I am," he replied.

"Do you intend to do something?"

"I don't see that there's anything to do," Nelson said in that infuriatingly smooth way of his that tells us nothing. "You asked him about it. He gave you his answer. I have no reason to believe his answer would be any different if I asked him."

"I'd like to say that's a relief," Mother replied, her tone clearly meant to belie her words.

"If that's all, I should get back to work."

"No, we didn't have anything more earth shattering than that," I snapped. I couldn't help it, I felt so let down. I didn't want James to be in trouble, but I was disappointed that Nelson didn't seem to think this was more important. "You're not the least bit surprised by this?"

"Not really," he replied. Then he added cryptically, "In fact, I wouldn't be surprised if he wanted to go back to the bar."

"What?" Mother and I exclaimed in unison.

Nelson gave me a smile so professionally sincere I marveled at the years of practice it must've taken to perfect it. "And if he does, I hope you'll take him."

With this he opened the bedroom door and went down the hall, leaving Mother and I gaping after him.

Mother interrupted the debriefing throughout the day again to ensure that James had the requisite rest periods, but this time she wasn't quite as imperious about it. In fact, she was downright tentative, which is very rare for her.

"It's like walking into a kennel, going in there," she said to me in low tones. "A kennel full of dogs you're not quite sure of, if you get my meaning."

"Yeah, I know," I said.

"And it doesn't help to know that the eager little black Labrador with the big sad eyes and the wagging tail may be the very one that'll turn on you."

"Yeah, I know," I repeated after a pause to worry about her sanity.

Mother and I had lunch with James in the kitchen. He kept up a surprising string of chatter about the previous night and what he thought of the freedom of Americans, particularly homosexual Americans. He seemed mindless of the strained response he was receiving from us. Mother watched him with cautious interest, her peerless scrutiny trying to divine whether or not he was genuine. We were both waiting for the same thing while hoping it wouldn't happen. When lunch was over and James had gone back to work with the agents without mentioning the bar, we were still too apprehensive to be relieved.

"We still have another meal to get through," Mother said as we washed the lunch dishes.

"And another evening," I added.

"Good job he's leaving tomorrow. I do feel for the boy, but honestly! I'd like to think Larry's wrong, but his attitude this morning didn't exactly inspire confidence, did it?"

"I hate to say I told you so—"

She cut me off. "Oh, no you don't!"

I ignored her. "—but didn't I say from the start that I thought Nelson was up to something?"

"Yes, you did, darling," she replied in her placating-the-child tone as she handed me a plate to dry. "You'll be able to take that knowledge to your grave."

"I hope not!"

While Peter changed after work that evening, I filled him in on what had transpired with Nelson, and what the rest of the day had been like.

"James never asked about going back to the bar?" Peter asked as he buttoned his jeans.

"Not a word. The day's not over yet, though."

He silently donned a purple T-shirt, tucked it into his pants, then shook his head. "I knew it! I knew Nelson had something up his sleeve."

"If I remember correctly, *I* was the one who knew it. I mean, not to put too fine a point on it, but every time we get involved in one of these cases, you and Mother always throw it up at me that I was the one who got us into it. I just want it on the record that this time *I* was the one reluctant to do it, and *you* were the one who thought we should go ahead."

He smiled at me. "It's duly noted." His tone was so exactly like Mother's had been earlier that I suddenly realized with a sinking feeling that the old adage is true: men really do marry their mothers.

"Of course," he added as we headed down the hallway, "the whole situation never would've come up if you hadn't gotten us involved with the CIA in the first place."

Following behind him, I swung back with my palm and gave him a stinging slap on the ass. He burst out laughing.

Dinner was even more strained than lunch had been. Listening to Mother carrying on polite conversation with a potential enemy spy was like watching a balloon being slowly overinflated and waiting for it to burst. When the tension got to be too much for her, she decided to stick a pin in the balloon herself.

"So," she said broadly, "what do you boys intend to do this evening?"

"I don't know," I said to my plate. "I haven't given it any thought."

"I hope—" James started tentatively, then broke off in an apparent loss for words. Mother, Peter, and I froze with forks halfway to our mouths and watched him. He tried again. "I hope . . . we could go back to bar."

"To Charlene's?" said Peter.

"Yes."

"There's a lot of gay bars in Chicago," I said carefully. "Why don't we try a different one?"

"I like this one," he replied eagerly.

"There's a whole world out there. You shouldn't limit yourself to one place."

He blinked his big brown eyes at me. "I tell Bob I be back."

"You did?"

He nodded. "He ask if he see me again. I say I come back tonight . . . I try to."

Mother, Peter, and I looked at each other. We all seemed equally disheartened.

"Okay," I said at last. "Fine. We'll take you there, then."

A cloud of concern crossed James's face. "This is all right?"

"Oh, yes! Of course!" I tried to sound jaunty.

Mother told us that we would have to take a cab to the bar because she had promised to take our neighbor Mattie to pick up something at some store that evening, but I barely heard her. I was trying to convince myself that this was another innocent action on James's part, and that he wanted to go back to the bar purely out of the desire to repeat an enjoyable experience. But I couldn't get myself to believe it. Nelson had called this one, so it now seemed clear that James was really up to something—and so was Nelson.

We left for the bar at a quarter to eight, with Mother waving us off from the front door: only this time she looked like a mother who's only half-witted child was going off to war and could be guaranteed never to return.

Finding a cab was no problem since Fullerton, the street on which our town house is located, is a major thoroughfare. Even in the dead of night with no visible traffic, all you have to do is walk to the curb and raise your hand and a cab will materialize out of nowhere.

On the way to the bar James kept himself plastered to the side window like a golden retriever watching the world go by. Peter sat silently beside me with his jaw set like a steel trap and his right leg solidly pressed against mine. None of us spoke. I had twisted this situation around in my mind until I could barely think. At that point the only thing going through my head was that damned marching music from the old *Flash Gordon* serials: the music that played while soldiers marched endlessly through caves.

As we got out of the cab in front of the bar, I reminded myself that Nelson really wouldn't ever purposely put us in danger. Purposely. And I reminded myself that he was having us watched, so we'd have backup (another word that stuck in my throat, given the dire situations it's used in in the movies). And I reminded myself that this was a crowded public place, so it didn't seem there was a lot that *could* happen. Of course, if I'd been able to share these thoughts with Peter, he would have accused me of having a very convenient memory. I sighed and opened the door. Peter and James followed me in.

A sinister haze hung in the air of the bar. Actually, it was the usual thick cloud of cigarette smoke; it just seemed sinister under the circumstances. It's amazing how a potential government sting can alter your perception: the people on the dance floor were gyrating with their usual fervor, but to me they appeared to undulate like the ripples in hot air, and the music took on a hallucinatory echo. The people scattered around the small tables didn't seem quite as Aryan as usual: they all looked dark and shifty-eyed and appeared to be taking special notice of our entrance. It was like being in a Middle Eastern production of *Cabaret*.

There were no stools available at the bar, so we were forced to stand grouped at the end of it, which left me feeling out in the open despite the crowd. James was very interested in the dancers and the other patrons, but it didn't seem like the naive awe he'd shown the night before. He was looking for someone. I could feel it. Of course, that someone could've just been Bob.

When Ernie had a second, he came to the end of the bar.

"Two nights in a row!" he said. "Where's that cutie pie of yours?"

"Right here," I said, motioning to James's back.

James turned around and Ernie shot him a lascivious grin. "Hi there."

"Hi," James replied.

"Three beers?" Ernie asked me.

"Yep."

The anonymous technopop music that had been blaring since we came in subsided, segueing into "Smooth Operator." The colored lights that speckled the dancers slowed in accompaniment. Once Ernie returned with the beers, Peter paid him and I handed a bottle to James, who drank half of it down in one gulp as he continued to scan the crowd. Even with his vigilance, I saw Bob approaching before he did. If I hadn't been so nervous, I would've smiled: Bob had gotten dressed up for his new friend. He was wearing white pants and white shirt, over which he sported a loose-fitting fringed vest. He looked like a loaf of Wonder bread in a suede sheath.

"Hi," he said over the music. "You're back!"

"Yes. Hello," James replied.

Bob jockeyed for position at the bar and called to Ernie for a beer. In the time it took him to get served, the music changed again. This time is was "Wanna Be Startin' Somethin'," a song that would've tap-danced on my last exposed nerve in the best situation, but then and there it seemed uncomfortably appropriate. The colored lights sprang back to life, picking up speed along with everyone on the crowded dance floor. In a matter of seconds, the entire bar had become a swirling mass of ear-shattering noise and movement.

I heard Bob yell, "I didn't think you would make it!"

James said, "Yes," and downed the rest of his beer.

It was then that I noticed the man who had just come in. He had short black hair and dark tan skin. He was wearing a black shirt and blue jeans under an unbuttoned, calf-length overcoat. But it wasn't his appearance that caught my eye, it was that he was heading in a beeline from the front door across the dance floor, straight for James. Without a pause in their gyrating, the dancers parted to let him pass. I nudged Peter and motioned to the stranger.

James had been giving most of his attention to Bob and was

the last of our trio to notice the new arrival. When he did, he tensed up noticeably, exactly as he did when faced with the agents at our house.

Bob finally turned to see what James was looking at, and stepped back in surprise when the stranger wedged himself purposefully between them without giving Bob a glance.

The man said something to James, presumably in Arabic, and James answered in such a halting fashion he sounded almost as if his command of his native tongue was as bad as his English.

Bob slunk back a few steps, apparently realizing that he'd been effectively cut out. But he continued to pay attention from a discreet distance, looking for any sign that he could insinuate himself back into James's attention. If I could've spared the energy, I would've felt sorry for him.

James and the newcomer continued to speak to each other in a manner I can only describe as fervent. Then the stranger glanced over James's shoulder toward the hall to the bathroom. He said something else; then, with a sidelong look at me, James turned and started for the doorway.

"Oh, Jesus!" I said to Peter. "What do we do?"

To my complete surprise, I heard Ernie yell "Hey!" above the din. He plunged halfway across the bar between two of the seated patrons, caught the stranger by the shoulders, and yanked him backwards.

It was then that in my head all sound stopped and everything went into slow motion. I was startled by the sudden attack, but not so startled that I failed to see that Bob was pulling a gun out of his vest. For reasons I'll never understand, I suddenly had an image of James the way he'd been when I'd watched him napping, all curled up in fetal position, and the words "tuck and roll" flashed through my brain. Without thinking, I dropped to the floor as I grabbed my knees, and rolled sideways toward Bob like a badly lopsided human bowling ball. Though he was only a few feet away, I managed to hit his legs with enough force that he flipped forward.

Then all hell broke loose.

I came to rest at the edge of the dance floor, but not before nailing two of the dancers in a seven-ten split. I had sent Bob sprawling into one of the bar stools from which he was having some difficulty extricating himself. Since he appeared to have lost his gun, I was stunned when I heard shots. Screams rang out as the crowd broke into a stampede, sending tables, bottles, and glasses shattering onto the floor. And still the shots continued. It was a matter of seconds before I realized where they were coming from: the stranger was on top of the bar, firing off to his right while people fled in all directions.

In the midst of the pandemonium, the stranger leapt from the bar and started for the back hallway. But before he reached the doorway, Bob rolled out onto the floor across the broken glass. He'd recovered his gun and was holding it in his outstretched right hand. Without a word, he opened fire.

The stranger convulsed, his back arching, then wheeled around, wavering like a drunk. He pointed his gun down at his assailant, but before he could pull the trigger, he froze for a split second, then crumpled to the floor.

Bob heaved a sigh of relief. After a moment, he turned his face to me.

"I hope you realize what you've done," he said.

James was nowhere in sight.

SIX

Peter!" I yelled. "Peter! Where are you?"

"Over here." His voice came from behind an overturned table about three feet from the doorway. His tone had that look-what-you've-gotten-us-into-now tinge to it. I was going to have to speak to him about that again. He rolled the table aside and added, "I'm all right."

Bob had gotten up and was brushing the loose glass from his clothes. Suddenly he looked up and said, "Where's James? Where is he?"

"He went that way," said Peter, motioning to the doorway.

"Stay here!" Bob commanded as he set off after him.

"Wait a minute!" I cried, jumping to my feet. "Don't you—"

"I'm FBI, you idiot!" he called over his shoulder as he disappeared.

I dropped my hands to my sides and sighed disgustedly. "Of course you are." Then I went over to Peter and helped him up. "You sure you're all right?"

"Oh, I'm just dandy!"

The colored lights were still cascading around the room, sparkling off the shards of glass and rippling across the body of the dead stranger. The music continued to pulsate, echoing hollowly in the empty room.

"Well, that's the fastest we've ever cleared out a bar," I said. "What the hell happened to James?"

Peter started to brush off his pants. "When the shooting started, I yelled 'Run!' and he took off. I wasn't as quick. I dove behind a table."

The music shifted from one song to the next, and during the momentary lull we heard a groan from behind the bar. We ran back there and found Ernie sitting with his back uncomfortably propped against a row of bottles. His hand was pressed against his right temple, and a thin stream of blood ran from beneath it.

"Ernie!" I said. "You're hurt!"

"No shit!" he replied, slewing his eyes at me. "Turn that fucking music off, will you?"

The receiver was on a shelf about four feet above his head. Peter leaned over and pressed the power button, and a blissful silence fell on the place.

"Were you shot?" I asked anxiously.

"No, that bastard just cracked me on the head." He removed his hand from his temple and looked at his palm, then let out a satisfied grunt. Apparently he thought there was enough blood to warrant the pain. The gash in his head wasn't deep, but it was impressive in its ugliness.

Peter climbed around us to Ernie's other side and we each grabbed one of his arms, hauling him up.

"What happened?" I asked. "What made you grab that guy?"

"He had a gun!" said Ernie.

"I didn't see one."

"I just saw a flash of it, for a second. I've had all kinds of things happen in here. I keep my eyes open. I didn't like the way he was talking to that friend of yours, so I watched him. When he started for the bathroom, his coat opened a little and I saw it, the gun."

"God, you sure took a chance," Peter said with admiration.

"I wasn't gonna let him hurt that kid, and he looked like he was walking him off to an execution. Only thing is, when I pulled him up on the bar, he nailed me with a beer bottle. Did he get away?"

"James?"

"No, the motherfucker with the gun."

"Uh, no—he's over there on the dance floor," I said. "Only he's not dancing."

Ernie looked over to where I was pointing, and instead of the shock I expected, he looked angry. "Oh, shit! A shooting! Do you know how much trouble that's going to cause?"

"We have a pretty good idea," said Peter.

Ernie put a palm back to his head, and with his other hand switched off the colored lights and turned on the work lights. It was then that we saw Agent Nelson. He was standing by the door.

"It looks like you've had some excitement," he said. "What happened?"

"The gunfight at Charlene's Corral," I intoned.

"Where's James?"

"You see those bullet holes over by that doorway? He went thataway. And your partner went after him."

"Fredrichs is not my partner," Nelson replied with his usual lack of emotion. He looked down at the dead man. "And this?"

"I assume that belongs to you, too."

Nelson glanced down at the prostrate gunman. "I don't know this one."

"What the fuck is going on?" Ernie said from behind his palm.

"Good question," said Peter, who looked as irritated as he usually does when he's been shot at.

We could already hear sirens approaching. Nelson ignored Ernie's question. "I'll handle the police. Your friend Frank O'Neil is still a commander, isn't he?"

"Yes," I replied. Frank was an ex-boyfriend of Mother's, and he had remained smitten long after the thrill was gone, a fact that had helped us out on the numerous occasions we'd found ourselves in a spot of trouble—which was a very mild way of describing our current situation.

Nelson knelt by the body and went through its pockets in a quick and efficient manner, but found nothing. While he was doing this, "Bob"—who I would now have to think of as Agent Fredrichs—returned through the hallway.

"He got away," he said to Nelson without preamble. "Through a window in the bathroom, out the side of the building. I couldn't find him. He got away thanks to this . . . guy of yours!"

"Really?" Nelson said, rising. For the second time since this affair had begun, I got the feeling he was trying not to smile.

"He knocked me over!" Fredrichs said angrily.

"You pulled a gun!" I exclaimed. "How the hell was I supposed to know you were an agent?"

"I was trying to save James!"

"And endangering everybody else? If you were trying to save him, why didn't you follow them to the back where there were fewer people?"

He jerked his thumb at Ernie. "Because Rambo here jumped him and he went for his gun. If you hadn't interfered—"

"If I hadn't stopped you, you would've had a shootout in the middle of the crowd!"

He replied with a snort. I had heard the term "acceptable losses" applied to government covert activities where innocent lives may be lost. From Fredrichs's contemptuous tone I had a feeling the term was relative when it came to the patrons of Charlene's.

"Gentlemen," Nelson said with a glance at Ernie, "I think we should continue this later."

Nelson sought to expedite matters by calling Frank on his cell phone. He asked me for the number and I was all too happy to supply it, figuring we could use all the help we could get. And Nelson was right to do it, because the first cops to arrive on the scene were a pair of uniformed officers, closely followed by another pair, all of whom greeted Nelson's announcement of being with the CIA with the blank-faced skepticism that the lower ranks sometimes fall into when faced with a situation where they know they're out of their depth. They clearly thought he was trying to put something over on them, and stared at his ID as if they suspected he'd had it knocked up at a novelty shop.

But Nelson's bearing makes him a hard person to doubt, especially when he told them that Commander Frank O'Neil was on the way. So they focused their attention on Ernie, with whom they already seemed familiar.

When Frank arrived about fifteen minutes later, he looked anything but happy. His square jaw was slightly askew as he approached us.

"Just once," he said, "just once I'd like to see you guys when you're not standing over a dead body."

"It's not my fault this time!" I said, tilting my head slightly in Peter's direction.

"I can guess who's responsible," Frank replied, eyeing Nelson with displeasure. I'm not sure if his resentment toward Nelson was because he blamed Nelson for continually getting us into danger, or because he would be jealous of any reasonably attractive man who comes within pecking distance of Mother. Or maybe it's just the natural animosity of the police for federal agents.

"Commander, thank you for getting here so quickly. Now let me fill you in," Nelson said, putting a hand on Frank's arm and smoothly guiding him away from us.

"I'd love to hear that explanation," I whispered to Peter.

"Why? He's probably telling Frank less than we know."

"Well, that's going to change soon," I said with determination.

It was almost two hours before we got home, escorted by Nelson and followed by Fredrichs. Mother greeted us with a narrowed glare that gave me the feeling she already knew something was terribly wrong. Of course, the fact that we were there with two agents and without James was probably a dead giveaway.

"Where's James?" she demanded as she closed the door after us.

"He escaped," said Fredrichs, "thanks to your son."

She eyed him coldly. "And you are . . . ?"

"Agent Robert Fredrichs. FBI."

She turned to Nelson with a raised eyebrow. "The two agencies working together? This must be worse than I thought."

"It *is* worse than we thought!" I said. "We were shot at!"

"What?"

"And by the way," I said to Peter, "remember when you said that we probably wouldn't get shot at for getting involved in this?"

He folded his arms across his chest. "You've just used up the number of times you get to say 'I told you so' on this case, all right?"

"Okay," I said sheepishly. It's not often he takes that tone with me, so I know it means I'm pushing the limit.

"You said this nonsense wouldn't be dangerous!" Mother said to Nelson.

"I didn't think it would be," he replied placidly.

"And now James is lost?"

"Lost!" Fredrichs exclaimed. "Huh! He escaped! He ran away!"

"Of course he ran away," I said loudly. "Somebody was shooting at him!"

"And while we're on the subject, what do you mean by 'He escaped'? He wasn't a prisoner!" said Mother sharply.

That effectively burst the blustering FBI agent's bubble.

Nelson was the one to break the silence that followed. "I believe what Agent Fredrichs means is that we don't know where James has gone."

"But you must have some idea," said Mother.

"None at all."

She sighed. "Larry, you must know who James called last night!"

"How would he know that?" I asked.

"The records for the pay phone," Nelson replied.

"But we only told you about that this morning." He merely looked at me without saying a word. It was several seconds before it dawned on me. "Oh, of course! You already knew about the call. Last night. From your pal Bob." Something else hit me—something I liked even less. I turned to Fredrichs. "By the way, are you really a faggot or do you just play one on TV?"

"I've been doing my job," he spat back, red-faced.

I looked to Nelson. "Oh, he's an agent, all right! Is there *nothing* you people won't do?"

"When you went into the bar last night, Agent Fredrichs followed. We wanted to keep an eye on you."

"Bob here kept more than an eye on James." I turned to Fredrichs. "What was that you were doing on the dance floor? A full-body search?"

"I was doing my job," he replied through gritted teeth.

"You were enjoying your job."

"Alex, please," said Mother.

"We have more important things to talk about than this," Nelson said. Fredrichs's head snapped in Nelson's direction. Apparently he felt Nelson was giving some veiled credence to what I was implying.

"Such as?" I asked.

"We need to figure out where James has gone."

Mother bristled. "How would we know?"

"You've spent three evenings with him. Has he ever said anything that would give us an indication of where he might have gone?"

"Like what?" Peter asked.

"Like mentioning knowing someone or someplace here?"

"Other than the cousin he said he called? No," I said. "And the only time he mentioned any locations was his first night here. He said he heard about New York and California."

"Hmm. That doesn't give us much to go on."

"Why do you need anything to go on?" I said. "You have the phone records. You know who James called, so you really haven't lost him. He'll probably go to whoever it was, won't he?"

"I doubt that very much," Nelson said.

"Why?"

"Oh, Christ!" said Peter, slapping his forehead.

"What is it?"

"That phone call," Nelson explained, "resulted in someone being sent to kill him."

"Larry, I think it's time you explain to us what this is *really* all about, don't you?" Mother said sternly. "It doesn't have anything to do with chemical weapons, does it."

"If we may sit down?" he said.

Mother sighed and motioned Nelson and Fredrichs to the couch. The three of us then pulled up chairs opposite them, forming a very tense little caucus.

"It does have something to do with chemical weapons," said Nelson. "Peripherally. What I told you was true. James did approach the UN team, and he did make the offer that I told you about."

"But there's much more to it than that," said Peter.

There was a beat before Nelson continued. "There was information that we previously believed you didn't need to know."

"Nelson! We were just in a shootout!" I said hotly.

"We didn't believe the information was relevant to your participation in the matter. Now, of course, things have changed."

"I don't see that anything's changed," Fredrichs protested. "They still don't need to know!"

Nelson didn't even glance at him.

"So what is it? Who is James?" I asked.

"Everything I told you at the outset is true. What I didn't tell you was that James was known to us *before* he approached the team about defecting."

Peter was already shaking his head. "I know I'm not going to like this . . ."

"We knew of him because he was a connection—not a very clear one—to a certain splinter group that we're interested in."

"A splinter group," Peter said flatly.

"A group called the Jihad Ahmad. Otherwise know as the Red Jihad."

My mouth fell open. "Jihad? Jihad? Are you telling us it's a terrorist group?"

"Yes."

I was on my feet in a flash. "James is a terrorist? You had us baby-sitting a terrorist?"

"Please," Nelson said calmly with a single wave at my chair. I dropped back onto it, but could feel steam coming from my ears. Peter was sitting beside me with his arms still folded and his lips flat, glaring at the agents with disdain. Mother looked curiously unmoved by this revelation. She was next to speak.

"I take it that you are unsure of exactly what James is."

"He could be exactly what he says: a young man who, because of his sexuality, wanted to defect. But he has relatives and friends who are known members of the Red Jihad. It's a connection, but we don't know how strong of one."

"You don't know?" I echoed with my mouth still gaping.

"No."

Fredrichs piped up: "This is covert information we're talking about. It's not like they're listed in the phone book under Terrorists!"

"Well, if he might be a terrorist, why would you let him into this country?"

"We have no concrete information that he is an active member of the jihad," Nelson replied.

"But still—"

"Nor did we know why one of its members would want to come here."

"But you don't know that he's—"

Nelson cut me off again. "We know that James does have a cousin, a cousin who is definitely a member of the Red Jihad. From our information, this cousin disappeared from Iraq several months ago. We suspect that he's come here, but we haven't been able to trace him. When James approached us about coming here, his motives may have been entirely innocent, but the fact that he has a close relative in the jihad made his request both welcome and suspect."

"Well, then why—" I broke off again.

Nelson stared at me impassively. I helplessly looked to Peter, whose jaw had squared and was set so hard I thought his teeth would crack. "You *wanted* him to come here, didn't you!" he said.

"We wanted to identify any of the Red Jihad that may be here, and know if they were planning anything."

"But you don't even know if James is actually a member!" I said.

"That's not the point, is it?" said Peter without removing his eyes from Nelson.

"What do you mean?" I asked.

"Finding out if James is a member of this crackpot organization of yours, that's not what really matters. It's his connections."

"What?" I still wasn't getting it.

He turned to me. "They know that he knows people in the group, and they wanted to find out who he would contact once he was here. It was a fishing expedition."

"You were using him!" I said in disbelief, although why I would find this any harder to believe than anything else the government has done in our own direct experience is beyond me.

"It's important that we find that out!" Fredrichs said defensively. He certainly had none of Nelson's stoicism. "If they're here, there can only be one reason."

"We have information that the Red Jihad may be planning a series of attacks in the U.S., but we don't know who they are or what they plan to do. It's imperative that we find them."

"You never did think he knew anything about chemical weapons, did you?" Mother asked accusingly.

"It was a possibility," Nelson replied with a shrug.

"If you didn't think that he knew, why go through all this debriefing business?"

"We had to go through the motions! He had to think we believed him," Fredrichs said, his tone implying we were fools for not realizing this.

"But why the elaborate charade?" said Mother. "He wanted asylum. Why not simply tell him that you would give him that in exchange for information about this jihad . . . assuming honesty is not completely foreign to you?"

"He's not an idiot," said Fredrichs. "He knows that betraying them would be to sign his death warrant."

Mother's spine stiffened. "It would appear that tricking him into betraying them has the same effect!"

I rose, shaking my head. "I don't believe this! A terrorist group! And you told us this wouldn't be dangerous!"

"I had no reason to believe it would be," said Nelson.

I screwed my face up. "For Christ's sake, Nelson! The Red Jihad even *sounds* threatening!"

He leaned forward, resting his elbows on his thighs. "Alex, we planned to have him here for three days. In a few months he would have been totally free of contact with the government."

"He would have?" Peter broke in skeptically.

"Theoretically," Nelson replied after a telling pause. He looked back to me. "Since he was staring into the face of freedom, we doubted very much that he would make any move so soon. There was no need for him to do that we know of. And the fact that he did make a move so soon is suggestive in itself."

"Wait a minute," I said to Fredrichs. "You went back there while James was making his call. Didn't you hear what he said?"

"The only place I could listen was from inside the john. I went in and stayed by the door, but there was too much noise. I couldn't hear him."

"You didn't try very hard. You came out before he got off the phone!"

"It wasn't the type of john where you could loiter without calling attention to yourself," he said defensively.

"I would think you would like that kind of attention."

"Look, you—"

"Don't bother," I said, then turned on Nelson. "Did you ever take into consideration the potential danger you were putting us in?"

"As I said, we didn't think there'd be any danger in this part of the process. I fully believed that his three days here would be . . ." His voice trailed off as he searched for the right words.

"Just part of the sham?" said Mother.

"I was going to say 'uneventful.' And a necessary delay. But we have had someone watching your house ever since James has been here, and following you when you took him out. I never believed there was any danger. There was no reason for James to harm you."

"But why did you want him with us in the first place, as opposed to with someone more experienced?" I asked.

"For the reasons I gave you at the outset."

I swear to God I could *feel* him thinking "I haven't lied to you." I wish he'd said it out loud. As angry as I was, I would've loved to debate whether or not lying and failing to tell the truth were the same thing.

Peter said, "Well, why didn't you tell us all of this to begin with?"

"Because you didn't really need to know. There didn't seem any sense in worrying you needlessly."

"Worry us?" Mother said. "Why would having a terrorist around the 'ouse worry us? We've entertained far worse than that!"

Nelson allowed enough of a pause to let her know he'd gotten her meaning. As he rose, he said, "Now that you've been filled in, we'll be going."

"Just a minute!" I said. "What about that guy that tried to kill James? Who was he?"

"We don't know."

"What will you do now that James has disappeared?" Mother asked.

"Find him!" Fredrichs said grimly. "I think it's clear now that he's a member of the Red Jihad. We might not have known it before, but we know it now."

"How on earth do you figure that?" Mother asked incredulously. "Didn't they just try to kill him?"

"That's right," he said, nodding his head significantly. "They did."

"Well?"

"Why else do you think they would try to kill him? A call to this so-called cousin of his is answered by a hit man. They wouldn't do that for nothing. They have to think he's betrayed them somehow."

"Why would they think that?" said Peter. "Even James doesn't know why he's really here."

"Who the hell knows! Maybe he's done something else to piss them off. It's easy enough to do! To get a death warrant so fast, he has to be one of them. One thing we know is, he ran away. If he wanted protection from them, he could've come to us."

"He ran because he was being shot at! He's already seen the kind of protection you can give him," I said.

"Do you feel that way?" Mother said to Nelson.

"My attitude is more wait-and-see. Of course, our first priority is to find James. We'll be searching for him, along with Fredrich's people. I've already talked to your friend Commander O'Neil, so the police are looking for him as well. All the bases will be covered."

"So you're looking for him and the police are looking for him? What about these Red Jihad fellows?" "Red Jihad fellows" is one of those phrases that simply has to be heard with a British accent to be believed.

"What about them?" Fredrichs snapped.

"Won't they be looking for him?"

"I don't know," said Nelson.

"I just wondered because if they are, mightn't they come here?"

"I don't think that would happen," said Nelson. "Since James told whoever he called to meet him at the bar, I think it's unlikely that he told them where he was staying. But I do intend to keep your house under surveillance for a while, just in case."

"Exactly what kind of surveillance?" Mother asked, her forehead creased with concern.

"We'll have a man in a car out front, and one out back."

"I see. Well, it's a comfort to know that at least."

Peter and I exchanged glances, and he looked as perplexed as I was. It wasn't like Mother to express concern to Nelson about our safety. Especially with so much sincerity.

The agents took their leave of us, and although they left practically side by side Nelson managed to keep himself aloof from Fredrichs, almost as if he were encased in one of those impenetrable blisters that protected the Martian spaceships in *The War of the Worlds.*

As Mother closed the door after them, I said, "Are you really that worried that those guys will come here?"

"The Red Jihad?" she replied incredulously. "Of course not!"

She started back toward the kitchen and Peter and I trailed after her.

"Then why were you so concerned about having someone watch the house?"

"I just wanted to know if they were doing it. He didn't tell us before that they were watching the house, and I simply had to know if they were still planning to do it."

She'd reached the far end of the kitchen and went directly to the door at the back of the pantry.

"Where are you going?" I asked with surprise.

"To the basement."

"Why?"

She pushed open the door, glanced over her shoulder, and said, "Come 'ead."

We followed her down the wooden stairs and I was surprised to find she'd left the lights on down there. I was even more surprised that the tiny black-and-white television set we normally kept in the kitchen was sitting on the dryer, the picture flickering and the sound turned off. The set was facing an old couch we'd long since retired to a corner of the basement. The room appeared to be empty.

"Were you watching television down here?" I asked, completely perplexed.

"Of course not!" she said. Then she called out, "You can come out now. We're alone."

There was a long pause, then someone very tentatively peeked out from behind the couch.

It was James.

SEVEN

I am sorry," he said fearfully. "I hear someone coming. I think they search for me."

I scraped my teeth up from the floor and looked at Mother. "What's he doing here?"

"Hiding."

"I can see *that*!" I said, gritting my teeth. "I mean, how did he get here?"

"In a taxi. I had to pay for it. He just showed up at the door about an hour after you went out. And I might add, darling, that when I send you out with a guest I do expect you to stay with him."

"I wasn't the one who left!"

"You weren't the one getting shot at," said Peter.

"I swear to God I'm going to kill you before this is over!" I turned back to Mother. "He took a taxi? How in the hell did he know how to do that?"

James answered. "I have been in taxis since I come here. I know you get in and say address."

"You remembered our address?"

He pulled a small white rectangle from the pocket of his pants. "You give me card with address on it."

"He's resourceful, I'll say that for him," Mother said with a degree of admiration.

"A little too resourceful, if you ask me! How could you let a terrorist in here?"

"I didn't know he was a terrorist then!" She caught herself and looked to James, who had climbed out onto the couch. "Oh, I'm so sorry, luv. I didn't mean it that way." She turned back to me. "I didn't know of the connection then."

"Well, you do now! Why didn't you turn him over to Nelson? How could you take a risk like this?"

"I don't think I'm taking a risk."

"After what happened at the bar? And after what Nelson and Fredrichs said? They knew—"

"I don't believe they really know anything. All Larry did was make it rather obvious he expected *something* to happen at the bar, but surely nothing so dramatic." I started to protest again, but she cut me off firmly. "Whatever you may think of Larry, I don't think he'd ever purposely put us in danger. We're the ones that do that."

"Then why did he tell us to take James back to the bar?"

"Probably he thought at worst James might make another phone call, that's all. And he wanted to give him the opportunity. I certainly don't think he believed someone would show up and try to kill him!"

"How can you say that after the way Nelson held out on us?"

"Because if he *had* thought something big was going to happen, don't you think he would've had more agents there?"

This stopped me. "I hadn't thought of that."

"You see, darling, they were expecting no more than a phone call. Larry sent that Agent Fredrichs in to watch and Larry came along and waited outside, more as a just-in-case measure than anything else."

"Well, now you know what happened! Doesn't that tell you something?"

"It doesn't tell me he's a terrorist."

"I am not one," James whimpered.

"Excuse us a minute," I said to him, then turned back to Mother. "You heard what Nelson said!"

"Darling, the words 'Arab' and 'terrorist' do not necessarily go together."

"Mother, if the password was 'terrorist,' the first clue would be 'Arab'!"

She narrowed her eyes at me. Had I been rational at the time I would've realized it was a bad sign. "You're going by what you've seen on television, and I won't have it! You know the danger of labeling a group of people!"

Her meaning wasn't lost on me. "Yes, but this goes beyond that. Nelson says there's a connection."

"But they don't know what it is!"

I was getting increasingly frustrated. Mother does have her little fads, but rarely ones that involve terrorists. "What makes you so sure he's innocent?"

She rolled her eyes. "Alex, he was hiding behind the couch!"

I looked over at James, who was sitting there staring at us with those big, dark Bambi eyes of his. He looked like he was going to cry.

"Yeah. That does seem kind of . . . kind of . . ."

"Yes, it does," said Mother.

"Then who did he call from the bar?"

"I've asked him about that. I think I'll let him tell it."

The three of us crossed the room to James. His eyes were still wide and his face was drawn. His hands were in his lap, fingers flexing together so fiercely I was surprised his knuckles didn't snap. He looked absolutely terrified. For the first time since he'd made that damned phone call, I felt sorry for him. One more about-face and I was going to run into myself.

Mother sat down next to him. Peter switched off the television and then he and I leaned against the dryer.

"Well?" I asked. "What's going on?"

He looked up at me and blinked. "I do not know."

I sighed with frustration, throwing my hands up in the air.

Peter said, "Alex, give him a break."

"I really do not know," James said. He was silent for a very long time, and was having trouble looking any of us in the eye. Finally, he looked down at his hands and said, "I lie to you."

"Aha!" I exclaimed.

"Alex . . ." Mother and Peter said in unison. Mother added, "Go on, James."

He cleared his throat. "I do not know where are chemical weapons. I lie."

"What have you been telling them for the past three days?" I asked.

"I give them locations. I know some. Little. Places they may be. Places they may . . ." He struggled for a moment, then found the tense he was looking for. "Places they may . . . have been. I only think maybe. The same as everyone. I know your people want to know this, so I tell them I know. Please understand. I have to leave my country. I do not know other way. So I tell them I know this."

If I hadn't been so astonished I would've laughed. Both sides were lying to the other and going through what Mother had aptly termed an elaborate charade to keep the farce going. The only difference between them was that Nelson and his crew had successfully deceived James, while he had never really fooled them.

I took a deep breath. "Well, if it makes you feel any better, they never did think you knew where the weapons were."

"What is this?" he said, his eyes growing even wider.

Peter explained. "They brought you here to use you. They were using you to flush out the Red Jihad."

"What?" he cried, bolting from the couch to a full standing position. It was so unexpected that all three of us flinched. The fear on his face before was nothing to the sheer panic it showed now. He breathed heavily, almost panting, and spoke fast and low. "The Jihad Ahmad? Why they think I can tell them about this?"

"It's a little late for that, don't you think?" said Mother.

James looked at her questioningly, but her meaning was clear even in a second language.

"I know people in the jihad," he said, "but I do not become one. You please believe me!"

"I do believe you, James," she said firmly.

"If they think I betray them, they will kill me!"

"They've already tried!" I said with a heavy sigh. I didn't know whether or not I could believe his ignorance of this.

"James," said Peter, "who was it you really called from the bar?"

"I call my cousin, like I say."

"What did you tell him?"

"Just what I tell you: that I am in United States and that I am good."

"Wait a minute! How did you even know his number?"

"My brother give it to me."

"So you told your brother that you were defecting?"

"Yes," he said guiltily. "I know I will not see them again, my family. So I tell them. Only those close. My brother give me the number and say to tell my cousin all is well." There was a pause, and his expression filled with emotion. "The sound of him . . . hearing him . . ." His lower lip began to tremble, and I could well understand why. He'd left everything he'd known and found himself in a very strange new world.

"I imagine hearing a familiar voice was rather like a tonic," said Mother.

"So you told him you wanted to see him?" I asked.

"No! No. He ask where I am, but I do not tell him I stay with you. I tell him if he wants to contact me, I try to be at the bar tonight."

"Why would he want to contact you?"

"I do not know why. Or how. I do not know where he is."

"What is the phone number?"

He pulled a slip of paper from his pocket and handed it to me. It was badly stained and wrinkled, but the numbers were still legible. "The area code is for New York."

"It is possible to come here so quickly from there?" he asked.

"Yes, but why would he need to?"

"I do not know," he answered helplessly.

"You could've just told him to come here to the house, you know. That would've been much easier."

"No! Because no one must know. Mr. Nelson . . . no one!"

"But why was it so terribly important to keep your call to your cousin a secret?" Mother asked pointedly.

He looked at her, then down at the floor. His hands started to shake. "I do not know where I am. I do not know who I am. I do not know who I can trust."

With this he began to weep, and in between loud sniffs he shot embarrassed glances at Mother as if checking to see if she was ashamed of him. The sight of this was almost too much to bear. Either he was a great actor, or he really was in a whole lot of trouble and knew it.

"We would've seen you together at the bar," I said.

"I do not know that anyone will come to the bar. But if so, you do not speak my language. I think we can talk and you not know."

That was a possibility, once I gave it some thought. We wouldn't have had any idea what they were saying to each other, and even if they had shown signs of affection, it wouldn't have seemed out of place at Charlene's. In fact, it might've seemed perfectly natural for him to be instantly affectionate with a fellow countryman, just out of the joy of discovering another one here. James might have been a bit more clever than I thought.

"There is another reason," he added tentatively, looking down at the floor.

"Another reason you didn't want him to come here?" I asked.

He raised his eyes to mine. "I do not want him to know you, or where you are."

From the look on Mother and Peter's faces, I could see they understood this as quickly as I did. I said, "So you *know* that your cousin is a member of the jihad."

"I knew he was in Iraq. I did not know now. I think maybe being here would change him."

"James, why would your cousin try to kill you?" Peter asked.

James's eyes widened. "He is not my cousin!"

"What?!" I exclaimed.

Peter said, "You mean you didn't know the man with the gun?"

"No! I never see him before!"

None of us knew what to say to this. Mother looked up at us from her place beside James and raised her eyebrows. The idea that his cousin had come to the bar to kill him had been hard enough to fathom; the idea that James had called his cousin and someone else had been sent to kill him was even more difficult.

"What did he say to you?" I asked.

"He tells me I am a traitor!"

"How could you be a traitor to the Red Jihad if you're not one of them?" I asked sharply.

He buried his face in his hands. "I do not know! I do not know!"

Peter said, "Remember, honey, that is why he was brought here."

In the heat of the moment I actually had forgotten that the government's purpose in bringing him here was to expose his relations, even if he wasn't an actual member. "That's true, but I don't see how they would know he'd done it so soon."

James whimpered. "He say I am a traitor and he shows me the gun. He tells me I must come with him. I am afraid! I do not want to go, but I think if I do anything he will shoot you, too!"

"Hmm," said Mother. "Did the two of you get on at all?"

He turned his tear-stained face to her quizzically. I translated this into American. "Didn't your cousin like you?"

"I do not know him so well. I do not understand."

"That makes three of us," I said.

Mother patted her legs with her palms and rose. "I think that's enough for tonight. You've had a very long day. It's time you should go up to bed."

"But what can we do?" he asked plaintively.

"Alex and Peter and I will try to figure that out. In the meantime, I don't want you to worry about it. We'll think of something."

We will? I thought.

Our newly expanded family went up the wooden steps, and I turned off the lights and shut the door. We said good night to James at the foot of the stairs to the second floor.

As James went up, Mother said, "You might want to keep from turning on the lights in your room. Larry Nelson has people watching the house. They might think it unusual."

"Yes," James said desolately.

The three of us went back to the kitchen. Peter and I sat at the table while Mother put the kettle on.

"I don't think tea is going to help this," I said.

"Oh, pother! Tea helps everything."

"I could just kill Nelson!"

"Why?" Peter asked.

"Because he knew damn well how dangerous this was."

"I don't see how he could've."

"He knew about the cousin. He knew about the jihad. He knew about a whole lot he didn't see fit to tell us!"

"Unless he was just telling us the truth." Peter was apparently determined to throw me completely off balance by defending Nelson, something that he had never done before.

I humphed lightly. Under these circumstances it was easy to believe the worst of Nelson. "The truth about what?"

"About the fact that they didn't think he'd try anything so soon."

"You *believe* that?"

He shrugged. "Oddly enough, I think I do. Why would he? It would've made much more sense if James had waited."

"Maybe," I said, puckering my lips after a pause. "But think of this: they would have had an agent breathing down his neck for the next few months."

"So?"

"James must've known that. He might've even thought they'd always keep an eye on him. So maybe our government buddies thought we'd give him an opportunity to make contact fast."

Peter reddened. "We did."

"That's not what worries me at the moment," said Mother, setting mugs out on the table with a loud thunk, apparently trying to divert us to a less infuriating train of thought. "What worries me is that fellow that showed up to kill James. When a call to his cousin results in an attempt on his life, something is dreadfully amiss."

"Spoken with true English understatement," I said.

She ignored me. "I mean, what could've caused that?"

"The most obvious thing is that they must know why James was brought over here," said Peter.

"You mean the real reason. To finger the mob."

"The jihad," Peter corrected.

"Whatever!" I was coming painfully close to sounding like Archie Bunker. "How could they know? Like you said, even James didn't know."

"It doesn't matter!" said Mother. "Whether they think he's giving away their secrets, or they think he's giving *them* away, it's obvious they're after him now!"

"Oh! So that's why you wanted to make sure the house was being watched. So we'll be safe?"

"Of course not! Darling, I've given up all hope of being safe as long as you're my son."

"I wasn't the one—"

She didn't give me a chance to finish this. "I wanted to know how hard it was going to be for us to get him out of here!"

"What? You're joking!"

"No! He can't stop here!"

"Why not?"

"It's far too dangerous!"

"Wouldn't this be the safest place for him?" Peter asked.

"I don't mean dangerous because of those jihad people. I wouldn't think they know where he is. I'm talking about Larry. He's no fool. He knows that James can't go to his cousin, and we're the only other people he knows in America."

"Come on, Mother! It would be crazy to think he's here!"

"He's 'ere, isn't he?"

"I'm afraid she has you there," said Peter.

"So the question is, how are we going to get him out of here, and where are we going to put him?"

"Yeah," I said. "With the government after him and this jihad after him, he's going to have to disappear. Permanently."

"But first things first," said Mother. "How do we get him out of the house?"

"It's not going to be easy," said Peter. "He stands out in our crowd."

I sighed heavily. "It's like Thunderdome."

Peter gaped at me. "What?"

"You remember: *Mad Max: Beyond Thunderdome.* Two go in, one comes out. Our guards don't know anyone else is in the house with us. We can't very well have three of us come in and four go out. Even if we could disguise him somehow, it would look awfully suspicious if they saw someone who never came into the house leave it." We fell silent for a minute, our minds running through a problem that on the surface seemed insurmountable. Then I felt my eyes widen as something completely fantastic—in the true sense of the word—came to me.

"Oh, my God! I've just had an idea!"

Peter folded his hands on the table and leveled his gaze at me. "You know how it scares me when either you or your mother say that."

"Well, I like that!" Mother said with comic archness. Then she added to me, "What is it?"

"Peter, do you remember Joe Gardner?"

"Joe Gardner?" He scrunched up his face as he searched his memory. "Oh, yeah! You mean that guy we worked with on the Clarke campaign? What about him?"

"He's interested enough in politics to want to help. And the last I heard he was still with Mickey Downs."

"So?"

I sighed and shook my head. "It's a really crazy idea, but it might work . . ."

"*You* think it's crazy? Now I'm terrified!" said Peter. "I'll probably end up naked and strapped to an anthill."

"Don't worry, honey," I said, playfully pinching his cheek. "You're not the one who's going to hate this one!"

On my way up to bed that night I stopped to check on James. He was lying on top of the bed in the dark, fully clothed, staring up out of the window at where the stars would be if they could be seen through Chicago's dome of pollution. I suffered another pang. By choosing to defect, he had even lost the stars.

"I do wrong," he said with a catch in his throat. "I do wrong to call my cousin."

I went to the bed and sat on the edge. "You were lonely."

"I cause much trouble. You and your mother and your Peter, you are all very good to me. I do not mean to cause you this trouble."

"Don't keep kicking yourself," I said kindly.

He looked at me quizzically. "What is this?"

Oh God, I thought, what a time for the language barrier to rear its ugly head!

"Do you know the word 'blame'?" I asked.

"Yes," he replied, turning away. "I know this."

"Well, I meant don't blame yourself. You're human. I don't think we took into account just how lonely you'd be. Maybe we could've done something more to help. I don't know. Probably not, because you've given up so much. But even in that you're not alone."

He turned his watery eyes back to me. "No?"

I wanted to assure him that he had us, but he would know that wasn't true: in order to ensure his safety, we were going to have to send him away, and in all likelihood he'd never be able to contact us again. But I wanted very badly to offer him some comfort.

"No, you're not alone in feeling you've lost everything. Even here in the U.S., some guys, when they come out of the closet, they—"

"What is this?"

"What is what?"

"This closet."

I took a deep breath. "I'm sorry, that is when you hide the fact that you're homosexual. 'Coming out of the closet' means admitting that you're gay. Deciding to be honest about it. Um . . . living honestly, like what you're doing . . . although most people don't do it quite so dramatically. When some guys here decide to admit openly that they're gay, they lose everything. They get disowned by their families. Turned out. Never see them again. Just like you. So even in the way you're feeling now, you're not alone."

"What do they do, these people?" he asked, blinking back tears.

"They make their own homes. Build their own families."

"This is what you do?"

"No, thank God! I was lucky. I was blessed with the best mother in gay civilization."

"And Peter."

"Yes, and Peter. But it was a long, long time before I met Peter."

He laid back on the bed and looked up at the ceiling. "I think when I come here, I will just be free."

I smiled. "Well, as my mother would say, we're none of us as free as we want to be. But things are better here. Really. No matter how things look now, things will get better for you."

He searched my face as if desperate to believe this was true. And I tried my darnedest to look like I was sure that it was.

EIGHT

The next morning Peter and I went out early to have a talk with Joe and Mickey. We'd met them when we were doing volunteer work for the senatorial bid of Charlie Clarke, an escapade that ended so disastrously I was pretty well assured that Peter would never press me to become civic minded again. I'd found Joe Gardner pretty repellent at first. He was an overly intense, politically active stick of a man who dressed like a color-blind longshoreman. But his lack of fashion sense was far overshadowed by the fact that he oozed internalized homophobia. At least I thought he did. So I was astonished when he fell head over heels for Mickey Downs, a slight and inoffensive little guy who dressed like a seventies disco queen and whose Keds barely had a nodding acquaintance with the ground. Joe initially gave every indication that Mickey was everything he hated in a man, only to do a surprise about-face and fall into his arms: which goes to prove something about love, though I'm not sure what. Shortly after the end of the campaign, Joe and Mickey moved in together.

Peter and I left at the crack of dawn to try to get to them before either of them left for work, although if I remembered correctly Mickey didn't have a job. But I was sure that Joe did: probably easing world hunger or healing lepers. I was relying on Joe's social conscience as a means to leverage his help. We decided to take the El because Joe and Mickey lived in Boys Town, where it's notoriously hard to park. We also figured it would make it harder for anyone to follow us. I didn't know of any reason the feds would have to do that, but there's something about having a foreign fugitive curled up on your daybed that makes you feel like everyone is watching you.

It's a short hop from Fullerton to Addison, and given the early hour and the fact that we were traveling in the opposite direction of rush-hour traffic, both the platform and the train were nearly deserted, which made it easier to ensure that we weren't being trailed, unless it was by a three-hundred-pound white man with dreadlocks whose lips never stopped moving. We got off the train at Addison and headed east. Joe and Mickey lived in a musty three-flat on Halsted directly across the street from Step Lively, one of the bigger dance bars.

As we mounted the stone steps, Peter said, "You realize what this means?"

I paused before ringing the doorbell. "What?"

"We're going to have to break a confidence."

"What do you mean?"

"If we explain to them what we want them to do, we're going to have to tell them that we work for the government."

He was right. We'd never purposely divulged our part-time status as agents, although I had once done it accidentally in a fit of pique. However, as betrayed as I felt by our boss at that point, I didn't care. "Right at this moment I don't feel a lot of allegiance to Nelson," I said as I pressed the bell.

There was such a long wait before our ring was answered that I was beginning to think we'd missed them, when finally the intercom crackled. Someone tried to speak, then broke off and noisily cleared his throat. "Hello? Who is it?"

"Joe? It's Alex Reynolds and Peter Livesay."

"What?" His thoroughly surprised voice rattled from the tin box.

"I'm sorry about coming here so early, but we have to talk to you. It's an emergency."

There was a long pause, then he said "All right" and buzzed us in.

Once inside, we heard a door crack open overhead. Joe called out, "Third floor."

"Of course," I said to Peter.

We mounted the stairs two at a time, and soon reached the third-floor landing. Joe was standing in the doorway. He hadn't changed much since we'd last seen him, although his dark hair had receded a bit more. He was wearing a pair of navy blue pants and a light blue shirt, and he was knotting a tie with red pinstripes as we approached. Although his outfit was not exactly outstanding, it was a sign that Mickey had been influencing him in the direction of color coordination.

"Do you know what time it is?" he asked.

I nodded. "I'm sorry. I know this is a surprise, but it really is important. Can we come in?"

"Sure," he said, stepping aside so we could enter. As he closed the door, he asked, "What's the matter?"

"Where's Mickey?"

"He was just taking a shower." He looked down the hall and called his partner's name.

"Just a minute!" The familiar singsong voice came from behind a door halfway down the hall.

"Why don't we go in here?" said Joe, directing us into the living room.

Mickey's influence was even more evident there. The wooden floor was polished to a shine, the furniture was attractively arranged mountain-cabin-style around a faux fireplace, and books were neatly lined up according to size on the built-in shelves along the walls. On the mantelpiece there was a framed photo of Joe and Mickey, both in tuxedos and smiling broadly as they sliced into a four-tiered cake with a huge knife.

Joe motioned us to seats and sat across from us. It was then that Mickey emerged from the hallway. His blond hair was still buzzed, and his slender body still taut. He was clad in an ankle-length robe of purple silk. In his hurry to join us he hadn't dried himself off completely, which caused some embarrassing clinging.

"My God! I don't believe it!" Mickey exclaimed happily as he dropped onto a chair next to Joe. "I don't mean this to sound rude, but what are you doing here? You're the last people I expected to see at this hour."

"Who's the first?" Peter asked.

He formed his lips into a tiny *o*. "Someone's mother." He gave a significant glance toward Joe. "She pops in unannounced from time to time at the oddest hours." He leaned forward and whispered conspiratorially, "She thinks we're sleeping together."

Joe laughed. "She's not that bad!"

"She's a Trojan warrior."

Joe reached over and lightly rubbed Mickey's head with the flat of his hand. I couldn't believe how this mismatched love had mellowed him.

"So, what's the emergency?" he asked.

"Well . . ." I began slowly with a glance at Peter. "First of all, what I'm about to tell you, we really need for you to keep it in the strictest confidence."

"Do tell!" Mickey said eagerly.

Joe patted his knee. "That's fine. What is it?"

"I know this will be a little hard to believe, but we . . . sort of . . . work for the government."

This announcement was followed by a protracted silence during which the two of them stared at me unblinkingly.

"Uh-huh . . ." they said in unison.

"As . . . well . . . secretly."

"Uh-huh."

"As . . . sort of . . . agents . . ."

"Um-hmm," said Joe.

"It's true," Peter said with a nod. I was glad he was there with me. He's a baritone. People believe them.

"You're the first people we've ever told about this—outside of the police—and we really need for you to promise us you won't tell anyone," I said.

"Wait a minute!" said Joe, finally animating. "You're serious?"

"Yes, we are. We really can't go into it in detail, we just do some minor work for them. Just odd jobs."

"Very odd," Peter added.

They both looked completely nonplussed, for which I couldn't very well blame them. Joe said, "So what do you need with us?"

"We need your help," I said. "You see, we were asked to take in this young man for a few days, and now we have to get him out of our house."

"Stop feeding him," said Mickey. "That'll get rid of him."

Peter looked at me. "I think it'll take a little more detail than that."

I launched into an abbreviated version of the story, explaining that James was gay and fleeing his homeland. I didn't tell them what he was supposed to be providing in return, the real reason he was being allowed into the country. I did explain that we thought the government was using him, and that he'd accidentally run afoul of both the government agents and a group of terrorists from his own country, and that Mother had chosen to take him in.

"Your *mother's* involved?" Joe asked incredulously.

"Of course she is. She lives with us."

"We live with her," Peter amended.

"Boy! Talk about a deviant lifestyle!" said Mickey.

"Anyway, now we have James at home and our house is being watched. We have to get him out of there and to someplace safe."

"You mean here?" said Joe.

I shook my head. "No. We're going to keep him someplace else. We just need your help in getting him out."

As I'd hoped, the idea of a gay man needing asylum and the prospect of political persecution won Joe over immediately.

"What do you want us to do?" he asked.

"Hey, wait a minute!" said Mickey, who'd gone quite wide-eyed and noticeably pale during my explanation. "This sounds dangerous!"

"I don't think so," said Peter. "So far the people from his country don't know where he is. We're actually only trying to get him past our own government agents."

"And," I said, smiling at Mickey, "we especially need you. You're the key player in this little caper."

He squealed with delight, which made me laugh. If Nelson didn't trust me when I was overly enthusiastic about getting involved in this, he would have fled at the sound that came out of Mickey.

"Cool!" he said. "What do I get to do?"

"Well, there's something you told me when we were working on the Clarke campaign . . ." As I explained, Mickey grew increasingly excited while Joe became very grave.

"You really think a stunt like that will work?" he asked.

"That entirely depends on Mickey," I replied with a shrug.

"Damn straight—you should excuse the expression," said Mickey. "I can do it! No, really! I can do it!"

"Are you sure?" asked Joe. "It's been a long time."

Mickey gave him a broad grin. "Baby, you never lose it! I'm making a comeback!"

"Just don't overdo it," I said.

"So you want us to get him out of your house and then what? Take him to where you're going to keep him?" Joe asked.

"No. Bring him here and let him change. I'm going to have someone come here and get him."

"Who?"

"I don't think you know him, and it's better if we keep it like that. That way, if someone comes here looking for James—which, if all goes well, won't happen—you honestly won't know where he is."

"Ooooh! Clever!" said Mickey, his eyes shining. "I like this!"

"Don't like it too much," said Peter, "because you can never tell anyone about it."

"Damn! My greatest role and nobody will ever know!"

Peter and I left Joe and Mickey to make preparations for their roles. We set seven o'clock, after Joe got home from work, as the time for the plan to go into action.

Once we were back out on the street, Peter said, "So, on to Stevie's place?"

"Uh-huh. He's just about four blocks from here."

We headed west, and despite the urgency of the situation, I enjoyed the walk. It had rained overnight, and the air was deliciously cool and damp, and full of the aroma of wet foliage: quite different from the neighborhood where we live, where a light rain makes everything smell like a flooded basement.

Peter said, "I don't understand why you don't want James to stay with Joe and Mickey. I think he'd be safe with them."

"I want at least two degrees of separation in this. The guys guarding our house might be able to identify Joe and Mickey. If they can trace them, I don't want them to find James there."

"You realize that the minute our guards see Mickey leave, they're going to know something's wrong."

"Yeah, but by then it'll be too late. James will be long gone."

Peter clucked his tongue. "You know, you're beginning to think more and more like Nelson. I don't think I'm going to let you play with him anymore."

"At the moment it's a good thing I can think like him."

"But why Stevie, of all people?"

"Because he's helped us before, and because you know as well as I do that no matter how goofy he acts, he would help anybody in trouble."

"Are we going to tell him the whole story?"

"Only if we have to. We had to tell Joe and Mickey because I didn't know how else we would've explained what we want them to do. But the fewer people that know the truth about us, the better."

"Especially Stevie," Peter said with a knowing smile.

"Yeah."

* * *

Stevie answered the door clad in a pair of shiny black lounging pajamas, the top of which wasn't buttoned, revealing a beefy but toned chest covered with dark hair. He was a dead ringer for Tim Curry in his younger days, only a little less flamboyant. His bug eyes seemed less alert than usual when he greeted us.

"Sorry, boys!" he said, waving us in with a flourish. "I was just about to go to bed."

"At eight in the morning?" Peter said.

"I'm on eleven-to-seven this week. I just got home and I'm so tired I could bite the wind. Take a pew!"

Stevie lived in one of the older high-rises in the area, so his apartment looked roughly the same age as Joe and Mickey's only with much smaller rooms. The pew he was referring to was a long, old couch that faced a Kmart entertainment center. He draped himself over a chair beside us.

"So you're still at the hotel?" Peter asked.

"Yes," he drawled. "And I'm just so fed up I could spit! Always switching my schedule. Always the same crap every day!"

"Sorry to hear it," I said. "You've been there a long time, though. Maybe that's why."

"Too long! And then what's there to do? You go out at night and see the same boring old queens everywhere you go. Oops! Sorry. No offense."

"None taken."

"Anyway, surely you didn't come here at this ungodly hour to discuss my general ennui!"

"No. The other night when we ran into you at the bar, you said you weren't going with anyone at the moment. So . . . does that mean there's nobody staying here with you?"

His nose wrinkled like a rabbit's. "That's right, Alex. I am alone. Sans husband. Without partner. Unattached. On my own. Loverless. Bereft, bedraggled, and bewildered. Did you just stop by to remind me?"

"Uh, no. We have a favor to ask," I said.

"Ask away!"

"We have a friend who needs a place to stay for a little while."

116

Stevie's eyes became more alert. He reached over to the occasional table a few feet from his chair and swept up a pack of Marlboro Lights and a lighter. He shook the pack and pulled a cigarette out with his teeth. Then he lit it and tossed the pack and lighter back on the table.

"This friend can't stay in that big old house of yours?"

"No. That's the problem."

"And you want me to put him up?"

"Yeah," said Peter. "It would really be a help to us, if you could."

He eyed us shrewdly. "The two of you want to stash a man over here. On the QT, I take it?"

"That's right."

He took a puff of the cigarette, dappling his pajama top with stray ash. "If I didn't know you two better, I would think you were involved in something a teensy bit sordid."

"We are, but not what you think," I said.

"Does Mother Reynolds know what you're doing?"

"She's with him right now. Look, Stevie, this is really important. This friend of ours, James, is in a little bit of trouble and we need to hide him for a few days, until we can figure out how to get him out of town."

This got him to straighten up. "Until you can get him out of town? Sweet Mother of Moses! What are you two up to?"

"It's just a little misunderstanding," I said.

"Uh-huh . . ." he said skeptically.

"The police are looking for him . . ."

"The police!" Now his eyes were fully bugged out. "What did he do?"

"Nothing," Peter said quickly. "They don't want him because he committed a crime—they're just trying to find him, and we'd rather they didn't."

"The police!" Stevie said again, taking another drag on his cigarette and sitting back in his chair. "Oh, God! The last time you asked me to help you it was to break into a room at the hotel!"

"We just asked you for a key," I replied weakly in our defense.

"I could've lost my job!" he said. After giving it a moment's thought, he added, "Not that that would've been a bad thing, but then again, my sweet boys, it would've been a little hard to start a new life with a record! And I would look terrible in prison whites!"

"They don't wear white in prison," I said. "They wear orange."

"Oh, delightful!" he said, rolling his eyes. "I'd look like The Gay Pumpkin!"

"Stevie, if we thought this would be dangerous for you, we wouldn't ask you to do it," Peter said sincerely. "James really hasn't done anything wrong. They're not looking to arrest him."

"Oh, of course not! They're just searching for him for the practice! Now what in the name of my sainted aunt Tillie is this all about?"

"We just told you," I said.

"Oh, puh-*leese*! You two want to stash someone who's running from the police in my apartment! This is a joke, isn't it? And I'm awfully tired!"

I looked at Peter helplessly. It had probably been foolhardy to think we could enlist Stevie's aid in something like this without divulging the truth, but I really had wanted to keep the number of people who knew to a minority. Peter shrugged, which I took as a sign to go ahead.

"Well, this is how it is . . ."

I gave him a much shorter explanation of our involvement with the government and our current mess than I'd given Joe and Mickey, carefully leaving out the bit about the terrorists for fear it would scare him off. When I was done, Stevie slid his leg back over the arm of his chair and took a couple more leisurely puffs on his cigarette, keeping his eyes leveled at me. "You know, a simple 'None of your business' would suffice."

"It's the truth!"

I'm usually a scrupulously honest person. So are both Peter and Mother, although they have a talent for lying very convincingly if the circumstances demand it. That's a talent I don't have, so it's no wonder that nobody believes me when I lie. I've just never understood why nobody believes me when I'm telling the truth, either.

"Of course it is, sweetie!" Stevie purred.

Once again I looked to Peter, who responded with another shrug.

"So, I take it you're not going to tell me the real reason the guy needs to stay somewhere other than your house."

This time I was the one that shrugged. "Not other than what I've already told you."

He sighed. "Is he at least cute?"

"You've seen him. He was the guy who was with us at the bar."

His face brightened measurably. "Really?"

For the first time I could see why Nelson found undue enthusiasm suspicious. "Yes, and he's been through enough."

"What's that supposed to mean?"

"It means his entire world has just changed, so he doesn't need any more new horizons opened up at the moment, if you get my drift."

He put his nose up in the air and put his fingers to his chest. "Are you implying that I would have my saucy way with any man who spends the night here?" His eyebrows suddenly flew up. "Wait a minute! That didn't come out right."

"All I'm saying is James is in a very fragile state right now. He needs our help. And yours. Are you going to do it?"

"Oh, all right, all right, I'll do it! Why not? It'll be something different. I'm due for a change. Bring him on over."

"Um . . . about that," I said. "We need you to pick him up. Don't worry, it's from someplace very close by."

"I have to pick him up, too?" he said with feigned indignation. "You can't deliver him?"

"No, it'll only work if you'll pick him up. Do you know Joe Gardner or Mickey Downs?"

"No."

I smiled. "Good. I'll give you their address. You'll be able to get James by nine tonight. Whatever you do, don't tell Joe or Mickey who you are. Oh, and one other thing: don't call us unless it's an absolute emergency. They may be tapping our phone. And if you do have to call us, whatever you do, don't call us from here. Use a pay phone. They may be tracing our calls."

Stevie stared at me for a very long time, his face a mask of incredulous amusement. "Do give it up, will you, sweetie?"

We had a very long wait until seven o'clock that evening, made all the longer by having to fight the urge to look out the window. When your house is being watched, it's hard not to want to watch the watcher. It didn't matter that Fredrichs's men only meant to protect us: since we were preparing to scam them, it made them seem like our jailers.

As I'd predicted, James was not at all happy with my plan. As new as he was to the idea of sexual freedom, my scheme was definitely pushing his envelope. But he agreed to go through with it, mainly through Mother's reassurances that it was the right thing to do. Frankly, I was surprised that Mother had liked the plan so much. It seriously shook my confidence when she told me she wished she'd thought of it.

We ate dinner at five o'clock to make sure that James had a good meal before leaving, but I barely touched my food. The butterflies in my stomach felt like bats. James's appetite, on the other hand, was unaffected, although he did have the good grace to look concerned while he shoveled the food into his mouth.

As the hour approached it got more and more difficult to keep from looking out the window, since I not only wanted to know if our guests were coming, I wanted to see if our guard was paying them any special notice. But to be seen peering out the window would've looked even more suspicious. Peter, James, and I sat on the couch staring like stupefied puppets at the evening news on the television. I don't think any of us took in what we were seeing. Mother kept herself busy in the kitchen.

It was about five minutes to seven when the doorbell rang, its double tones startling me into a spasm that nearly cost Peter a limb. Mother came out of the kitchen and headed for the door, but I got there first.

"I'll get it." I paused with my hand on the knob. "Oh, God. I feel like the guy in "The Lady or the Tiger?," except I know what it's going to be!"

I opened the door and found Joe standing on the stoop with an arm around the waist of a young woman so striking she could've been an Egyptian goddess. She was wearing an electric blue dress with long sleeves and a high neck, and a matching band that circled her forehead and disappeared under her long black hair. Her ears sported large blue hoops, and she had a huge satchel-like purse slung over her shoulder.

"Hi, Joe," I said loudly.

"Hi, Alex," he replied. "I don't think you've met my girlfriend. This is Marlene DuBois."

She held out her dark hand to me and in a deep, sensual voice said, "I am very pleased to meet you."

I kissed the proffered hand, which seemed to be what was expected. "Come in, come in!"

They went into the living room and I closed the door. When I joined them, I said, "Jesus Christ! I'm surprised you didn't wear a veil!"

"You said not to overdo it!" said Mickey from beneath the black wig.

"Marlene DuBois?"

He laughed. "Of course! Marlene for Dietrich, and DuBois for Blanche. I hope you know the risk I was taking! I could get arrested for this, couldn't I?"

"For going out in drag?"

"No, silly, for going out in blackface. Isn't that against the law?"

"This is hardly a minstrel show," I replied through curled lips.

"Good lord!" Mother exclaimed, fairly glowing with delight. "You do make a lovely woman!"

"Doesn't he?" Joe said with pride. I was perfectly astonished by his reaction. When we'd first met him, he'd shown a marked disdain for drag, which was another one of the reasons I was so surprised when he took up with Mickey. The change that had come over Joe really was a testament to the power of love.

"Thank you very much," Mickey replied, "but I think this'll be my swan song!"

"Whatever for? You look fantastic!" said Mother.

"It's been years since I've done this. These heels are murder! I don't think we've met. I'm Mickey Downs."

She shook his hand. "I'm Alex's mother. Please call me Jean."

"And I'm Joe Gardner," said Joe, shaking her hand in turn.

"I'm very pleased to meet you both. It's so wonderful of you to do this for us."

Mickey gave a royal wave. "It's nothing!"

"Alex explained the situation to us. We had to help," Joe said soberly. "Is this James?"

"Yes," said Peter, bringing him over to them. James shook their hands but said nothing. He seemed mesmerized by Mickey.

Mother waved a hand up and down Mickey's costume. "Do you think you'll be able to do this with him?"

Mickey pursed his lips and looked James over. "It's a cinch! It'll be much easier to do him over. He doesn't need this damned body makeup!" He took James's chin between his thumb and forefinger and turned his head sideways. "I got as near as I could to the shade from your description, Alex, but it's not a match."

"It's close enough. It'll be dark when they leave."

"Hmm." He let go of James's face and then pulled the rings from his ears with a grimace. "These are clip-ons. I sort of figured he wouldn't have pierced ears."

"Mickey thought of everything!" Joe said.

"We'd better get started," said Mickey, heading for the dining table, where he began to unpack his shoulder bag. "I'm going to need to take a shower to wash this muck off first."

"That's fine. It's upstairs," said Mother.

"I have my street clothes in here and all the stuff I need to do his face. You can pack his belongings in this so he can take his own clothes with him."

Mother picked up the now empty bag. "I'll get his things."

"I'll just get washed up, then I'll slip into something a little less comfortable and get started on you, young man!"

James turned his doe eyes to me. "Alex?"

I shrugged and managed a smile. "It'll be fun!"

Once Mickey had cleaned up and changed into his usual attire—a T-shirt and jeans that both looked as if they'd been painted on—he had me bring a stool up to the hallway bathroom. He instructed James to take off his shirt and sat him on the stool facing the mirror over the sink. He then opened a case that was lying on the counter and spread out its contents. It was a larger array of cosmetics than I've ever seen outside of Marshall Field's.

"I didn't know what I'd need," Mickey explained when he saw the look on my face. He turned around, rested his butt against the counter and considered James, whose face at that moment bore a striking resemblance to an attentive greyhound. The only thing lacking was the splayed ears.

"Now that I see you," said Mickey, "I don't think it's going to take much. Your skin is fine. You've shaved your cute little face. I just have to powder you off so you don't shine. Then I'll do your eyes and lips. You'll look stunning!"

I sat on the counter and watched as Mickey worked. Although he'd said it wouldn't take much, he labored over James's face as if it were a canvas for over half an hour. James stared at his slowly changing reflection with a deep sense of fascination. A few minutes into his transformation, he said, "Alex, why do you do this?"

"We explained all that," I said patiently. "It's the only way to get you past the surveillance."

"I do not mean this. I mean why do you do all this for me? You do not know me."

I swallowed hard. "We're doing it because we want you to know that there are good people in the world. There are people who care about you. Peter and I, and Mother, we care about you."

James turned his eyes to Mickey, who was carefully lining his left lower lid. "Why do you do this?"

He shrugged. "I wasn't busy tonight."

"Mickey . . ." I said warningly.

He rolled his eyes. "All right. I'm doing it because you need help. When a guy needs help, this is what you do." He glanced at me and added, "You turn him into a woman."

James turned back to me. "You risk your life for me. The Jihad Ahmad, if they find you help me, they will kill you."

"Don't worry about that. There's no way they'll find out about us."

"The jihad are people who will want . . ." He searched for the word but couldn't find it.

"Revenge?" I offered.

He replied with gravity, "Yes . . . this is it. Revenge. If they think you help me, they will find you."

Mickey slowed in his work and looked over at me with a great deal of concern.

"Don't worry," I said to James. "They won't find us."

He looked extremely doubtful. "You do not know these people." There was a long silence; then he added to his reflection, "Because of me, there is much danger for you."

"I know, but what else can we do? We have to help."

His eyes brimmed with tears. Mickey yelled "Shit!" and snatched a wad of toilet paper from the roll on the side of the counter. He pressed it carefully under James's eyes. "Look, it's all right to get all weepy on your own time, but don't do it now. You'll ruin my work!" He dabbed James's eyes, then when it appeared that our soldier had regained control of himself, Mickey tossed the tissue aside. I noticed that Mickey was looking a bit misty himself.

"Now, close your eyes," he said, "I need to do your lids."

James complied, and Mickey went to work with a blue shadow that was a close match to the dress.

"Alex," said James, "I still do not understand. You are against the government if you do this for me. But you are with the government."

I hung my head and sighed. I knew what he was saying, and from time to time I'd wondered about it myself. The escapades in which we'd gotten involved had provided me and my loved ones with a lot of excitement, but this wasn't the first time I'd found myself wondering if we should have anything to do with them, despite the dimension they'd added to our lives. Like jeopardy. Within myself I had come to understand that there was more to our involvement than mere thrill seeking.

"James, I don't know if I can put this in a way that you can understand, because it's hard to explain. Our government—the American government, I mean—sometimes they're more interested in the ends than they are in the means."

"What does this mean?"

I sighed again, because it would've been difficult for me to explain how I felt even to someone who spoke perfect English.

"When our government—I mean, like the FBI or the CIA—find something bad happening, they try to do something about it. Sometimes they don't care so much about *how* they do that. In this case they see the Red Jihad as a real threat to our security, and they want to do something about that. Along you came. They saw you as a means to find them. I don't think they realized the kind of danger that would put you in. Or maybe they did and they just thought that finding the jihad was more important than your safety. So they used you. We've seen them do this sort of thing before. I don't think they just do this with gay people, I think they would use anyone."

"You can open your eyes now," said Mickey.

He did, and turned them on me. "But if they use people like this, how can you be with them?"

I took a deep breath. "Because of the look on your face when we took you to Charlene's for the first time."

"I do not understand."

"We have a lot of problems here," I said. "A lot of problems. But we're still free. You saw that yourself when we took you to Charlene's. For all the stuff that's wrong with our government and our country, we're still better off here. I may think the way they've used you is despicable, but at the same time, the Red Jihad *is* a threat. They *do* have to do something about them, even if I don't

125

agree with the way they're going about it. So I guess the answer to your question is that me and my mother and Peter are with the government because *somebody* has to keep them honest!"

"If you're done singing 'Yankee Doodle Dandy,' " said Mickey, "I have to do his lips."

Just before Mickey started, James said, "But your Mr. Nelson, does he think as you do?"

"Lips together!" Mickey ordered, and James complied.

"Larry?" I could feel a dark cloud passing over me. "I don't know what he's thinking right now. There's a lot he needs to explain. But . . ."

Mickey was smoothing the color over James's lips with the pinky of his right hand. When my voice trailed off, he paused and James looked at me. "But what?"

I raised my eyes to him. "But I have to believe he's one of the good guys."

Mickey wiped the red off his finger and tossed the tissue onto the ever-growing pile on the counter. He then took up a pencil and carefully ran it along the outlines of James's lips. When he was done, he stepped back and surveyed his work.

"There! Doesn't look exactly like I did, but what do you think?"

"It's close enough to pass in the dark."

"Now let's do the wig." He gathered it up from beside the sink and fitted it onto James's head, pulling it down and shifting it into position.

"This," said Mickey, picking up the blue headband, "I'll bet you thought was just for decoration, but it's not!" He slipped it onto James's head, across his forehead, and under the back of his hair. "It has a dual purpose: it's tight enough to make sure the wig stays in place, and the way it covers the front—you see? It makes him look even more generic. *Voilà!*"

I had to admit, he had successfully transformed James into a near-copy of himself. Mickey stepped aside so that James could see the end result in the mirror. I was worried about how he'd react, but I certainly didn't expect what happened: For a moment, he didn't appear to recognize himself, as if he were looking through a glass at someone else instead of his own reflection. Then his lips curved into a smile, and at last he broke into laughter. I was stunned to realize it was the first time I'd heard him truly laugh.

Mickey gave me a puzzled smile and shrugged. "Now we've got to get you dressed. Slip out of your things."

"I'll take them to Mother," I offered, preparing to give them some privacy.

I picked his shirt up from the counter as he stripped off his pants. He gave them to me as Mickey held up a rather skimpy undergarment that looked like a thong and appeared to be the consistency of a girdle.

"What is this?" James asked with a dubious frown.

"That, my dear boy, is a gaff. It'll tuck everything away nicely and see that you don't go poking through my lovely dress. I'm afraid your shorts will have to go, too."

James hesitated a moment, then stepped out of his briefs.

"Oh, my God!" Mickey gasped. "I don't think the shoes are gonna fit!"

James handed the briefs to me and took the gaff from Mickey. When he started to step into it, Mickey stopped him and turned it around. "This way! We only want you to be a woman for a little while!"

I left the bathroom and took the clothes to Mother, who was waiting in James's room.

"These have seen better days," she said, eying the ragged briefs as she began to fold them. "How's he doing?"

"Better than I thought. We may have found him a new career. Where's Peter?"

"Downstairs with Joe," she said as she neatly folded the clothes. "Honestly! This is the craziest idea!"

"That's something, coming from you!"

"Oh, I'm not being critical, darling. I'm proud of you!"

"Hmm. I'd always hoped to make you proud by coming up with a vaccine or bringing about world peace, not for turning an Iraqi soldier into a Nubian princess."

"Well," she said, putting the pants into the bag, "we all have to make our mark in our own little corner of the world."

I laughed. "I'll go see if they're finished."

Back in the bathroom, the transformation was complete. James was in the dress and Mickey was adjusting the sleeves.

"How's it going?" I asked.

Mickey stepped back. "Well, you told me he was about my size, but he's a little thinner. He doesn't fill the dress quite as well as me—he doesn't have my child-bearing hips—and he's a tiny bit taller. I hope they don't notice the bit of hair that's showing down there. But all in all, I think we have a match."

James turned to me. "Is okay?"

Mickey was right, the dress hung more loosely on James than it had on him, but with a little darkness and a little distance, I didn't think anyone would notice the difference.

"It's more than okay. It's great!"

James looked in the mirror and smiled at himself. "Okay."

"What about the shoes?" I asked Mickey.

"His feet are much bigger than mine, as I guessed," he said ruefully, "which will work to his advantage. The shoes won't fall off. Of course he might break his ankles . . ."

"Let's keep a good thought," I said wryly, then added to James, "Maybe you should take them off before going downstairs."

"Is okay," he said, taking a few tentative steps forward.

"No, he'd better not," said Mickey. "There's four steps outside your house. He should try them on the stairs to get used to navigating them before going outside."

James was only slightly wobbly as we walked him down the hallway. He moved carefully but not too slowly, which actually made his gait seem rather regal. At the stairs he grasped the banister with his right hand and went down the steps one foot after the other, maintaining his balance so skillfully it was hard to believe it was his first time in heels.

Peter and Joe were seated on the couch and rose when they saw him.

"You look great!" Peter said encouragingly.

"Look how well he's doing on the heels!" I said.

James reddened slightly. "It's not so much different from army training."

"Really?" Joe said with surprise.

"Yes. It hurts, but it must be done."

Mother came downstairs with the shoulder bag and smiled with wonder at the sight of James. "You look smashing! Here's your purse."

"Thank you." He slipped the strap over his shoulder.

"Your duffel bag and all of your other things are in there." There was a short silence, then she added, "Well, it's no use standing about! We'd best get on with it."

"Yes," said James hesitantly. "But . . . I must . . . I thank you. Nobody do so much for me before."

"That's quite all right."

Mother put her arms around him and he held her tightly for several seconds.

"Look, you!" said Mickey. "Don't you start blubbering again! You ruin your makeup and I'll be forced to kill you!"

He released Mother, then hugged Peter and me in turn, very nearly cracking our ribs. We walked him to the door and as Mother opened it Joe said, "Put your arm through mine. Like this." He demonstrated, and James followed suit.

"Stay back," I said to Mickey. "They can't see you yet."

"Okay," he replied, a bit disappointed.

Mother stayed by the door and Peter and I stepped out onto the stoop and watched as Joe and James went down the stairs. James faltered only once, when they reached the walk, but regained himself almost immediately. We called our goodbyes as they headed for the El.

Mother went back into the house and Peter and I followed her after a moment.

I closed the door, then said, "He came in a soldier and went out a drag queen. I think our work here is done."

"Not by 'alf," said Mother.

* * *

As prearranged, Mickey waited at our house for an hour before leaving. When the time came, he said, "I haven't been this nervous about walking down the street since I had to go past Wrigley Field at night."

"Not in drag!" I exclaimed.

"No. In baseball season."

"Just act naturally and everything will be all right," said Peter.

Mickey grimaced comically. "Exactly what my father used to say!"

We didn't see him off at the front steps, because we figured the less attention we drew to his exit, the better.

Once he was gone, Mother heaved a sigh. "Such a bother having company! I love having people here, but it's always nice when things return to normal."

"Normal," I said flatly. "Yes, why don't we have some tea and figure out how to smuggle our accused terrorist out of the city."

"Good idea!" Off she went to the kitchen.

I looked at Peter. "I was being facetious."

"She knows that, honey," he replied with a smile.

We followed her into the kitchen where she was already filling the kettle with water.

"Actually," she said as she turned off the tap, "the *means* of getting him out of town isn't really a question. I already have that figured out."

"I should've known," I said. "How?"

"By car, of course. I'm sure Agent Fredrichs will have people watching the airports, train stations, and such, but now that James is away from our house, we should be able to drive him out of the city quite easily."

"You think so?"

She placed the kettle on the stove and turned an indulgent smile on me. "Darling, despite what some writers would have you believe, Chicago is not a small English village. They can't very well put up road blocks at both ends of the city and stop every car that comes through. What we have to do is decide where to take him."

"You mean who to take him to," said Peter. "Because he'll need someone to take care of him. At least for a while."

"Quite right," Mother said vaguely. She sounded as if she was already running this through her mind and was distressed that a solution wasn't more forthcoming.

As the discussion wore on, our options dwindled. Surprisingly enough, it's difficult to come up with someone in the normal course of one's life who'd be willing to take in a foreign fugitive and instruct him in how to live in the New World. Every possibility was brought up and shot down. Peter first suggested housing James, at least temporarily, with his parents or his sister in California. But we realized at once that the first place the feds would look for him would be among our relatives. Then we dredged up the names of every friend and acquaintance we'd ever had outside of Chicago, but each one was negated in turn, for a variety of reasons.

At last Mother heaved an exasperated sigh. "I think we should sleep on it. Maybe we'll come up with something in the morning."

"You don't have any ideas?" I said with shock. "You're going to have to resign as head of Lucy Ricardo Incorporated."

"Go to bed, dear," she said flatly.

Peter and I went to our room and undressed. In the distance I could hear the faint clink of mugs knocking together as Mother cleaned up the tea things. She could never go to bed while something was out of place in the kitchen. Aside from that, an overpowering stillness had fallen over the house. Mother was right: no matter how little trouble guests may be, they unsettle your home while they visit, even if it's just that their breathing is creating unfamiliar ripples in the air. I think that's what causes that weird sense of ennui you get when company leaves. It's not so much letdown as relief. And James had brought with him a few more problems than the ordinary guest.

We climbed into bed together and Peter leaned over and gave me a gentle kiss. When our lips parted, he drew back slightly and furrowed his brow.

"What's wrong?" he asked.

"Huh? Oh, I was just thinking, I wish there was some way that Joe and Mickey could've let us know that they got James home all right."

Peter tilted his head. "I'm sure they did. If just from the negative standpoint."

"What do you mean?"

"If something had gone wrong, we would've heard about it by now."

"That's true."

"Is that all that's bothering you?"

"No. I'm still worried about where we're going to send him."

He sighed. "You should try to put that out of your mind and get some sleep. We're all too tired to think."

He started to lie back against his pillow, but stopped. He brought his face close to mine and scrutinized it. "Are you sure that's all you're worried about?"

"No," I said. "I was just thinking about a talk I had with James while Mickey was fixing him up."

"Yeah?"

"Do you ever regret getting involved with Nelson and the government?"

"Only when I'm trying to get some sleep."

"No, really."

He laid his head on my chest and was silent for a very long time. I could almost hear the wheels and gears clicking in his head. I knew that Peter had had some serious issues with the way some of this work of ours had panned out, but I'd always believed—or wanted to—that on a gut level he believed in what we were doing. At least enough to go along with it. I was just beginning to think he wasn't going to answer when he raised his head slightly and looked at me.

"Really?" he asked.

"Yeah. I want to know. Do you ever regret it?"

"No," he said after a beat. Then he laid his head back down and quickly fell asleep.

Even though I was exhausted, I still couldn't sleep. I lay awake most of the night, staring at the ceiling and listening to Peter softly whistling through his nose, and thinking about what James had said would happen if the jihad ever found us.

NINE

As usual when I have a sleepless night, I finally fell asleep about twenty minutes before it was time to get up. Peter was already taking a shower. I went into our bathroom and looked at myself in the mirror. There were rings under my eyes and my face looked like a cake that had fallen. The nerve endings all over my body felt like they were misfiring. I sighed, realizing that I was going to have to resign myself to feeling like a ferret on crack for the rest of the day. I ran some cool water and splashed it on my face, which helped a little, but not much.

Through the frosted glass of the shower stall I could see Peter vigorously rubbing soap over his legs. I went over to the stall, pulled open the door, and stepped in.

"Bad night?" he said, righting himself.

"Uh-huh." The warm water flattened the hair on my chest and started to relax my muscles.

He started to say something else, then changed his mind. He put the soap back in its dish, moved closer to me, and gently pushed me back against the tile wall.

"Let me see if I can make it better." He pressed his wet flesh against mine and we kissed deeply.

A shower stall isn't exactly a cascading waterfall, but it'll do in a pinch. Despite the fact that we were vertical, there was a surprising tenderness in the way we made love that morning. After several days of dealing with James, the poster child for abandonment, we needed to reassure each other on a cellular level that we were not alone in this world. It was like having a large glass of brandy: it didn't change anything, but for a while I didn't care. I have to admit, though, when I got around to actually showering, I caught myself humming.

When we went down to breakfast, we found Mother pensively frying eggs. She stood holding the spatula to one side and staring down at the contents of the frying pan as if she thought the yolks held a secret code.

After exchanging good mornings, she said, "Did you think of anyone we might send James to?"

"No," I replied. "And it wasn't for lack of trying. I must've only gotten five minutes sleep."

She gave me a sympathetic *tsk*. "Poor darling. But you know, 'sleep on it' means you're supposed to let go of it for the night and let the answer come to you."

"Did *you* sleep?"

"Like a top."

"And did you get an answer?"

"Not for what to do with James, but I did remember where I put the good scissors."

I rolled my eyes and Peter laughed. He retrieved the pitcher of orange juice from the refrigerator while I laid three plates on the counter beside Mother. She was just starting to dish out the eggs when the doorbell rang. The three of us stopped what we were doing and looked at each other.

"Who on earth could that be so early?" said Mother.

"I don't know," I said, "but I have a feeling it's not good news."

Mother put the frying pan to one side and turned off the burner, then we went to the front door together through some sort of unspoken understanding that we were all in for it. Mother opened the door and Agent Fredrichs stormed in, almost knocking her aside, which didn't endear him any further to us. Nelson followed him in the calm manner he maintains even in the worst situations.

"Where is he?" Fredrichs demanded.

"I beg your pardon?" said Mother, her tone conveying that she was affronted by his manner.

"Where is he?"

"Where is who?" I asked.

"You know who! James Paschal!"

"Agent Fredrichs," Nelson said evenly, "control yourself."

Fredrichs glared at him. "You know what they've done!"

"No, I don't. That's what I've come to find out. These are my people, and I'm the one who will handle this."

"We're on American soil! This is an FBI case!"

"James is a guest of my branch here. We're responsible for him."

"Not anymore! Once he took off, he became my problem."

"That may be," said Nelson, "but I'm responsible for my people, and I will handle this."

Although Nelson said all of this with perfect equanimity, I got the feeling that he was working at controlling himself. We had witnessed this type of tension between the two agencies before in our ongoing career with the CIA, but this time it was worse.

"What's this all about, Larry?" Mother asked.

"Agent Davidson, who was on duty in front of your house last evening, reported something unusual that warrants an explanation."

"What's that?" she replied with perfect innocence.

"He reported that last night at nine-thirty a young man was seen leaving your house."

"So?" said Peter.

"The odd thing is that he has no record of the young man coming *into* your house. You can see the problem."

"Obviously, he missed him coming in," I said.

"Davidson is one of my men!" Fredrichs boomed.

"That explains it."

"He didn't miss a thing! You smuggled that kid out of here!"

"Smuggled!" Mother exclaimed with wide eyes. "You just said that your man saw this person leave our house, right through the front door!"

"You know damn well I'm not talking about that! Where is he? What have you done with him?"

"Do you mean James?" Mother said, deepening her British lilt for emphasis. "You must be mad!"

"The guy your agent saw leaving here was just a friend of ours," said Peter.

Mother said to Nelson, "Did your man happen to note what the young man looked like?"

"Yes!" Fredrichs snapped before Nelson could reply. "Blond. Crew cut. About five-six. And obviously—"

"Obviously what?" Peter said sharply.

Fredrichs caught himself and looked to Nelson.

"I would think the one thing that's obvious is that that is not a description of James," Mother said haughtily.

"That's true," said Nelson. "However, an hour earlier Davidson noted a couple leaving your house, a man with a dark-skinned woman."

"And was Davidson awake to see them arrive?" I asked quickly.

"Davidson is a good man!" Fredrichs said loudly. "He saw what he saw!"

Nelson said, "Agent Fredrichs thought it possible that one of those people might have been James."

"I didn't think he was that clever," I said under my breath.

Peter leaned close to my ear and whispered, "Shut up!"

Mother folded her arms under her breasts and leveled her eyes at him. "And what are you suggesting? That James was the white man or the black woman?"

"That still leaves you one up on visitors," said Nelson.

"Honestly, Larry! Your man saw them come in and leave. He simply missed seeing our other friend when he came over. And I must say it doesn't give me the least feeling of security to know that one of the people who is supposed to be watching to make sure someone doesn't *sneak* into our house doesn't even see someone who enters through the front door!"

Fredrichs looked like he was about to burst. "Look, lady—!"

I cut him off. "Don't you call my mother a lady!" They all looked at me. "You know what I mean!"

"I don't know what you think you're doing, helping this kid, but he's a terrorist and a danger to the country—"

In my irritation, fueled by lack of sleep, I had to fight the urge to say, "Says you!"

"—and we've got to find him."

Mother produced her most condescending smile. "Oh, I think I'm beginning to understand now. It was you who lost James, what with your rough handling and your gunplay. He ran away from you at that bar and now you're trying to shift responsibility to anyone else, no matter how potty your accusation might be!" She looked to Nelson. "James knows we work with you. I should think we'd be the last people he'd come to for help."

Nelson gazed back at her so impassively that I swore he could see our entire plot laid bare. I almost shivered.

"That is, of course, a valid point. And when Agent Fredrichs brought up the discrepancy in the number of your guests, and suggested the possibility that you were somehow engaged in assisting James, that was my first consideration. However, it did occur to me that having run away, James is in a dilemma. He couldn't very well go to his friends, who apparently have tried to kill him. The only other people he knows in this country are you."

"Like Mother said, he knows we work for you," I said. "So he wouldn't think he could trust us, would he?"

There was a beat before Nelson replied. "I couldn't say."

"Oh, for Christ's sake!" said Peter. "He could've just as easily gone off on his own! He could be anywhere."

"I've spent a considerable amount of time with him over the past several days. He didn't strike me as the type of person who has it in him to fend for himself on his own in a strange country. Did he strike you that way?"

I had in my mind the picture of our little guest cowering

behind the couch in the basement. "Of course he could," I lied with my usual lack of conviction. "He's a soldier!"

"Look, I don't know why you're standing here making polite conversation with these people," Fredrichs said to Nelson. "They're assisting a fugitive!"

"Even if we were in a position to do that, why would we?" Mother asked.

"Helsinki syndrome," Fredrichs pronounced authoritatively.

"What?" said Peter, his jaw dropping.

"You heard me. That's when prisoners start sympathizing with their captors."

"Stockholm syndrome," said Peter.

Fredrichs stared blankly. "What?"

"That's Stockholm syndrome. Common mistake."

"I don't know if you've heard," I said, "but James wasn't holding us hostage."

"It can happen in reverse," said Fredrichs.

"We bloody well weren't holding *him* hostage, either!" said Mother.

"This wouldn't be the first time this type of alliance was formed. You could easily have gained sympathy for your . . . for him while he was staying here. And if he managed to win you over, then I've got to warn you: these people are nothing to screw with!"

" 'These people'?" Mother said archly.

"The Red Jihad! They'll say and do *anything* to get what they want. If you're feeling sorry for him, they have you right where they want you!"

"Assuming you're right about James being one of them," Mother said, "which I very much doubt."

Fredrichs displayed the type of smile you immediately want to wipe away with a lawn mower. "So you do sympathize with him."

"I'm not being sympathetic," she replied down her nose, "I'm being rational."

His smile disappeared. "One thing I'll tell you now: if you're helping a fugitive, you're going to be in some big trouble."

"You give us an awful lot of credit," Peter said. "How do you think we helped him?"

"It's obvious."

"Obvious?" I said, forgetting for the moment that it probably wasn't a good idea to sound offended that he didn't think my plan was ingenious.

"We already said it! You got him out of here in disguise."

"In disguise!" Mother exclaimed with a sardonic laugh. "Are you actually suggesting that we took a soldier newly arrived from Iraq, dressed him up like a woman, and sent him out on the street? Do you actually think we would do something that daft?"

Only my mother could manage to sound so indignant when accused of something we'd actually done. It was a gamble, but it worked. Fredrichs looked as if he was realizing for the first time how incredibly crazy that *did* sound. When he hesitated, I looked over at Nelson and my heart almost stopped at what I saw: he was smiling.

"No," Nelson said. "I'm sure Agent Fredrichs doesn't believe that you would do something like that." He looked to Fredrichs and cocked his head toward the door. "Agent?"

"Hey, wait a minute! I want the names of the people who were here last night!"

"For what?" I asked.

"So I can question them! I intend to find out what happened to that fugitive!"

"Well, you're damn well going to have to do without!" Mother said, sounding increasingly incensed. "I'll not have you pestering our friends with your wild ideas!"

"Let's go, Fredrichs," said Nelson as he opened the door.

Fredrichs looked like he wanted to question us some more—probably with the aid of bamboo shoots or hot pokers—but knew it wouldn't do any good. Instead, he said, "Believe me, this isn't over! I'm going to find out what you've done with him!"

"Be sure to check all the 7-Elevens," I said.

He growled at me and marched out the door.

Nelson paused in the doorway and gave us what was perhaps

the most significant look I've ever received. He left without a word, closing the door behind him.

"Dear Lord, we're in it now!" Mother exclaimed.

"I can't believe they put it together so fast!" I said. "I didn't think they were that smart."

"What did you think they would think when they saw an extra person leaving our house?" Peter said loudly. "That we were practicing some sort of magic trick?"

"You know what I thought!"

"Yeah, I know! You thought you could play watch-me-pull-a-faggot-out-of-my-hat and nobody would notice!"

"That's not fair! It was the only way we could do it! And it doesn't matter if they think we pulled something over on them! They only suspect! They don't know who was here! They don't have any way of finding Joe and Mickey, or Stevie, for that matter. We're perfectly safe!"

His jaw dropped even lower than it had before. "Perfectly safe? The FBI thinks we're aiding a terrorist!"

I gritted my teeth. "They think we're aiding somebody they *think* is a terrorist! But he's not!"

"But they don't know that! And we *are* aiding him!"

"Are you both quite finished?" said Mother, sounding exactly as if she were scolding Jane and Michael Banks. "Because if you are, we can consider the much bigger problem we have now."

"What?" I asked.

"What are we going to do about James?"

I heaved a sigh. "For heaven's sake! You know we haven't thought of anywhere to take him yet!"

"I don't mean *that!* I mean, how are we going to get him out of town now?"

"I thought you said we'd just drive him."

She raised her eyebrows at me. Peter said, "Oh, no!" and dropped down onto the couch.

"What?" I said irritably.

"They think we're involved," Mother explained. "Now they'll be watching us. We can't go anywhere near James."

"Oh, God!" I said when I realized what she was saying. I slowly lowered myself onto the couch beside Peter.

"Yes! It's not just that we don't have anywhere to take him, we can't take him there when we *do* have somewhere to take him! I hardly thought it possible, but we're in a much bigger mess than before. Does Stevie have a car?"

"I wouldn't think so," said Peter. "Not where he lives."

"What about Joe and Mickey?"

"Same thing. Hardly anyone in that neighborhood owns a car."

"Oh, God!" I repeated, burying my face in my hands.

After a moment Peter put his arm over my shoulder affectionately. "I'm sorry I snapped at you, honey. It's just, you know, the way I get when I think I'm going to have to spend the rest of my life in a federal penitentiary."

I raised my head and looked him in the eye. He was grinning at me lovingly.

"And," he continued, "I know I was the one who wanted us to get involved in this business to begin with."

"Along with me," said Mother.

"Now let me get this straight," I said, sitting up in my chair. "You're both finally admitting that I didn't start all this?"

"That's right," said Peter.

"Well, darling," said Mother, joining into the spirit of conciliation as she sat on the arm of the couch, "if it makes you feel any better, not only did your plan work—even if they did catch on a bit soon—but it appears it was even more necessary to get James out than I first thought."

"What do you mean?"

"You heard Larry. It *did* occur to him that James might come back here, just like I said. We had to do it as quickly as possible."

"That's not the only thing that occurred to him. I got the distinct impression that he really believes we're helping James."

"I got that impression as well," said Mother. "Funny, that."

"You think so?" I unconsciously lapsed into a Yiddish accent.

"Well, yes. Only that Larry usually goes rather out of his way to show nothing. I wonder if he was trying to tell us something."

"Fredrichs told us something that makes me awfully nervous," I said.

"What?"

"That stuff about how James would try to win our sympathy. How the jihad would do anything to get what they want."

"What are you saying?" Peter asked.

"Is it possible that James really is part of the jihad, and he's charmed us just so we would help him get away from the feds? We did everything we could to make him feel as if we weren't . . . well, totally in sympathy with Nelson. Maybe he's a lot smarter than we think he is."

Mother and Peter glanced at each other, looking very much as if they didn't want to believe this, but couldn't dismiss it out of hand.

"Then why bother with the gay thing?" Peter asked.

"What do you mean?"

"I can see him using it to get our government to believe he wanted to get out of Iraq, but why tell us about it?"

I spread my palms. "To win us over. To make us think we were all sisters under the skin."

He was silent for several seconds, then turned back to Mother, the one person in our lives who was usually an infallible judge of character. "Jean?"

She thought for a long time, apparently replaying the last few days in her head. Finally, she rested her palms on her legs, looked up, and said, "I really don't think that boy with the tattered undies is that good an actor."

"I don't know," I said with a sigh. "That boy in the bra and panties was giving an awfully good performance when he left here!"

Our family, now reduced to its normal size, found that it puts a damper on the day to be berated by the feds before breakfast. What followed was one of our worst days. Nelson had certainly understated just how much allowing James in our house would disrupt our lives, but of course that was before the shootout, and the escape, and before we started aiding a fugitive, so I suppose he could be excused.

We spent the day being uncharacteristically uncommunicative as we worried the problem in our various ways. Peter and I converted James's room back into my office, then wandered around the house looking concerned and bumping into each other. Occasionally I peeked out through the curtains of the living-room window to see if our guard was still on duty, always knowing that he would be.

Mother did what she always does when something's fretting her: she cleaned. I took it as a bad sign that she did it with nary a hum or a whistle. By mid-afternoon you had to wear sunglasses to tolerate the gleam in the kitchen.

It wasn't until afternoon tea—something that we usually don't have with such formality—that we settled down to try to work things out.

"I've been thinking about it," I said, pausing for a sip from my mug.

"*Rah*-ther!" Mother said ironically.

"Actually, I don't think the who is much of a problem."

"You're going to have to explain that one," said Peter.

"I mean who we can get to take James out of town. I'm sure Joe and Mickey would be game."

"From what I've seen of them so far, they'd be game for anything," Mother said with a sly smile.

"They could always rent a car."

Peter shook his head. "Too risky. Too easy to trace. Car-rental companies clock in the mileage before and after your trip. If Fredrichs traced them, he'd know exactly how far they went."

"I suppose if needs be I have enough money that I could buy one for them. A used one, I mean," Mother offered.

"You're not Janet Leigh, Mother," I said. "And it's not as easy to do that without being traced as it was when they made *Psycho*."

She wrinkled her nose. "Quite right. And look what happened to *her*."

Peter added, "We still don't have any idea where to take James once we figure out how to do it."

"Oh, bother!" Mother exclaimed with frustration. "I'm absolutely stymied!

My heart sank. I'd come to rely on my mother's endless stream of ingenuity when it came to espionage—something that not every son can say. To see her at a loss was more than disheartening, it was almost scary.

"You're not throwing in the towel!"

"Certainly not! But it is a dilemma. I'd thought of Joe and Mickey myself. The trouble is, how could we even work it out with them?"

I shrugged. "All we'd have to do is talk to them."

Mother raised her elegant eyebrows at me.

Peter cleared his throat. "How, honey?"

"Oh, that's right." I said after a beat.

"We can't very well call them," Mother said. "Fredrichs will be tracing our calls, if he's not actually listening in."

"And I'll be willing to bet he's going to have us followed," said Peter. "We not only can't contact James, we can't safely contact anyone else."

I suddenly felt the walls closing in around me. "If I ever start thinking I'm clever again, remind me of this. I've really gotten us into a hole."

The rest of the evening was much the same, the three of us seeming to have disappeared inside our own heads, searching for a solution with no luck. Mother's temporary answer that night was the same as the night before: to sleep on it. I went to bed feeling certain of only one thing: that things couldn't get any worse.

I was wrong.

TEN

Mother was sitting at the kitchen table when Peter and I came downstairs the next morning. She was clad in one of the many silk kimonos she'd bought on the trip to Japan she took after my father—her ex-husband—died, leaving her more than reasonably well off. This one was shiny black with appliqués of Japanese lettering in white, like an ankle-length happi coat, only not quite as busy.

"I haven't started breakfast yet," she said as we came into the room. "I will in a minute."

"Thank you, honorable Mother-san," I said with a bow. "You look very serene this morning. Have you been meditating?"

"I've been having a bit of a think," she said, setting her cup in its saucer. "And I may have a little idea."

Before she could tell us what it was, the phone rang. I answered it and was confronted with a familiar voice that sounded panicked.

"Alex? It's Stevie."

"I know who it is!" I said quickly, trying to cut him off. I hadn't wanted him to say his name. I'd told him not to call us unless it was an emergency, but he was flaky enough that I wasn't sure he knew what an emergency was. After yesterday's scene with Fredrichs, it wasn't safe to call us at all.

"Gee, it's been a long time," I continued.

"What?"

"Since we've heard from you! What have you been up to?" I said a silent prayer that he would catch on.

"Oh, for pity's sake, Alex! This is no time for your spy games! I just got home, and—"

"This isn't a game!" I said loudly, cutting him off again. "Everything I told you was true!"

He sighed. "I just got home, and Ja—"

"Don't tell me now! Not on the phone! Tell me in person!"

There was a tense pause. "Okay, okay, if we have to play, I can do that, too. When do you want me to meet you?" Although he still sounded impatient, there was a bit of uncertainty in his voice now, as if he was just beginning to believe in the "spy games."

My mind raced. Whatever had happened, it really must be bad. I tried to think of a way to meet with him without the feds being able to monitor us.

"Well . . . the thing is, Peter is working today . . . so I don't think we can see you until late. Very late. After eleven . . ."

"But you know I—"

"Yes, I know!" I said loudly. "But listen to me! Peter is working today, so we can't do it until after eleven."

He huffed. I could almost see him rolling his bug eyes. "Alex, you know I—"

"Yes, I know!" I said quickly. "But we can't see you until after eleven. Peter is working today . . ."

Come on . . . come on . . . you can do it, I was thinking.

"Oh," he said at last, "I see."

"Do you?"

"Uh-huh."

He didn't sound very sure, but I said goodbye and hung up anyway, feeling that if I tried any harder to get it across, I might as well just come out and say it.

"Please, please, please, God! Make him understand!" I said to the ceiling.

"What is it?" said Peter.

"There's a problem."

"Another one?" said Mother.

"That was Stevie."

"Lor', what's happened now?"

"I don't know. I stopped him before he could say anything. But he wasn't doing his Trulamae Lipshitz routine, so it must be bad. We're going to meet him."

"How can we do that?" Peter asked.

"I think . . . I think I was able to set it up," I said slowly. "I think he's going to come to us. Or at least, to you."

"What?"

"I gave him a not-very-gentle hint that I think he got. At least I *hope* he got it."

"I heard you. You told him we'd see him tonight after eleven. But that's not even possible. Didn't he say he's on the late shift?"

"Yep," I said.

"Then wha—"

"I was trying to tell him that he could meet us where you work. At Farrahut's."

Peter squinched up his face doubtfully. "You think he got that?"

"I'm not sure. I hope so."

"Why on earth would you want to meet him there?" Mother asked.

I shrugged. "There's nothing but gay men in and out of that place. The FBI can't follow them all!"

At nine o'clock Peter left for work, and I went with him. We didn't know if Fredrichs's men were prepared to follow one or both of us, but it didn't matter, since either way they'd end up at Farrahut's. We just had to hope that if they'd listened to Stevie's call, they thought our meeting was at eleven that night. If they didn't, then we were banking on the fact that they wouldn't be able to tell our caller from the rest of the customers.

"Did you notice anyone?" I said as we went up the stairs to the Fullerton stop on the Red Line.

"Nobody in particular," Peter replied. "But who can tell? It's still rush hour. There's too many people on the street."

The same was true of the El platform. Although there were fewer people than there would've been an hour earlier, there were still enough to constitute a crowd. We couldn't very well scan them to see if anybody was paying particular attention to us without looking like we were looking for someone, if you know what I mean. That would've only made what we were doing look more suspicious. So we agreed to try to put the idea that we were being followed out of our heads and try to act naturally, as much as that was possible.

We got off the El at Division and joined the minor surge of people up the endless stairs to the surface, then walked down Rush to Oak Street. I tried not to look behind me, but given the fact that it would've been a little more unusual for someone to be following this exact route, my curiosity got the better of me. A couple of times as we passed shops I looked sideways as if something in the window had caught my eye, and let my head turn as we passed until I got a glimpse over my shoulder. About half a block back there was a guy in a pale yellow polo shirt and a pair of gray slacks. He looked so casual and unassuming I was sure he was a Fed.

We turned onto Oak Street and headed east. About midway down the block is the Esquire Theater, which was once one of Chicago's movie palaces but has long since been Ginzued into a cineplex, saving only the beautiful Art Deco facade. As we passed it, I grabbed Peter's arm and stopped.

"Wait a minute!"

"What?" he asked with surprise.

"Pretend to look at that." I pointed at a poster for some generic Julia Roberts movie.

"Why?"

"I just want to see something."

The box office was to our left, and a placard listing the show times for all the films was suspended just inside the window. I turned toward it and tried to appear as if I were searching for a show time. Out of the corner of my eye, I looked back down the street. The unassuming guy had stopped at the store on the corner and was giving the impression of being fascinated by the window display.

"That does it," I said. "Let's go."

"What does it do?" said Peter as we continued down the street.

"We are being followed."

He naturally started to turn around to see for himself.

"Don't look!" I said.

He snapped forward and sighed. "I'm married to Laura Petrie."

"I'll point him out when we get inside."

Farrahut's is just a couple of doors east of the theater. Nobody knows where the store got its name, except perhaps for owner/proprietor Arthur Dingle, who isn't telling. Peter's theory is that Farrahut was the surname of one of Dingle's long-lost loves. I personally believe it's German for "fairy house."

The building that housed Farrahut's had undergone a change a decade earlier that was exactly the opposite of what had been done to the Esquire: the interior was spared any renovating atrocities while the facade had been torn off and replaced with a floor-to-ceiling mock bay window. In the window three ghostly white, anorexic mannequins stood sporting obscenely expensive Italian suits in colors that ranged from olive green to olive drab, which is probably why Italian suits always look like you can squeeze oil out of them. We went through the door to the musical accompaniment of an old-fashioned overhead bell.

The store was long and narrow, with carpeting roughly the same shade as the suits in the window. The walls in the front two-thirds were lined with racks of suits, carefully spaced to avoid wrinkles. At gaps in the racks there were huge monochrome vases from which sprouted enormous dry reeds, a sure sign that Dingle had never heard of feng shui. The remainder of the store has shirts, ties, and underwear, all bearing price tags that have actually caused wallets to go limp. A glass case across the back of the store held an array of accessories ranging from gold cuff links to diamond stick-pins. The place smells like old money—Old rotting money.

"Good morning," called Benny Harper, one of the other sales-men. He was spritzing the case with Windex. Benny was a tall, wil-lowy man with fashionably oiled black curls. He was wearing a black knit shirt and black pants, which made him look like an upscale stagehand.

"Good morning, Benny," said Peter.

"Hi," I added.

When Benny saw me, he dropped the Windex on the counter with a thud and his eyes widened. "Alex! I don't believe it! There is a God! I haven't seen you in a hundred years! Don't tell me you've finally decided to stop being the fashion disaster that you are and let us dress you properly!"

I hadn't realized until that moment that I hadn't given any thought to what I was wearing: a coral-shaded gauze shirt and a pair of jeans. I looked down at myself and then back up at him.

"Um, I haven't decided."

"I would *love* to get you out of those clothes!"

"That's my job," Peter said with a smile.

Benny smiled back and snatched a paper towel from a roll behind the counter, then started to wipe the blue mist from the glass counter. "Well, Alex, don't you worry none about how you look. You're dressed better than at least ten percent of the guys that come in here!"

I laughed. "Thanks a lot!"

"Is Art here?" Peter asked.

"Uh-uh. He called in and said he's not going to be in all day."

"Is he okay?"

Benny puckered his lips. "She sounded like she was calling from just south of death."

"Is he sick?"

He leaned over the counter toward us. "Just between you and me and anyone else who cares to hear about it, Grandma had a date last night with someone half her age. And she can't even burn the candle at *one* end anymore without landing herself in a wheelchair, much less burn it at both ends. She'll be in tomorrow."

"Look," I said to Peter. My attention had wandered back to the front of the store.

"What?"

I nodded toward the window. The guy I thought had been following us had paused there to light a cigarette, although he wasn't giving any indication of looking in.

"Look at what? That boy?" said Benny, craning his neck to see past us.

The guy stuck his lighter in his pocket and moved on.

"What's the big deal?" said Benny, puzzled by our interest. "I wouldn't clean my teeth with a boy like that!"

"That's the one following us," I whispered to Peter.

"Hmm. Let me show you something in the window."

We went to the front of the store and Peter went through the motions of drawing my attention to the suit on the first mannequin. I pretended to be interested. We both knew what we were looking for, and we found it: the guy had crossed the street and seated himself on a fire hydrant, where he seemed to be contemplating the gutter.

"Could just be innocent," Peter said doubtfully.

"I don't think so. But I've only seen one. I was expecting one for each of us."

He smiled. "You sound disappointed."

"Maybe they thought since we left together we'd stay together," I said distractedly.

"Alex . . . what are you thinking?"

I gave him an impish smile. "It might be fun to try to lose him."

"For what? If he is watching us, hopefully he's just going to think Stevie's a customer, assuming Stevie shows up. Wasn't that the plan?"

"Yeah, but if I could lead that guy away from here and lose him . . ."

"If you did that, wouldn't he just come back here?"

"Oh. Yeah. I hadn't thought of that," I replied, somewhat crest-fallen. I hadn't tried to lose a tail since Mother and I ditched a Russian at the zoo. Not everyone can say that.

"Just relax and go with the simple plan, will you?" said Peter. I noticed for the first time he sounded a little tense.

"All right."

He straightened the mannequin's collar, and we were about to return to the back of the store when he said, "Hey, look."

I followed his gaze. The guy had stood up and was crushing out his cigarette. He then looked both ways and crossed the street at a diagonal heading away from us.

"Well!" I said, feeling even more deflated, though I don't know why I should have. We certainly didn't *want* someone following us. "Either he wasn't tailing us or . . . or he's just changed to this side of the street. I think I'll go see if he's standing down there."

"I think I'll have you committed," said Peter, taking me by the arm and ushering me toward the back of the store. "We're in enough trouble without you acting like Charlie Chan's number two son."

My anxiety level rose as the minutes ticked by without a single customer entering the store. Benny continued cleaning and Peter spent his time straightening the suits with an unerring eye for symmetry. I stayed at his side.

"I wish you had a few customers," I said.

"So do I."

"I don't mean that! I mean for cover. I was hoping there'd be a few shoppers for Stevie to blend in with."

"Hmm," said Peter, "We're probably better off without."

"Why?"

"Remember how easily Agent Fredrichs passed himself off at Charlene's?"

"Oh yeah. You know, I wonder if the feds have a whole stable of reasonably attractive young men who can pass for us. It makes you wonder what they need with us at all."

"There's no substitute for the real thing," Peter said wryly.

It was five after eleven when the door swung open, sending the gentle shop bell into a violent spasm. Stevie rushed in looking like I'd never seen him before: his normally florid skin was pale and drawn, and his eyes were blank.

"Thank God you're here!" he said, heading straight for me. "I didn't know if I understood your silly—"

"Stop!" I kept my voice low but urgent. "Pretend you don't know me!" I snatched a suit off the rack and made a pretense of examining it.

Stevie came to a halt at my command and crossed his arms. "For heaven's sake, Alex!"

"I'm not kidding! We're being watched from outside."

"What?"

"Don't look!"

He stopped just short of wheeling around toward the front window, then turned halfway back to me. "Okay, I'm not supposed to look at you, and I'm not supposed to look at whoever's outside. May I ask you exactly what I should look at?"

"A suit!" I said.

He sighed dramatically. "Oh, all right!" He stamped forward to the nearest rack and began to finger the material of one of the jackets.

"Okay," I said. "Now I'm going to take this one back to the dressing rooms. You look around for a couple of minutes, then pick out a suit and come back there."

"Hey, is this silk?"

I clenched my teeth. "Are you listening to me?"

"Yeah, yeah, yeah," he said wearily. "Wait a minute, pick up suit, go to dressing room."

"Good!"

"Do I get to keep the suit?"

I hissed at him then headed for the back of the store. On the way I told Peter what we were doing.

"Fine. I'll come back there with him," he said.

I went to the curtained entryway just to the right of the glass cabinet where Benny was sipping coffee and leafing through a copy of *GQ*. He looked up as I passed and did a double-take.

"All these years I've been trying to get you in fashion, and you're gonna buy *that?*"

I looked down at the suit draped over my arm and stifled a gasp. The one I'd haphazardly plucked off the rack was a bizarre shade of purple that was awfully vivid even though it was fairly dark. I wasn't only surprised to find it was the one I'd grabbed; I was surprised they had it in the store.

"Uh . . . yeah," I said vacantly. "I like the color. I just thought I'd try it on."

He shook his head slowly as he went back to his magazine. "You'll look like a fag pimp."

I passed through the curtains.

The elegance of Farrahut's didn't end in the front of the house, it was carried on to the dressing rooms. There were four of them, each large enough for two with padded, L-shaped benches and full-length mirrors. They also had proper doors for privacy rather than those idiotic saloon-type doors that are the staple of tacky stores.

While I waited for Stevie to come back I stood in front of the mirror in the first dressing room and held the suit up in front of me. Benny was wrong. I didn't look like a gay pimp; I looked like a tall glass of Welch's Grape Juice. I quickly hung the suit on a hook when I heard someone coming through the curtains.

Stevie appeared carrying one of the olive suits—away from the others I couldn't tell which shade it was—which he hung up without even looking at it. Peter was right behind him and shut the door, closing the three of us in.

"You didn't call us from your apartment, did you?" I said to Stevie.

He pursed his lips. "You know, up until I got home this morning, I thought you were just pulling my chain—not that I would've minded that, either—with all this stuff. But after what happened, I'm not so sure."

"What happened?" I asked anxiously.

"So no, even though I don't believe it myself, I did not call you from my apartment. I went out and called you from a pay phone on Clark. Because if James was really just some friend of yours who needed a place to stay for a few days, I don't know why he'd do what he did."

"What did he do?" I said loudly, losing my patience.

Stevie glared at me and emitted a huff as if he'd already explained everything and I was just being slow. "He's gone!"

"What!" I exclaimed.

"What do you mean, he's gone?" Peter asked.

"I mean, I got home from work at a quarter to eight this morning and found myself home alone. He was gone."

"Maybe he just . . . went out for a little while," I said weakly.

Peter looked at me as if I'd finally suffered the mental collapse he's always expected. "Where?"

"I don't know!" I turned to Stevie. "Are you sure he just didn't . . . step out?"

He shook his head. "He took all of his things. Lock, stock, and duffel bag!"

"Was there any sign of a break-in?" Peter asked.

Stevie shook his head. "No. He was just gone. The place was quiet as a mouse."

"Jesus Christ, Stevie!" I said. "You were supposed to watch him! How could you let this happen?!"

"Well, excuse me for having to make a living," he replied haughtily, "but I have a job, you know! You didn't tell me I'd have to chain him to the radiator before I went to work! I thought he was supposed to *want* to be in hiding!"

I was brought up short again. Once more James had managed to throw doubt on his real motives by his own actions. "You're right, he is supposed to. I'm sorry I yelled."

" 'Sall right," he said with a flip of his wrist.

We fell silent for a minute, then Peter said, "Did anything unusual happen?"

"What do you mean, unusual?"

"I mean, you didn't notice anybody watching your place or hanging around or anything like that?"

"Oh, no, nothing like that," he replied with a nervous laugh.

I narrowed my eyes at him. "Was there something else?"

"Huh?"

"Did something happen between the two of you?"

He looked down at the floor. "Alex, you know I'm not the kind of person who would . . . who would . . ."

"Take advantage of a situation?" I suggested. "Betray a trust?"

"I was going to say 'kiss and tell.'"

"You slept with him!" I exclaimed in shock.

"Alex, keep your voice down! Benny's out there!" said Peter.

"You slept with him?" I said in a lower but no less intense tone. "How could you do that?"

"It's not like I forced myself on him!" he said defensively. "I made up the couch for him to sleep on, just like a good little hostess! But hell, I wasn't in bed fifteen minutes before he came into my room and crawled into bed with me. He said he was scared!"

"He said he was scared, so you slept with him?"

Stevie drew back disdainfully. "Well, I've done a lot of things with guys in bed, but I've never scared anyone!"

"That's not the point! We left him in your safekeeping, and you took advantage of him?"

"All I did was try to comfort him! He climbed into my bed, and I held him. Before I knew it, he was all over me like a cheap suit!" He paused for a second, then added, "A cheap suit that fit very well!"

"I don't believe this!" I said, sinking to the bench. "We leave someone in your care and you . . . and you . . . Stevie, I told you he just came out of the closet! He's in a strange land!"

"Aren't we all?"

"There's no telling how much you might've traumatized him!"

"Traumatized him?" Stevie said, his voice cracking. "Traumatized *him!* What about *me?*"

I was thoroughly lost. "What about you?"

"What about my feelings! I can be traumatized, too, you know!"

"By what?"

Tears welled in his eyes. "You cast that waif on me out of the blue and expect me to know what to do with him! You didn't warn me how sweet he was!"

"He's an endearing little refugee, I know," I said.

"He just . . . he just . . . sleeps with me and then runs off without a word! I know my batting average has been bad, but they don't usually flee in the night!"

"What are you saying?" Peter asked.

"You've got to find him and make sure he's all right! I don't want to think I . . . that I was the reason . . ."

I suddenly felt abashed when I realized what he was thinking. I got up and put my arms around him. Peter stood behind him and rubbed his neck.

"No, no . . ." I said quietly. "It's not your fault."

His tears were flowing freely now. "It's just . . . you know how some guys can be about their first time. I didn't mean for it to happen, it just did!"

"There's more going on here that embarrassment over sex," said Peter.

Stevie pulled away from me and looked at him. "You really think so?"

"Um-hmm."

"Because . . . well, you see, it happened the first night, and then, you know, I was off yesterday, so I was with him all day. Talking and talking. He wasn't out of my sight until I went to work last night, so I thought maybe . . . he was just waiting for his chance to get away from me."

"He might've been waiting for his chance to get away, but not from you."

Stevie managed to convey his gratitude through his tears, then seemed to realize how damp he'd become. He fished in his pocket for a tissue. "He's so sweet! I just can't bear the thought of him being out there alone." He paused to blow his nose. "Jesus! He's gay and at large in Chicago! It sounds like my youth!"

I hated to sound like Nelson, but I had to ask the next question. "Do you have any idea where he might have gone? Did he mention anybody or anyplace?"

158

"No, nothing."

"What did you talk about?"

"Have you ever tried to have a conversation with him? It's not that easy, even as darling as he is." There was a short silence, then he added, "He talked about the two of you quite a bit."

"He did?"

Stevie nodded. "Yeah. All about how wonderful you are. I wish . . ." Whatever he was wishing brought on a fresh onslaught of tears. "You guys just have to find him and make sure he's all right!"

"We intend to," I said.

"How?" Peter asked.

"I don't know, but . . ." My voice trailed off because I really had no clue as to how we'd go about it. But after a few moments, I began to see a glimmer. "Wait a minute! Stevie, did you really call us from a pay phone?"

"Yeah," he said with a sigh. "Why?"

"Did you make any other calls when you got home from work?"

"No, I got home, found he was missing, then went out and called you."

"And since then?"

"No, I didn't call anybody!" he said, impatient for me to get to the point.

"Hmm. Does you phone have automatic redial?"

"Yeah."

"Then do me a favor: when you get home, do that and see what happens."

"What are you thinking?" Peter asked.

"That maybe James didn't just run off on his own. He might've called somebody before he left. Maybe we can find out who that was. We can't get Stevie's phone records without telling Nelson what we know—"

"What about Frank?"

I shook my head. "He may be an area commander, but he's not going to get phone records for us. At least not without an explanation. And the minute we explain, he'll have to do something about it. Look, it's just a chance, but we should take it."

"What if somebody answers?" Stevie asked.

"Hang up."

He reared back slightly. "Then what the Sam Hill is the point of doing it?"

"I'm hoping you'll get a machine. After all, it's the middle of the day. And a lot of people say their number in their message."

"Boy, that's a long shot," said Peter.

"Maybe, but it's about all we have."

Before leaving, Stevie made a stop in the bathroom to wash his face and generally pull himself together. Peter waited for him in the back while I went into the front of the store so that it wouldn't look as if the three of us were together. Much to my dismay, I found that a couple of would-be customers had come in while we'd been in the back. They could've been innocent shoppers, especially since neither of them was the guy I thought was following us, but in our present circumstances I had to view the timing of their arrival as suspicious, even if just for safety's sake.

One of the customers was a tallish man of about thirty with dusty blond hair who was lingering uncertainly by the first rack of suits. He was dressed in a tan cloth jacket and a pair of light-blue slacks and was slowly touching the shoulder of each of the suits, shifting them slightly for a better view. His puzzled frown made him look like he'd never seen a suit before.

Benny was waiting on the other customer, a fey young man who was slightly over five feet and had dyed white hair. There were three diamond studs pierced through each ear, as well as dangling earcuffs. He wore a skintight white T-shirt and denim cutoffs. He looked like an even less likely candidate for an Italian suit than the other customer. However, the attention with which Benny was serving him meant that he was known to the shop, so I figured he could be ruled out as a potential agent.

Benny inadvertently helped me maintain the illusion that I was shopping. He smiled over at me, pointed to the suit I'd grabbed for cover, and said, "What did you think?"

"You were right," I said with a laugh. "I don't know what I was thinking!"

He immediately returned his attention to the little guy, and I wandered to the front of the store. I didn't know how long it would be before Peter and Stevie came out from the back, so I seized the opportunity to find out if this guy was really a shopper or was an agent. As I got closer to him, I happened to glance out the window and saw that the guy in the pale yellow shirt had returned to his perch on the fire hydrant and was lighting another cigarette. Fighting an increasing feeling of claustrophobia, I sidled up to the would-be customer as nonchalantly as I could, trying to seem as if I were still making some decision about the suit. When I was fairly close to him, I held the suit out at arm's length and tsked loudly.

"What do you think?" I said, turning my head slightly in his direction.

He glanced at me, then looked the suit up and down. "It's kind of a weird color."

"I know. That's why it caught my eye, I guess. Under the lights in the dressing room it looks even worse. Ah, well." I hung the suit back on the rack with a sigh. "The stuff here is a little out of my league."

"Yeah."

"Do you usually shop here?"

He shot me a sidelong glance. I hoped I wasn't being too obvious.

"Uh, no. This is the first time I've ever come in here." He paused, then added. "How about you?"

"Oh, I come in from time to time. I don't know why. What brought you in?"

He hesitated. "I don't know. I just wandered in. No reason in particular." He was attempting to sound casual, but there was a tenseness in his voice that gave him away. For an agent, he was awfully unprepared.

"You weren't . . . looking for anything?" I asked.

"No," he said slowly, "but you never know what you might find."

He certainly was being cagey. Although I'd set out to feel him out, I got the feeling he was very subtly trying to turn the tables on me. "I don't know how much luck you'll have here. I never seem to find anything I want."

"Maybe your luck will change."

"Maybe."

He took a deep breath. "My name is Tony. Tony Davis." He offered his hand and I shook it confusedly. I hadn't known another agent to take such a direct approach. Out of the corner of my eye I saw Peter and Stevie emerge through the curtains. Tony didn't show any sign of noticing them, which in itself was suspicious, since if he was an agent he would make a point of ignoring them.

Peter said, "Sorry we couldn't help you," as he took the suit from Stevie, who then left the store.

As Peter went to hang up the suit, I realized that Tony still had hold of my hand. I slipped it away.

"Um, you know, there's a Starbucks just around the corner from here," he said.

"Yeah, I know."

"Uh . . . want me to buy you a cup of coffee?"

"You want to buy me coffee?" I asked with surprise.

"Uh-huh."

It took a moment for this to break through. "Oh! Oh, no, I'm sorry! I wasn't . . . I'm married!"

"Oh," he replied, looking flustered. "I thought you were—"

"No, I wasn't!" I stammered. "I was . . . I was . . . just looking for . . . you know, an opinion on the suit."

"Uh-huh."

"No, really! You see that guy over there? He's my husband."

Tony glanced over at Peter, then turned to me and a little smile appeared. "Oh, I get it."

"You do?"

"Uh-huh." He reached into his pocket and pulled out a business card, then took my hand and pressed it into my palm. He leaned forward and whispered, "Call me when he's not around."

Before I could try to explain, he waggled his eyebrows and headed for the door. I looked down at the card, then nearly jumped out of my socks at the sound of a throat being cleared behind me. I turned around and found Peter eyeing me with one raised eyebrow.

"Can I ask you something?" he said.

"Sure."

"Were you just making a date with one of my customers?"

"Well, to be perfectly accurate, he was making a date with me. I mean, trying to. I mean—" I broke off. I could feel my grave getting deeper.

"Yes?"

"I was just . . . you know I would never—" I stopped again and took a deep breath to calm myself. "I was trying to find out if he was an agent."

"Of course you were."

I was starting to go red in the face. "You know I love you more than anything!"

Benny and the little guy stopped what they were doing and looked over at us. Peter put his lips close to my left ear. "I know. I just wanted to hear you say it!" He kissed my earlobe and laughed. "Jimmy Chan!"

"Honest to God, one of these days I'm going to kill you!" I said. "You know, I'm not just being paranoid."

"I know."

"Look." I cocked my head toward the window.

"At what?"

I looked across the street. Our tail was gone. "Oh, no! He was there! He was back!" I sighed. "All that trouble we went to and he found Stevie anyway."

"Maybe not. He was following us, remember. He might've just gone out of sight again."

"I hope so. Did you get anything more out of Stevie?"

"Nope."

"I can't believe how broken up he is about this."

Peter shrugged. "It can't be easy to have lost somebody he was supposed to be taking care of."

"I don't know about that. *We've* done it twice in the past three days!"

"You *know* what I mean!"

"Yeah, I know." I shut my eyes and put a palm to my forehead. "I can't believe James has run off!"

"What I can't believe is that you told Stevie we intend to find him!"

I opened my eyes. "Why wouldn't we?"

He glanced at Benny and the customer, who were deep in conversation, and lowered his voice some more. "You must understand what this means!"

"No, I don't!" I didn't say this very convincingly, because I really did think I knew where he was going.

"Alex, he ran away when he was perfectly safe where he was. And he didn't come back to us. That doesn't look good. I think it's time we entertain the idea that Agent Fredrichs might be right about James, no matter how unpleasant that idea might be."

"I don't know about that," I said, finding myself in the uncomfortable position of arguing against something that in my heart of hearts I knew was a possibility. Hell, I'd suggested it myself. "There could be other reasons for him running off. Maybe he didn't feel safe with Stevie! I don't mean—"

"I know what you meant," Peter said, rolling his eyes.

"For all we know, despite the precautions we took, that jihad might have found him and taken him."

"You really believe that?"

I sighed wearily. "I don't know what to believe!"

"Alex, if you're right, and he called somebody before he left, it'll mean—"

"All it'll mean is that he made a call!"

He stared at me for several seconds. "Look, honey, I've felt as much sympathy for James as you have, but I think we have to face facts."

"That's just it! We don't have any facts! Since we don't know what's happened, I think we have to find him!"

Peter looked at me for a long moment, then relented. "All right. How do we start?"

"By calling Mother."

ELEVEN

Mother arrived in the dark blue Saturn about twenty minutes after I made the call. She pulled up into the loading zone in front of the theater and honked the horn in a ladylike manner. I'll never know how she manages that.

I gave Peter a peck on the cheek and went out to join her. Of course, I hadn't told her anything over the phone other than the fact that I needed her to pick me up, so she was bursting with curiosity when I climbed into the car. I told her everything Stevie had said. Well, almost everything. She greeted the news of James's disappearance with grave displeasure.

"Good lord! What *can* that boy be up to?" she said, staring out through the windshield.

"I don't know. Peter's inclined to believe the worst."

"At this point you can hardly blame him. You were the one inclined to feel that way before. What d'you think now?"

I shook my head and sighed heavily. "It's like the phone call. I can't see any good reason for him to do it. But . . ."

Mother picked up for me. "But he's been treated shabbily and despite the way things look, you don't want to believe ill of him."

"Idiotic, isn't it?"

She smiled lovingly. "P'raps. But it does you credit. As long as it doesn't get us killed."

"The question is, what do we do now?"

She thought about this. "I think we should go to the Imperial Inn. We need to talk to Larry."

"Why?"

"To see if they found out anything. In all your ideas about what might've happened to James, one thing has escaped you. Perhaps our own agents found him."

The Imperial Inn was built in the fifties and looked it. Perched on a corner of Lake Shore Drive just north of Navy Pier, the hotel roughly resembled a large pile of old-fashioned hatboxes, sort of in the mode of the old Capitol Records building out in L.A. It looked like the kind of place the Jetsons would stay on a weekend jaunt to Chicago. A multilevel parking lot was tacked onto the back of the hotel like an afterthought. Each level of the lot was a maze of dangerous blind angles that the builders tried to mitigate by the use of round mirrors suspended at each corner, which had the unfortunate effect of startling drivers into thinking they were about to collide with themselves. I considered it very lucky that Mother found an empty space on the second level, before either of us had a heart attack.

We took the stairs down to the first level, bypassed the side door of the hotel, and went to the main entrance. The lobby was swarming with twentysomethings all headed in different directions, each one dragging along sets of matching luggage on wheels.

Mother clucked her tongue at the sight of them. "You know, when I was younger we were more adventurous. We used to travel the world with barely a change of linen. Now people aren't satisfied unless they're toting along all their earthly possessions wherever they go. It's rather like the beautiful person's version of a trailer home, don't you think?" She stopped when she noticed my expression. "What on earth are you looking at me like that for? You don't agree?"

"No, I'm horrified at the thought that you were *more* adventurous when you were younger than you are now. What did you do, fly combat missions with the RAF?"

"I'm afraid I'm not allowed to discuss it," she said. Given some of the things Mother has done over the past five years, I wish I could've been more sure that she was joking.

"Come along," she said a bit impatiently. "We've got to find Larry."

She swept up to the front desk where a crisp, energetic young woman in a bright blue blazer was talking on the phone.

"Yes, yes, we do have that available," she said as her fingers scampered across the keyboard of her computer. "Would you like that? I can reserve it on a credit card." She typed in the number, repeated the information, then said, "Yes, we'll be looking forward to seeing you. Bye-bye now."

She replaced the receiver and squared a pair of light brown eyes at Mother as if she would be the most important person in the world for the next thirty seconds. "Yes, and may I help you?"

"We're here to see Lawrence Nelson. Could you give us his room number?"

"Yes, I'm afraid I can't do that."

"Yes, you can't?" Mother said after a beat.

The young woman reached for the phone. "Yes, but may I tell him who's calling?"

"Yes, I suppose you may," Mother replied with a touch of loftiness. "The names are Jean and Alex Reynolds."

"Yes? Mr. Nelson?" the woman said into the phone. "There is a Jean and Alex Reynolds to see you. May I send them up? Yes? Thank you." She hung up the phone and looked at Mother. "Yes, you may go up. Mr. Nelson is in room 501. The elevators would be around the corner to the left."

"Would they?" said Mother with a coy smile.

The young woman blinked blankly. "Yes."

Mother glided away from the desk and I followed close at her heels.

"You were a bit peculiar with her, weren't you?" I said as we waited for the elevator.

"I'm feeling a bit peculiar." She gave the already lighted Up button another couple of thumps. "Honestly! I can't abide officious people, especially when I'm in a hurry." She pressed the button again. It was very unlike her to be so outwardly impatient, a sure sign that she was more worried than she would've liked to let on.

She gave a silent snort when the doors opened, expressing her annoyance with the recalcitrant conveyance. We rode up to the fifth floor and stepped into a hallway that was narrow and circular with a very low ceiling. There was a row of insistently identical doors on the outside wall. It was like being in the middle of some sort of warped luxury liner. Room 501 was the first room to the right of the elevators. The door opened just as I raised my knuckles to knock.

As always, Nelson looked like he was on his way to chair a meeting of the Fortune 500. He was wearing a navy blue suit, white shirt, and blue tie with thin maroon stripes. I'll never understand how a government agent can always look so urbane—especially on his salary.

"Come in," he said, stepping aside to allow us to enter.

The room was surprisingly bright and airy, despite the dark brown carpeting. The desk and table were made of fake wood in a light shade, and the spread on the double bed was a nubbly cream. White sheers were rustling in the lake breeze through the open windows.

"Our tax dollars stretch to this?" I said as he closed the door. "You don't look at all surprised to see us. Could it be you already knew we were on our way here?"

"The front desk told me," he replied without inflection.

"Oh. Right." I'd meant that as a challenge on the fact that we were being tailed and only managed to embarrass myself. I could feel my cheeks going red.

"What brings you here?"

"That should be obvious," said Mother. "We wanted news of James. Have you heard anything?"

"Have a seat," he said, motioning to the two chairs by the table. He pulled the desk chair over to join us. If he believed that we knew where James was, he didn't show it in the matter-of-fact way he addressed us. "Fredrichs's people and the police are combing the city, as much as that is possible. As far as I know they haven't come up with anything yet."

"As far as you know?" I said. "Wouldn't they tell you?"

"We're supposed to be cooperating in this matter, yes."

"Aren't they?"

"To the best of my knowledge."

"What are you, Ronald Reagan?" I said irritably. "Can't you answer anything directly?"

He took a long pause before he responded. "James has not been found yet. I would have been informed of that."

· I sat back in my chair, my mouth hanging open. "Oh, my God! They've taken you out of the loop, haven't they? They're not telling you anything!"

"I'm sure you've noticed that there's a certain amount of . . . strain . . . between the FBI and the CIA."

"You mean distrust, don't you?" Mother asked.

Nelson looked across the table at her without emotion. "Not on my part."

"Of course not," I said.

Mother's face lost some of its color. "It's us, isn't it? We're to blame. This Fredrichs fellow thinks we're helping James, and you're guilty by association. Is that it?"

"I can't tell what Agent Fredrichs is thinking. I don't believe he's ever been exactly trusting."

Mother frowned sympathetically. "Larry, I'm so sorry if anything we've done . . . I should say, I'm sorry if we've caused you any trouble."

"No trouble. I've worked with a lot of agents over the years. In my experience they generally come in two types: those who think everyone is lying, and those who don't show you that they think everyone is lying."

"Are you saying you fall into the latter category?" Mother asked after a lengthy pause.

"I like to think of myself as special."

"Oh, that you are!"

"Look, Nelson, Fredrichs told us flat out that he thought we were aiding James," I said. "And if that wasn't enough, now he's having us followed. What we want to know is what do *you* think?"

His head pivoted in my direction. "I know you well enough to rely on you to do what you believe is the right thing."

"Thank you very much, Larry!" said Mother. "That tells us absolutely nothing."

He folded his hands on the table and leaned in slightly. "I can tell you this: if I didn't think I could trust you, I would cut you loose."

Mother's eyebrows went up, as did mine. Ever since Fredrichs made that scene at our house I'd had the distinct impression that Nelson believed we were helping James. If that was true, then from what he'd just said either he also thought we were doing the right thing, or he had an agenda all of his own that nobody, including Fredrichs, was in on, and we were playing into it.

"While you're in such a straightforward mood, would you tell us something else?" I asked.

He inclined his head.

"Do you think James is a member of the Red Jihad?"

Nelson sat back in his chair. "I don't know."

"Oh, come on, Larry!"

"What do you expect me to say? Initially, I would've said no, I don't think he's a member. But making that phone call, disappearing from the bar, these things have cast some doubt, so the most accurate answer I can give you is I don't know."

I heaved a frustrated sigh. "But you must *think* something!"

Nelson leveled his eyes at me. "I *think* that you want to believe

James—and perhaps go a bit further for him than would be strictly prudent—because he's gay."

It was several seconds before the full sting of this hit me. "That's not true!"

"I'm not saying it's the only reason," Nelson continued calmly. "Only that it's a factor for you where it isn't for me." I started to protest again, but he held up a palm. "Think about it for a minute, Alex. If James wasn't gay, if he was just another Iraqi soldier who said he wanted to defect . . . if you'd taken him to a different kind of bar and had caught him making that phone call, what would you have done?"

I did give this some thought, a little reluctantly, and I didn't like what I was seeing. Under the circumstances he'd just described, I don't think we would've asked James to explain the call first; we would've gone straight to Nelson as we'd been instructed and reported it a lot more forthrightly than we did. As I quickly ran through the events of the past few days in my mind, I began to see something that made me uncomfortable: we *had* been more inclined to cut James some slack because he was gay. Even with all my doubts about him, without realizing it I hadn't handled things the way I would have otherwise. It didn't make me feel much better to think that Peter and Mother had done the same as well. The astounding thing was, it wasn't as if I didn't know any gay people who are absolute shits. There was no rational reason to err on the side of faggots.

However, the fact that Nelson was right wasn't something I was prepared to admit to him. Unfortunately, he seemed to read the truth on my face. I was grateful that he was enough of a gentleman not to say it.

"That aside," he said, "whatever other reasons you may have for believing in James, I think that some of the things Agent Fredrichs said to you yesterday may have planted doubts in your mind, and you've come to me for reassurance. But the only answer I have for you is I don't know if he's a member of the jihad, and at the moment it doesn't matter. My job now is to try to find him."

"Like Tommy Lee Jones," I muttered.

"I beg your pardon?"

"In *The Fugitive*. When he caught up with Harrison Ford in the tunnel, Ford said that he didn't kill his wife, and all Jones says is 'I don't care.' "

"Not exactly like that," Nelson said.

"Larry, believe it or not, we didn't come to you for reassurance," said Mother. "We want to find James just as much as you do."

There was a pause before Nelson spoke. "Then you don't know where he is?"

"Oh, my God! I do believe you've surprised our Larry at last!" I exclaimed. "We'll have to mark this day in red on our calendar."

"Alex, please!" said Mother. She turned to Nelson. "I can honestly say we have no idea where James has gone."

"Interesting," he said, reverting to his usual maddening composure. "Then it would seem that your part in this episode is over."

"Not quite, Larry. After all, we are concerned about the boy."

It seemed to be our day to surprise Nelson. There was another pause before he spoke. "You're not planning to try to find him on your own."

Mother let out a laugh that couldn't have sounded more phony if she'd sung it in the middle of an aria. "Don't be daft!"

Nelson continued, mindless of the interruption. "Because it would be very foolhardy for you to do that. So far the Red Jihad knows nothing of your involvement. If you were to put yourself in their way . . . Just say that that is one area in which Agent Fredrichs and I are in agreement. It would be extremely dangerous."

"We're not completely barmy," said Mother. "And we'd have no way of seeking James out on our own, even if we wanted to."

"Then I am confused. What did you want with me?"

"We'd like to clear up some loose ends. After all, Alex was shot at and our home life was turned upside down. We'd like to have some idea of what it was all about."

Even with Mother's unnerving expertise at fabrication, she hadn't managed to sound very convincing. I don't think that could've escaped Nelson, but he didn't challenge her.

"You know what it was about."

"I mean the specifics of what happened."

"What do you want to know?"

"Who was it that James called?" I asked. It was the one question that kept nagging at me, because somehow I felt that if James had told us the truth about this one thing, I could put my complete faith in him. Despite his sexuality. "Was it really his cousin?"

"I'm afraid I don't know that. The call was made to a cell phone registered to a man living in an apartment in New York. His name is Joe Smith."

"You're kidding!"

"Not very imaginative, if it's an alias. One thing that makes a very, very slight connection is that the real name of James's cousin, the one we know was in the Red Jihad, is Yusuf bin Akeel bin Salem al-Ansari. Yusuf al-Ansari, for short."

"Why is that a connection?"

"Yusuf is one of the Arab equivalents of Joseph. Joe Smith."

"Oh, great!" I said, rolling my eyes.

He shrugged. "I said it was slight."

"What was James's real name?"

"In short, Kahil al-Kaabi."

"How did that phone call result in the shootout?" Mother asked.

"I'm afraid I don't know that, either."

Mother pursed her lips. "Larry, is it your intention to allow us to ask you questions only to answer everything with 'I don't know'?"

"I'll be glad to answer anything I can."

Mother looked heavenward and sighed. "Well, did you find out who the man was who tried to kill James?"

"Yes."

"Oh, goody! We've hit the jackpot!" I said wryly.

"He was a waiter."

"A *waiter!*" Mother said with disbelief.

He nodded. "At a restaurant called The House of Persia."

"A waiter tried to kill James?"

"Would you be happier if it'd been a social worker?" I said.

"I'm just surprised," she said at me through her nose. Then she turned back to Nelson. "It's puzzling, isn't it?"

"To a certain extent," Nelson replied. "After we identified him we checked his phone records. He received a call from Joe Smith's number the morning after you first took James to the bar."

I said, "So, James called Joe Smith, and the next morning Joe Smith called this guy . . ."

Nelson filled in the name. "Samir."

"Samir, and put a hit out on James? Why?"

"That's another one of the things I don't know. We're left with conjecture: that either the jihad or his cousin want him dead because of something in their prior history, or something transpired over the phone that made him a marked man. Did James tell you what they talked about?"

I shook my head slowly. "Only that he told his cousin he was all right, and that his family was all right. And that he'd try to be at the bar the next night. Nothing earth-shaking."

"Nothing that would make anyone want to kill him, you would think," Mother added.

"Assuming, of course, that James was telling you the truth," said Nelson.

"Yes," I replied tersely. "But in his defense—and by the way, I would defend anyone under these circumstances—James has never really lied to us." Of course, I knew he'd lied about knowing exactly where the chemical weapons were at the outset, but I understood his need to do that to get out of Iraq, so I wasn't counting it.

"He hasn't lied that you know of," Nelson said.

I sighed heavily. "All right, that we know of. I mean, he didn't tell us that he wanted to make a phone call. His doing it might've been going against your instructions, but it wasn't lying . . . per se."

There was a smile behind his eyes. "Granted."

"Have you talked to him?" Mother asked.

"To who?"

"To Joe Smith, of course!" she replied, her tone implying that she thought he was being purposely obtuse.

"Mr. Smith disappeared after making the call to the hit man."

"Wait a minute!" I said. "How do you know that?"

"They had a tail on him. They lost him."

"They had a tail on him? How did they even know about him?" Nelson responded with a raised eyebrow. "Oh. Of course. James's phone call."

"So," said Mother, "James is gone and this Joe Smith person is at large."

"While the FBI wastes their time following us when we don't know anything," I said.

"They're doing other things as well," said Nelson.

"And the restaurant, The House of Persia. Did you talk to the people there?" Mother asked.

"Yes. Nobody knows anything about anything."

"Are any of them in the Red Jihad?"

He shook his head. "We have no way of knowing."

"Nelson," I said after a short silence, "there's one thing you haven't told us. Well, there's a lot of things you haven't told us, but only one I'm interested in at the moment. How did you know about James?"

"I'm afraid I don't know what you mean."

"About his connection to the terrorist group. And about the group itself, for that matter. I mean, nobody knows what's going on in Iraq."

He considered me a moment before answering, apparently weighing whether or not this was another matter to be divulged on a need-to-know basis. "James was not the first person to want to defect. There have been others who we've helped in exchange for information. We'd been told about the Red Jihad and that they were planning to infiltrate the country and begin their acts. One of the few people identified to us by name was Yusuf al-Ansari. So a little digging revealed the names of his family."

"That's how you knew the connection to James."

"Yes."

"What a stroke of luck when he came to you," Mother said, her tone very ironic.

"That's just the problem. Perhaps it was more than luck."

The implication wasn't lost on us. If James's request for asylum hadn't just been a coincidence, then he was here on a mission.

"But if James had come here to get involved in terrorist activities, why would he do it in a way that would put him under government scrutiny?"

Nelson shrugged slightly. "Just another missing piece to the puzzle. Then again, he's proven it's not exactly difficult to disappear here, even if you are under government scrutiny."

I could feel my face going red again.

"Hmm. So there really is nothing for us to do," Mother concluded.

Nelson eyed her for a moment. "That's correct."

She rose from her chair. "You understand, Larry, we feel somewhat responsible for James's welfare. Indirectly, at least. After all, he was in our care when he disappeared."

"From the bar, she means," I said quickly as I got up.

"I knew what she meant," Nelson said.

Mother glanced at me as if disappointed to discover she'd raised the village idiot, then turned back to Nelson. "But you see, we did want to tie up the bits of information we didn't know, and make sure there was nothing we could do to help."

"I understand," he said as he walked us to the door.

"What will happen if you find James?" I asked.

He looked at me in a way I can only describe as disquieting. It was as if the suspicion that we knew where James was had just come back to him. "I don't know. That will be in the hands of the FBI or the State Department."

"What do you *think* will happen?" I said with increased impatience.

"If I were to hazard a guess, I would say that most likely he'll be deported."

"Sent back? To Iraq?"

"If Fredrichs really believes he's a terrorist, yes."

"He'll be murdered the minute he gets there! But then again, James was dead the minute he got on the plane to the U.S., wasn't he? You people tried to trick him into fingering the jihad. If he did, and it turned out he was a member, then Fredrichs's people would put him away. If he fingered them and it turned out he wasn't a member, the jihad would kill him. Either way, his life was over when he boarded that plane—just when he thought he was starting a new life. And now, if you find him, you're going to send him back, where he'll surely be killed."

Nelson stared at me for a moment. "As Agent Fredrichs so eloquently put it, once James fled he became an FBI matter."

"And that's that?"

"I'm afraid it is." He reached for the doorknob, then paused with his hand on it. He looked Mother directly in the eye. "Jean, whatever you're planning to do, I very strongly advise against it. It wouldn't just be dangerous. If you got into any trouble, I don't know that I could do anything about it . . . and if I found James, I would have to take him into custody."

She returned her coyest smile. "Larry, I can assure you that we have absolutely no plan whatsoever."

"You know, as time goes by I like Nelson less and less," I said as we walked back to the parking lot.

"Any reason beside the obvious?" said Mother.

"Yeah. He makes me feel like a clunky, middle-aged Gypsy Rose Lee. No matter what we're saying to him—whether it's the truth or not—I feel like I'm doing a striptease against my will."

"You never were very good at lying, darling."

"You always make that sound like a bad thing!"

"And after all, we weren't exactly lying to him. At least not entirely. I did want the facts filled in. I just wasn't completely honest about why." She paused and sighed. "Larry really is being very perplexing about this whole matter. He's got me in a dither."

"Perplexing? How can you tell? He's always been a blank wall!"

"I know, but this time he seems like a very unhappy blank wall.

It's so unlike him to show us anything, let alone tell us anything. I can't tell where he stands in this case!"

We reached the lot and started up the stairs to the second level.

"I'll tell you one thing, he has a hell of a lot of nerve saying that he would cut us loose if he thought he couldn't trust us! Trust *us*! After the way he's used James he'll be lucky if I can ever trust him again!"

"Shocking," Mother said distractedly.

"Don't you agree?"

"What? Oh, of course I do. But I'm still puzzled. I can't get away from the feeling that something's up with Larry. Everything he's done in the past—accepting all that need-to-know non-sense—has been rather aboveboard."

"Oh, come on!"

"No, honestly! You've said it before yourself. Whatever else one may think of him, we've always been pretty sure of his veracity."

"Uh-huh," I agreed reluctantly.

"It's unlike him to take part in something so underhanded. I mean something that would put an innocent person in so much peril—this business of fooling James into exposing these people."

"That's assuming he thinks James is an innocent person."

We'd reached the second-level landing, and Mother came to a stop. "You know what I think? Whether or not he'll admit it openly, I don't think Larry believes for a minute all that chat about James being in the Red Jihad. Which is what makes it even more of a muddle. I can't believe Larry would put that boy in danger . . . unless . . . unless he didn't know the real reason James was being brought here until it was too late."

"Oh, please! You give him too much credit!" I opened the door and we walked out into the lot.

Mother said, "It's possible. Of course, I doubt he'd ever admit to that, either."

"Don't be so willing to put such a positive spin on it. Nelson probably just seems off because he's pissed over having the case taken out of his hands."

"Hmm."

When we got to the car, Mother unlocked the doors and climbed in behind the wheel, while I got in on the passenger side. Before putting the key in the ignition, she turned to me and scrutinized my face.

"You know, if you keep talking like that I'm going to start thinking there's something up with you. What's bothering you?"

"Besides everything that's happened?" I replied, screwing my face up.

She peered down that aristocratic British nose of hers, and in her most toffied accent said, "I think you know what I mean."

I looked down at my hands for a minute and sighed. "Do you think I've been prejudiced in James's favor because he's gay?"

Her expression immediately softened and she lowered her nose. "I think you've been prejudiced in favor of someone you know has been sorely used. As you would for anyone you felt that way about."

I only managed a weak smile. I wasn't sure whether or not she was just being kind. I had too many doubts about my own motives to fully accept this. "Thank you. Now what are we going to do about him?"

"To quote Larry, I don't know."

"We have to find him before they do! If the feds or the Red Jihad get him first, he's dead! What are we going to do?"

She stared at me unblinkingly for several seconds, then stuck the key in the ignition and turned it. "I don't know how to tell you this, darling, but I wasn't lying to Larry about that, either. I haven't the foggiest!"

TWELVE

When Peter got home from work I spirited him upstairs for a private conference. While he changed clothes I filled him in on what Nelson had to say. By the time I'd finished Peter was in jeans and a wine-colored T-shirt, sitting on a corner of our bed and staring up at me soberly.

"They would send James back?"

"Yes," I replied. "If you can believe it, Nelson didn't sound very happy about it."

Peter's right eyebrow arched attractively. "Really?"

"He's one surprise after another."

He thought about this for a second, then said matter-of-factly, "Nelson's a good man."

I folded my arms. "That does it!"

"Does what?"

"If either you or Mother give me one more shock on this case, I'm going to have to start taking nitroglycerin! What the hell do you mean, 'Nelson's a good man'?"

He looked genuinely surprised. "You don't think so?"

"That's beside the point! You're the one who's always so distrustful of Nelson! Now you sit here and tell me he's a good man!

Next thing I know you'll be telling me Saddam Hussein is just mis-understood."

"Alex, we've been working for Nelson off and on for a long time now. I don't agree with everything he does. I don't like a lot of what he does. But I think he's proven to us that he's at least honest."

I dropped down on the bed beside him. "You're right. It really is like *Murder, She Wrote.*"

"What?!" Peter exclaimed, laughing.

"I mean, all those years Jessica Fletcher was solving murders week after week, and the police still didn't take her seriously. I always thought one day some detective would tell her he didn't want her interference, and she would come back with, 'Do you know how many cases I've solved?' "

The bemused expression didn't leave his face. "What are you talking about?"

"Just that you're right. Nelson has proven himself."

"He still doesn't usually tell us much. But I think he's honest."

"Yeah. If only we could trust him," I said with a sardonic laugh.

"This whole thing seems to be about trust."

I rested my cheek on my left hand. "I know. Nelson said if he found he couldn't trust us, he'd cut us loose. And I don't even know what he means by that, because I'm sure he believes we've helped James, so you would think he'd already know he can't trust us. And no matter how he feels about James personally, we can't trust Nelson to help us because he would have to take James in. He told us that much. I don't know whether or not we can trust James—I've done so many about-faces on that one that I've prac-tically given myself whiplash. And I'm not even sure I can trust my own judgment anymore." I paused for a second to martial a little courage. "But Peter, I have to go with what I feel, and I really feel we need to find James and help him."

"Even though he might have run off to join his friends in the jihad?"

"Until I know what happened to him, I'm not going to know what to believe."

He looked me in the eye. "All right."

I breathed a sigh of relief. "If we're going to go on, then there's one thing I'm sure of: the one person we can't trust is Mother."

"What?!" Peter exclaimed. "You've got to be kidding!"

"No, I'm not. Nelson made it damn clear how dangerous this is. I didn't tell Mother about asking Stevie to try the redial thing. After dinner we'll go over to his place and see if he came up with anything. But I don't want Mother to know anything about it. We have to protect her."

"We have to protect *her*? May I remind you how many times she's pulled your nuts out of the fire—and mine because they happened to be with yours at the time?"

"Oh . . . shut up!" I said. "And don't say anything. To Mother, I mean."

The awkwardness of our meals with James were nothing compared to the Felliniesque dinner we had that night. It was like the first time I'd eaten with Peter's family, about six months after we first met. I felt I was under Divine scrutiny for any sign of flaws, lest I prove to be an unfit companion for their cherished son. As a result, I developed an irrational fear that one of my elbows would jut out involuntarily and knock over a serving dish, or that I would miss my mouth with my fork and gouge out my eye. The fact that his parents are lovely people and did absolutely nothing to make me feel that way made no difference.

That's the way it was with Mother at dinner that evening. She didn't do anything out of the ordinary, but I just knew she was keeping me under observation. We opted for takeout Chinese that night. Over the fried rice and moo shu pork, Mother conducted something of a postmortem of the case as it stood. Peter occasionally interjected something, and I mutely nodded in agreement, thinking it was better not to say anything at all rather than run the risk of betraying something by the tone of my voice.

Though my eyes never left my plate, I could feel Mother's boring into me as the meal wore on. Finally, she laid her fork down on her plate, rested her elbows on the table, and propped her chin on her hands, turning an inquiring eye on me.

"You're very quiet this evening."

"I am?" I said, looking up and attempting to appear surprised.

"Yes, unnaturally so. Is anything the matter?"

"No. No. I was just listening to you. And thinking."

"About what?"

"Just about what you were saying."

"I see," she said, narrowing her eyes at me. Then suddenly she brightened and reached for the bowl of fried rice. As she spooned some onto her plate, she said, "Well, all in all I think we've come to an end."

I frowned. "You do?"

"Of course, darling. Much as I hate to admit it, I think Larry is right."

"You do?"

"Yes! This is much too much for us. And this business of James disappearing! I have to agree that it doesn't look good for him."

"But . . . you've never shrunk from danger before."

I cried out when I received a sharp kick in the right shin under the table. It was Peter's way of reminding me that I didn't want Mother to be involved.

There was a gleam in her eye when she said, "That's true. But you see, part of wisdom is knowing when you're in over your head. This is just too dangerous for us. We need to leave it to Nelson and his lot."

"Yes . . . yes, you're right."

I was surprised (and suspicious), but if her reluctance to continue was genuine, it would make it infinitely easier for us to go on without her.

After dinner we helped her with the dishes, trying to appear as if we weren't in a hurry, then I announced that we were going to visit Stevie.

"He was really in a state about losing James," I explained. "We should spend a little time with him. Make sure he's okay."

"Are you sure that's wise?" Mother asked. "We're still being watched. I thought you didn't want anyone to know about Stevie."

"It doesn't matter now. They've had a tail on him ever since he left the store this morning, so they already know about him. Besides, James is gone and Stevie doesn't know where he is."

"Ah, well," she said with a faint smile. "Whatever you think is best."

I looked at her long and hard. "We really are going to Stevie's."

"I understand that," she said, knitting her eyebrows.

"Because I agree with you . . . you know, about the danger."

"I know."

"And we don't have a way to find James anyway."

"I know."

Peter applied a gentle pressure to the small of my back, guiding me away as he whispered, "Say good night, Gracie."

"Have a nice time," Mother said with a wave.

As we headed down the front steps I said, "I don't like the way she said that."

"All she said was 'Have a nice time.'"

"I know, but it was *way* she said it."

Despite what I'd said to Mother about not caring if we were followed, we kept on the lookout for a tail. Unfortunately there were still enough people on the platform and the train itself that it would've easily been possible for someone to follow us without our knowing it, which only made me feel more apprehensive. Believing someone was watching us and not being able to see him was worse than seeing my tail smoking on a fire hydrant. It gave me that over-the-shoulder, angels-with-tablets-marking-down-all-your-sins feeling.

"Well, at least I know one thing: Mother's not following us. I would've spotted her."

"She doesn't have to follow us. She knows where we're going," said Peter.

"She *thinks* she knows."

"Aren't we going to Stevie's?" he asked with surprise.

"Yes! But that's not the point!"

It was no better when we got off the train and walked over to Clark Street. With the unceasing pedestrian traffic, an eight-foot gorilla could've followed us without our knowing—especially since in Chicago an eight-foot gorilla could walk up the street without causing comment. As usual, the street was lined with cars parked bumper-to-bumper on both sides.

"I don't see him," I said, pausing in the doorway to Stevie's building.

"Who?"

"The guy that was following us this morning—the one that picked up Stevie at the store."

Peter looked up and down the street. "Neither do I. Maybe he really wasn't an agent."

"He had to be one. He was trying too hard to look normal."

After being buzzed in, we rode the creaky elevator up to Stevie's place.

"Have you heard anything yet?" he asked anxiously as he let us into the apartment. He looked paler than usual.

"Nothing," I said. "But that could be good news. At least we know the authorities haven't got him."

We sat in the places we'd occupied on our last visit. Stevie's hands kept moving in a way Mother would've referred to as "nervy." He would drum them on the sofa cushions, then on his legs, then on the cushions again, always keeping them in motion.

"Has anyone been here to talk to you?" Peter asked.

"No. Why?"

"I hate to tell you this," I said, "but you were followed from the store this morning."

"No way!" His eyes widened.

"You *might* have been," Peter amended.

"You didn't notice anyone?" I asked.

"No!" Stevie said. "Is he still there?"

"We didn't see anybody," said Peter. "I think you were wrong, honey."

"Why?"

"Because if they'd followed him home, they would've questioned him."

"Questioned me?" Stevie looked not unlike a startled puppy.

"Maybe not," I said to Peter. "They might've just wanted to see if James came out."

"They wouldn't wait if they think he's a terrorist."

"A terrorist?" Stevie exclaimed, going noticeably whiter.

"Don't worry, he's not a terrorist," I said, suddenly feeling like I was on the wrong end of my own conversation. "At least, we don't *think* he is."

"We don't know," said Peter. "We're trying to find out."

"It's just, since that gunman tried to kill him, the feds seem to think—"

"A gunman! There's a gunman?" There was now no color whatsoever in Stevie's face.

"Don't worry, he's dead," I said offhandedly.

"Oh, that makes me feel *sooo* much better!"

I looked at Peter. "You know, I don't think I realized until just now how commonplace the ridiculous situations we get involved in seem to us anymore."

"Someone tried to kill him?" Stevie said, trying to bring me back on track.

Peter sat forward in his chair and took charge of the explanation. "Yes. A few nights ago. Someone who may have been in a terrorist group tried to kill him."

"Oh, my Jesus in heaven! What have you guys gotten me mixed up in?"

I suddenly had a sour feeling in the pit of my stomach. Another thing I had only just realized was how blithely we'd gotten our friends into something that was so potentially dangerous. I'd have to find time to feel guilty about that later.

"We told you!" I said.

"Yeah, but I didn't believe it!"

I shrugged. "I can't help that. We told you the truth."

He shook his head. "This is crazy!"

"Now you know what married life is like," said Peter.

I wrinkled my nose at him, then turned back to Stevie. "Look, you're not in any danger. You never were. That group doesn't even know about us, so they couldn't possibly know we delivered James to you."

This seemed to calm him somewhat. "But you think that sweet young thing is . . . is . . ."

"We don't know," said Peter. "We didn't believe he was. But then he disappeared from here. We don't know why else he would do that."

"You're sure nobody broke in and took him?" I asked.

"You've seen the door! Nobody battered it down!" Stevie said with a *tsk*.

"Then we don't know why he would leave. You see, Stevie, the only things we know about James are what the government has told us, which is questionable, and what James has said himself, which is also questionable, because we don't know if he was telling us the truth or just saying anything to win us over." I heaved a frustrated sigh. "It would help if we knew for certain that he told us the truth about *something*."

"Well," Peter said after a slight pause, "we know he didn't lie about being gay."

I glanced at Stevie, then back at Peter. "I don't know. Agent Fredrichs said these guys would do anything to get what they wanted."

Stevie was shaking his head again. "Oh, no, he's gay all right. Terrorist or not, there's some things a straight boy would not do even if he thought he had to. So when James—" He broke off and looked from Peter to me. The color rushed back into his cheeks. "Let's just say he's gay."

"All right, so he's gay," I said.

"And, in case you haven't noticed, he's very, very sweet, and very, very vulnerable."

"I know. I hope he's not a terrorist."

Stevie huffed. "Alex, you're always so gloomy! I prefer to think the best. I couldn't . . . well, I just can't. I can't think he's one of them. And I don't want to think of him out there in this city all alone and not knowing where to turn!"

"I know," I said, not sure whether or not I really did know. "Did you try your automatic redial?"

"Yes!" he replied with a roll of his eyes. "But all I got was a machine with someone babbling in one of those skippity-doo languages."

"Damn," I said. "The message didn't say what phone number it was?"

He curled his lips at me. "I don't speak skippity-doo."

I was at a loss for a minute, then had an idea. "Wait a minute! Have you gotten any calls since you got home?"

"No."

"And there were no messages on your machine?"

"Alex, if you're trying to imply I'm unpopular, I really don't need—"

"It's important!"

"No, there were no calls, no messages."

"Good! Hand me the phone!"

He picked it up from the end table and passed it to me.

"What are you going to do?" Peter asked.

"Stevie got a machine when he redialed the number. Maybe James did, too! If the person had to call him back, maybe we can star-sixty-nine his ass!"

"Hey! There's a charge for that!" said Stevie.

"I'll pay it!"

He handed me a pad and pencil as I punched the three buttons. I said a little prayer of thanks when the mechanical voice rattled off the last number dialed. I scribbled it on the pad, then hung up.

"Look familiar?" I said, holding the pad up for Stevie to see.

"Uh-uh."

"But that doesn't mean anything, honey. It could be someone that just didn't leave a message."

"No, my machine would blink if somebody did that," said Stevie.

We sat and looked at each other for a few seconds, then I said, "Well, we could call it and see if we get the same machine that Stevie got."

"He called during the day," Peter said. "You might not get a machine, you might get a person."

I sighed, then perked up again. "Oh! Wait!" I picked up the receiver and began to dial.

"Who are you calling now?"

"That number the phone company has—the one that gives you the name and address that goes with a phone number."

An automated voice answered the phone and instructed me to enter a number. I tapped the number into the dial. After another pause, a second automated voice, this one spliced together, provided the information. I jotted it down.

"Who was it?" Peter asked as I hung up.

"The name that goes with the number is Al Faisel. The address is 631 North Kestler."

"Kestler? Where's that?"

We both looked to Stevie. He did one of his Tim Curry eye rolls and said, "Oh, I suppose now you want a map."

He got up and went into the kitchen, then reappeared carrying a street map of Chicago, which he handed to me. Peter and I opened it and scanned the street guide for Kestler. When we found it, we did a quick search of the map.

"Here it is," said Peter, tapping his index finger on the spot. "Just north of Grand Avenue, next to the river."

"No wonder we've never heard of it. It's only a block long."

I thought for a minute as I looked at the map. "We'll have to take a cab."

"You're not going down there!" said Stevie.

I looked up. "Of course we are."

"That's insane! You can't do that!"

"We're only going to look around, we're not going to storm the battlements single-handedly."

"Have you lost your ever-lovin' mind? Terrorists? Gunmen? Hello?"

"What do you think we should do?" I said, challenging him to come up with a better idea.

"Call the authorities! Tell them to go there!"

"The authorities are one of the groups after James."

He went blank for a moment, then faded back onto the couch. "Oh, darn, that's right. But couldn't you tell them what you know? Then maybe they'd go and see if they can find him and everything else could get worked out later."

"They believe he's a terrorist. We tell them anything and they'll arrest him."

"But Alex, sweetie! You can't go there alone!"

"Oh, I won't be alone. Peter will be with me."

Peter gave Stevie his most long-suffering look. "Now you *really* know what married life is like!"

Once back on the street, we quickly caught a cab and told him where we wanted to go. The driver grunted and started the meter, then made a U-turn and headed back to Belmont to get on Lake Shore Drive.

"I wish I could say this is the craziest thing we've ever done," said Peter as the cab wove in and out of traffic, "but there's just too many to choose from anymore! What exactly do you hope to find at this place?"

"James in a pink pinafore cooking dinner for the man he fell so madly in love with that he ran off with him on the spot and simply forgot to tell anyone that he was going."

He looked at me. "Barring that?"

I shrugged. "An arsenal?"

"How are we even supposed to find out if he's there? Knock on the door and ask for him?"

"I don't know," I said wearily. "Look, I really just want to see the place . . . at least for the time being. Somehow I think I'll know if James is inside."

Peter raised an eyebrow. "That's sort of pushing the limits of gaydar, isn't it?"

"You know what I mean! We'll just have to play it by ear."

"Oh, God!" he moaned.

We reached Grand Avenue and the cab driver headed west. Both sides of the street seemed to be lined with giant cranes amidst massive, swiftly rising building projects from the lake all the way to the river. I'd been aware that there was a lot of building going on in this area, but I had no idea of the extent of it. It looked like Chicago was rapidly being turned into New York. If that stretch of road was a surprise, my teeth almost fell out of my head when we crossed the river. What used to be a run-down industrial neighborhood was now peppered with luxury high-rises and wildly expensive lofts, all with a panoramic view of train yards, expressways, and the river, which at that locale looked not unlike the Black Lagoon.

The gentrification ended abruptly just before Halsted, where we had the driver let us out. We didn't want him to take us all the way to the address, or even to Kestler, for fear our arrival would be noticed. That area of Grand was deserted except for a few derelicts who were either too drunk or too nuts to even bother us for money.

We walked west and found Kestler a couple of blocks over from Halsted. We stopped beside the dirty red brick building on the corner and cautiously peered around the side to check the layout of the street. As it had appeared on the map, Kestler was barely a block long, truncated by both railroad tracks and the expressway, a concrete canal from which a glow emanated upward. It was a good thing, too, because the streetlights were out.

"I don't see anybody," I said.

"Me either."

I looked back down Grand. "And no cars behind. At least we know Mother hasn't followed us."

"Under the circumstances that doesn't make me feel better."

"Shall we?"

Peter sighed. "Go on."

We skirted the corner of the building and cautiously headed up Kestler. On the left side there was a deserted, low-lying factory of some sort, and on the right were three houses so ramshackle they looked like the last ones left after a nuclear war. The first two were boarded up with plywood, much of which was rotted and falling away. We stopped at the edge of the second one to look at the third. It was separated from the other two by a broad dirt lot, and wasn't boarded up but looked like it should've been. There were lights on in the front room of the first floor. Tattered curtains hung limply in the windows, and every now and then a human shadow would glide across them, waffling in the folds and tears. The windows were low enough that we could see inside if we stood on tiptoe, but I didn't know if I had the courage to do that. The second floor and the back of the house were dark. Two cars, which could've been politely referred to as jalopies, were parked by the curb.

"So much for the pinafore theory," said Peter.

"Christ! It looks like something out of *Sleepy Hollow!*"

"Somehow I don't think Tim Burton's in there. What now?"

"Get a closer look."

"I was afraid you were going to say that." He gestured toward the lot. "How do we do it? This approach is awfully public."

I thought for a minute. "Let's try the back way."

We doubled back and ducked into the narrow, dark path between the first two houses. This was the one place on the forsaken properties where there was grass growing, even though it was tall and dried out. I almost took a header when my foot came in contact with a soft mass on the ground. I stopped and nudged the mass with my foot, and it let out a soft groan.

"Oh my God! Are you all right?" I said to the prostrate figure that I could barely see.

He moaned, smacked his lips, and turned over on his side. The unlovely aroma of alcohol and urine wafted upwards, sending me reeling backward onto Peter. Once I'd gotten my heart to calm down, I stepped over the drunk and Peter followed me. Just before reaching the back of the building, I heard a scurrying noise inside the second house. It made my heart leap again, something I certainly didn't need it to do while it was pounding so loudly.

There was no more cover behind the houses than there had been in the front, but at least there was a little less glow. What once had been fairly vast yards were now expanses of dirt spotted with clumps of dead grass, sliced at a diagonal by the expressway. Behind the occupied house was a large, dirty white truck, not unlike a dairy truck only without any logos. Its cab was facing the back of the house.

"I don't like the look of that," said Peter.

"I don't suppose they can be delivering milk in between terrorist attacks," I said.

We stayed as far away from the incessant aura as we could, keeping close to the back of the second house until we worked up the nerve to cross the back lot.

"Come on," I said, hunching over as I started across.

It wasn't easy to do that stealthily. I had a feeling that if we went too fast the movement would attract the attention of whoever was in the third house, and if we moved too slowly we'd be left out in the open longer. Peter moved quickly behind me. Although the rough dirt crunched beneath our feet, the sound was masked by the continual drone of traffic on the expressway. When we reached the back of the truck, we waited and listened for any sign that we'd been heard. Once we were fairly certain we hadn't, I started to examine the latch on the back of the truck. It had a large metal lever that opened by being pulled upward. I put my right hand on it and tugged.

"What are you doing?" Peter said, putting his hand on the scroll-like door.

"I want to see what's inside."

"Are you crazy? Do you know how much noise that'll make?"

"It doesn't matter," I said with a disappointed sigh. "It's locked."

He didn't exhale until I let go of the lever.

"What now?" he asked.

I turned one eye around the corner of the truck. "Come on," I said, waving him after me.

We ran to the back of the house and plastered ourselves against the back wall of a porch whose torn and twisted screens belied the term "screened in."

"I feel like I'm on The Rotor," I whispered.

Peter turned to me in the quasi-darkness. "Alex, if you make me laugh, I'll kill you before they have a chance."

"You know how I get when I'm nervous."

"Yes, I do. What do we do now?"

"Try to see inside." This idea was met with pointed silence. "You didn't think I was going to settle for just looking at the outside of the place, did you?"

"I thought you said you could feel James's presence." The mildly snide tone betrayed his own tension. "How do you intend to do it?"

I did a slow take. "How do *I* intend to do it? Don't you mean *we*?"

"That was implicit," he said after a beat.

"Well . . . I suppose if we're going to look in, we're going to have to move. Hold on."

I turned around and slowly inched my way up so that I could just see over the ledge through the screen above me. The porch itself was empty, the floor badly warped. On the interior wall there was a good-sized window looking into the kitchen, visible in the dim glow seeping in from the front of the house. Next to the window was a door with another window, a little higher up. I lowered myself back down.

"There's a window in there. I think we might be able to see into the front."

"Okay."

With me in the lead, we edged our way around the corner of the porch where four wooden steps led to a screen door. I crawled up the stairs and reached for the handle, which was badly rusted. Even though I tried to be very careful, it made a deep grating noise as I turned it.

"Alex . . ." Peter whispered warily.

"I know."

When the handle was halfway down, the door unlatched. I

pulled it open cautiously. Unfortunately, there was a large spring running from its left side back to the jamb, meant to snap the door shut. At irregular intervals, the spring let out a metallic *poing* that probably wasn't as loud as I thought it was. But even so each *poing* made my heart skip a beat.

When the door was open enough for me to pass through, I looked over my shoulder at Peter and whispered, "Stay here and hold it open while I go in. I don't want to risk moving it too much."

"Be careful."

I crept onto the porch, the floor of which creaked under my weight so loudly that I was sure the occupants of the house couldn't help but hear it. But when I stopped and held in place I realized that I'd been so focused on the noise I was making, I hadn't noticed the noise coming from inside. Voices were raised to a shouting level in a very heated argument that sounded as if it involved several people, all apparently speaking Arabic—or whatever it was; it wasn't English.

I moved up to the window and peered inside. The kitchen looked dusky in the scant light coming from a doorway in the far-right corner. Beside the doorway was a door which was closed. Dirty dishes were heaped in the sink and pots caked with food were piled haphazardly on the stove. I couldn't see James or anyone else from that vantage point, so I decided to move up to the window in the door, which gave a clearer view of the inner doorway.

Once at the door, I slowly inched my eyes up to the window. From there I could see the interior wall of the room beyond, across which wildly gesticulating shadows were dancing. With the uncomfortable half-crouch I had to maintain in order to see through the window, I wasn't sure how long I could stay there, but I hoped I could hold out long enough to see at least one of the people inside, if not James.

I was just about to lower myself when one of the shadows shifted, then suddenly its owner came into view. He was shouting angrily as he reached the wall, then he turned around and rested his back against it. He was an incredibly intense man about thirty years old, wearing black pants and a white shirt that was soaked with sweat. The shirt clung to his body, revealing a muscular if underfed torso. He had wavy black hair down to his shoulders, a thick beard, and skin about the color of a football.

He spat words like a rapid-fire machine gun at the unseen occupants of the room. Then with an abrupt, dismissive gesture at them, he turned toward the kitchen.

I dropped down in terror, my back pressed against the door. After a second the kitchen lights came on. I looked over at Peter, who was still holding the screen door. If the man happened to look out the window, he would surely see that the screen door was open. But I was in no better position: if he opened the back door I would fall at his feet. I made a mental note that if we got out of this case alive, I should have an EKG. My heart skipping had been bad enough, but now it had completely stopped.

I heard the sucking sound of a refrigerator door opening, and the rattle of bottles within. Then the door closed and the lights went off. The man's heavy footsteps retreated. I heaved a sigh of relief and could see Peter doing the same.

"Alex," he whispered anxiously, "let's get out of here!"

I hesitated. I'd really hoped we'd see some evidence of James's presence, although at the same time I was hoping we wouldn't. I wasn't ready to give up yet, but couldn't see how we could go any further. We certainly couldn't go inside.

Peter's brows were knit with concern. With a shrug, I moved back over to him and went down the steps. He lagged behind, closing the door more slowly than I thought humanly possible. Then he joined me at the foot of the stairs and we edged back around the corner of the porch.

"Could you see anything?" Peter asked.

"Just a guy who looked like Jesus, only masculine."

"Any sign of James?"

"Uh-uh."

"Then let's go. There's nothing more we can do here but get killed."

"I've just got to find out if James is in there."

"You've tried. Now we should call Nelson and tell him what we know. He can take it from there."

"And if James is in there, they'll pick him up as well."

His eyebrows almost touched. "If James is in there, he deserves to be picked up."

I pursed my lips and sighed. That was probably true. But I still wanted to prove it. Too much of what James had done didn't make sense.

"Just because he called here doesn't mean he came here," I said softly. "I just . . . I just want to find out."

"How? You couldn't see him."

"Let's go around the other side of the house. Maybe there's a window over there we can use."

He sighed, but he followed me. Keeping low, we moved across to the other end of the porch. I peeked around the corner, and when I saw that the coast was clear we went around it. Just past the end of the house was an oblong black hole with concrete steps leading down to a door. Although shielded from the expressway's glow, I thought I could see a pane of glass near the top.

"Look!" I said, keeping my voice low. "A cellar!"

I started down the steps, but Peter grabbed my arm. "What are you doing?"

"I'm going down to have a look."

"Alex, your mother isn't Janet Leigh, and you're not Vera Miles! Remember what happened to her when she went down in the cellar?"

I smiled. "Have I ever told you you bear a striking resemblance to John Gavin?"

His eyes narrowed. "You know, it's hard to accept flattery from someone I think is insane."

"I'm just going to look!" I pulled away from him, but not in time to miss seeing him roll his eyes yet again.

I went down the steps quickly and quietly, and despite his protests Peter was right behind me, much to my relief. The narrow pit smelled like dank earth. My heart sank when I found that cardboard had been taped up over the inside of the window.

"Well, that's that!" said Peter.

I put my hand on the doorknob. It was so loose it jiggled in my hand.

"What are you doing now?"

"Thought I might as well try, see if it's—"

I broke off as the door fell open about an inch.

"—locked."

Peter looked startled and even less pleased than he had a moment earlier. "Alex, you know how bad a sign that is!"

"Maybe it doesn't lock. Look at this place!"

"Let's pretend for a minute that it does lock," he said, insisting on being rational. "Why would a group of terrorists leave this door unlocked?"

"Is this a riddle?"

"I'm serious!"

"I don't know! Maybe they just forgot."

"Or maybe they're planning to move something out," Peter said. "Maybe into a waiting truck?"

I looked at him for a moment. "Maybe we should see what's inside."

"You *are* crazy."

"We've come this far."

I pushed the door open a little more and carefully stepped inside. The cellar was nearly black. All of the high-up half-windows were covered with cardboard. The only light coming in was the little that could get through the door. I could just barely make out piles of sacks forming an aisle down the center, leading to a wooden staircase to the first floor. The air was choked with a heavy chemical stench.

Overhead we could hear footsteps walking to and fro as if several people were pacing chaotically. The sound was limited to one area that I guessed corresponded to the room where the lights were on. The argument was still going on, although coming from above the voices were a bit more muffled. Peter and I stood in the darkness near the door and listened for several seconds.

"I don't hear James," I said.

"You can't tell from down here."

We slowly moved into the room, going down the aisle and struggling to make out the writing on the sacks. But it was impossible to see anything, let alone read.

"We could strike a match if we had one," I said with a low laugh.

"You know what happens when they do that in the movies."

"What is that smell?" I said, wrinkling my nose. "It smells like shit!"

I could feel Peter freeze behind me. His hand shot out and grabbed my shoulder, stopping me in place.

"Not shit, Alex. Fertilizer."

I turned around. "Well, fertilizer is—" My mouth dropped open. "Oh, shit!"

"Exactly."

"Unless these guys are farmers who've *really* lost their way, they're planning *big* trouble."

"That's why they call them terrorists, honey. I think we should get out of here!"

"I think you're right."

We were just turning around when suddenly the door at the top of the stairs opened, casting on the floor a shaft of light that ended a few inches from the tips of my shoes and dimly illuminating the room. Peter and I were instantly frozen in place. From where I was standing I could just see the man's legs, blackened with backlighting.

Peter was the first to thaw. He took my arm and slowly backed us to the nearest opening between rows of sacks. We ducked behind the piles and waited. A long silence followed, finally broken when we heard the man take one tentative step down.

"Come on," Peter said almost inaudibly. "Down here."

We sidled silently down the row and turned the corner, secreting ourselves at the end with me standing behind Peter. Now that we were back by the wall the darkness seemed even more encompassing. I could barely see anything of our surroundings, except that the piles of sacks stopped far short of the back wall. Despite this, we seemed to be in a very tight space. I sensed something behind me pushed up against the wall. I reached back and my hand lighted on something cold and metallic standing about four feet high. I choked back a gasp.

"There're metal drums back here."

"I'm not surprised," Peter replied quietly.

We listened for quite some time for further movement from the staircase before the man took another step down. Then after a short pause, he descended the stairs to the concrete floor. He walked very slowly down the center aisle, and I could practically hear his head swiveling from side to side, looking down the rows.

"I don't suppose it would help if I sang 'My Favorite Things,' " I whispered to Peter, who responded by digging his fingers into my arm.

The man paused at the opposite end of our row. I was seized by the insane desire to peek around the corner to see who it was, and was only able to resist with a surprising degree of difficulty. After what seemed like an eternity the man passed on.

I was about to allow myself to feel relieved when to my shock he turned down the next row and headed in our direction.

"Christ! What'll we do?" I whispered frantically to Peter.

"Go around the other way."

"He'll hear us, and if he cries out it'll bring them all down here." My mind raced. I didn't like the idea it finally lighted on, but it was the only one I had. "When he gets close enough, I'll grab him."

The man drew nearer, my heartbeat speeding up with each approaching footfall. Finally, he stopped at the end of the row, just out of what would've been our sight if we'd been able to see. In the silence that followed, I could feel him craning his neck around the corner.

I lunged forward, my hand shooting out to where I imagined his mouth to be, and I managed to mush somewhere around the middle of his face. I was able to slide my palm over his mouth before he could let out any real cry. His hands went up to my wrist and struggled to pull it away, but I slid my left arm around his waist and held him tightly.

"Shut up," I said in his ear. When he continued to struggle and emit muffled noises, I summoned up a more serious tone. "Shut up and stop struggling or I'll snap your neck like a twig!"

I could feel Peter smiling in the darkness. I don't know what movie I'd heard that in. It sounded hopelessly melodramatic even to me, but it worked. My prisoner suddenly went limp with surprise, and after a beat his lips moved beneath my hand.

"Umphrx?" was what it sounded like. It wasn't a language that was recognizable to me, but the voice was.

"James?" I said.

He nodded.

"Okay. I'm going to take my hand away from your mouth. But if you cry out, I swear I'll kill you."

"He means it." Peter was letting James know that I wasn't alone, but he still sounded like he was trying not to laugh.

Slowly I slid my hand away.

"Alex! Peter! What do you do here?" he said in a panicked whisper.

"The question is, what do *you* do here?" I asked.

"I had to come."

"No, you didn't! You were safe where we put you."

"You must leave here now. They will find you!"

"Did they take you from Stevie's?"

"No. I come myself. Now go!"

"You came yourself?"

"Yes. I decide I must. It is the only thing to do."

"No it isn't! Come with us," I pleaded. "It isn't too late. You don't have to do this!"

"Yes I do."

There was urgency in his tone. I suppose I shouldn't have been surprised by this, given all the signs that had been there all along, but the realization that he really had wanted to be with these terrorists broke over me like a sickly rain cloud.

202

"Then you are one of them."

There was a long silence. "You are good people. I do not want you to be hurt . . . or Stevie to be hurt. Now you must go."

"No! First tell me what this stuff is for!"

He blinked. "It is for to make explosion."

"I know that!" I intoned. "What are you going to blow up?"

"I have to go back up. They will look for me."

"James! Jesus Christ! We took you into our home! Into our family! We tried to help you!" I faltered. I was coming close to reminding him that he was one of us, but after Nelson's accusation, I was determined not to let his sexuality be an issue. "We cared about you."

He swallowed. "And I do for you."

"Then for Christ's sake, tell us what they plan to do with this stuff! What is the target?"

"I . . . I . . . I don't know."

"Goddammit, tell me!"

"I really don't know . . . I only know they are going to explode . . . I don't know word for it . . ."

My eyes rose heavenward. "Oh, for God's sake, this is no time for your English to fail you!"

"It is place you eat . . ."

I looked at him with disbelief. "A restaurant?"

"Yes! This is it."

"They're going to blow up a restaurant? Oh, come on! There are enough explosives here to level a city block!"

"All they talk about is restaurant. I do not know name or which one. I cannot tell anything more. Now please, please, go!"

"Kahil!"

The voice boomed James's Arabic name from the top of the stairs, startling the three of us. James's hand reached out in the dark and landed on my heart, where it stayed, willing me to keep still.

"Who is that?" I asked.

"My cousin. Yusuf al-Ansari!"

"Joe Smith!" I exclaimed softly, realizing at once that it sounded a hell of a lot scarier in Arabic. "He's here?"

"Kahil!" The voice commanded again.

James moved away from us to the center aisle as the voice spouted something in Arabic. James answered. I don't know what he was saying, but the tone was very apologetic. Peter and I had plastered our backs against the sacks and listened. But I almost cried out when a cockroach crawled onto my shoulder and into my collar. It was then I realized the sacks were crawling with bugs. I shivered and tried not to jump as the bug made it's way down my shirt, which fortunately I hadn't tucked in.

The man said something else and received a short reply. Before I could even think about where this was going, the man came tramping noisily down the stairs. Several times he angrily shouted a word that sounded like "Gha-bee-ya! Gha-bee-ya!"

"Oh God, oh God, oh God!" I only just managed to say it quietly.

"Don't panic!" said Peter.

We heard the sound of a pull chain, and suddenly there was light. Apparently the man had been chastising James for not having turned it on. The cellar wasn't exactly flooded with light; there was only a single bare bulb hanging overhead at about the center of the aisle. But the man had yanked the chain so angrily it went swinging wildly back and forth, sending shadows rising and falling everywhere.

"They're determined to turn this into *Psycho!*" I whispered to Peter.

The man yelled something else at James, then we heard him march to the outer door and slam it shut; then he shot the deadbolt. He and James held a hasty conversation, heated on the part of the man and frightened and placating on James's side. Then they fell silent, and we heard footsteps moving in two directions, one set away from us and one set toward us.

Both Peter and I heaved abbreviated sighs when James appeared around the corner.

"He asked what I am doing down here. I tell him I hear noise. I say, 'Look that way, I look this way.' I cannot help you anymore. He is away from the door. Now go!"

The footsteps that had been heading in the opposite direction stopped abruptly.

"Kahil!"

James spoke a single word in reply, then al-Ansari barked something else. James froze.

"What is it?" I whispered.

"He ask who I am talking to!"

"Oh, Jesus! Tell him you were talking to yourself!"

He stammered this out in his mother tongue, then the man spoke more sharply. James began to tremble.

"He tell me to stay where I am."

James had barely gotten this out when I realized that footsteps were headed in our direction down one of the rows between us and the back door. We ducked behind the row to our right and heard al-Ansari say something else. It didn't take much imagination to realize he'd heard us moving, thought it was James, and ordered him to freeze. But we couldn't risk staying where we were, so we tried to be even more silent as we crept our way down the row toward the center aisle. James was awaiting al-Ansari just one row back at the opposite end. The two of us stood pressed against the pile of sacks at the end of our row, leaving us in an even more vulnerable position than before. We were obscured from al-Ansari's view for the moment, but if anyone came down the steps they would see us at once, aided by the fact that we happened to be under that damned lightbulb, which had finally stopped swinging.

And there was another problem: If Al-Ansari decided cross to the center aisle to go back upstairs, we'd have to move quickly to escape being seen, and that would mean making noise. If he decided use the rear aisle, we might be safe.

Al-Ansari was speaking very hotly to James, who answered repeatedly in a frightened, innocent tone. I wished to God I knew what they were saying. Then there was the sound of a slap, followed by another, faster flow of words from James that sounded even more pathetic. He was slapped again and again, all the while pleading. Even though we had finally settled the matter of whether or not James was one of the terrorists, it made me sick to hear him being knocked around.

At last it stopped. The worst part about the silence was that I didn't know whether or not that meant James had finally given us up. After a lengthy pause, al-Ansari said something to James in that conciliatory tone abusers use on their victims.

They started to move. I was relieved that it sounded as if they were going up the back aisle, but once they'd gotten a couple of rows past us, one of them started down a row toward the center aisle. I looked at Peter, then we both looked up at the lightbulb. As quietly as we could, we went around the corner and pressed ourselves into the sacks.

The light was just barely in view. I could see a hand reaching up for the chain. The sleeve looked like it belonged to the guy I'd seen up in the kitchen, but I didn't dare lean out to see if I was right. He switched off the light, and we heard him go tramping back up the stairs, followed by the lighter steps of James. The door at the top of the stairs closed, plunging us back into darkness.

Peter and I both heaved rattling sighs. It was all I could do to keep myself from breaking out in hysterical laughter.

"I'm glad I inherited Mother's rock-hard bladder control," I said.

"Let's just get the hell out of here!"

We made our way to the back door. There was a simple deadbolt that fortunately didn't require a key to open from the inside. I turned it slowly with my right hand, keeping my left hand against the mechanism to try to muffle the sound a bit, which thankfully worked. The bolt sprung with less volume than when al-Ansari had closed it. I then pulled the door open cautiously, and Peter and I slid through the opening. The noise of the traffic on the expressway was practically a full roar after the relative silence of the basement. We went up the cement stairs and around the back of the house, keeping close to the wall.

"Okay," I whispered to Peter. "Let's make straight for the back of that house." I gave a nod toward the house across the lot.

Keeping low, we started to move hurriedly across the back of the dirt lot, but we hadn't gone fifty feet before a voice yelled, "Halt!" This was followed immediately by the metal snap of a gun being cocked.

"Hands up! Turn around!" said the heavily accented voice.

Peter and I had stopped dead in our tracks. We turned around slowly and found ourselves facing the man I'd seen in the kitchen. He was standing in the doorway of the porch pointing some sort of automatic weapon at us that looked like it'd been borrowed from Arnold Schwarzenegger.

"Joe Smith, I presume?" I said.

"It's nice of you to come to us," he said with the same kind of smile King Kong wore when he chewed the natives. "You have saved us the trouble of tracking you down."

So that was what James had meant when he said he didn't want us to get hurt. Of course they would want to get rid of anyone who could identify one of their members. I suppose we owed something to James for not having given us up to them already.

"James . . . Kahil is one of you," I said, emboldened by the belief that we didn't have much to lose anyway. "You didn't need to track us down."

His smile grew more malevolent. "Kahil is a liar! Anyone would be a fool to believe him. Now come inside." He gestured toward the house with the weapon.

Peter and I glanced at each other. I knew that doing as he said was not a good idea, because once we were out of sight anything could happen to us. Besides, I knew he was going to kill us one way or the other, and I wasn't sure that I wanted to prolong that. At the same time, cutting and running might at least give us something to do for a few seconds before getting shot.

"Come in!" he commanded in the same tone he'd used on James.

I felt myself moving forward almost as if compelled to with Peter by my side. I still didn't think this was wise, but somewhere inside me I believed that prolonging this might somehow afford us some opportunity to escape. All I know is, I was in such a daze that I didn't immediately notice the sound of the car: or maybe it was just that I didn't initially hear it over the drone from the expressway. I didn't fully realize that something was wrong until al-Ansari's attention was drawn to something behind us. I wheeled around and jumped out of the way, pushing Peter down, as a car tore across the dirt lot like a dark monster sending out a cloud of dust. It headed straight for al-Ansari. He was so startled that he didn't aim his automatic until the last minute. The car crashed into the back steps, causing the dilapidated porch to collapse and sending al-Ansari flying backward, releasing a volley of shots into the air.

Cries rang out from inside the house, and the tattered curtains were ripped aside, revealing a sea of dark faces.

The porch had been almost completely dislodged from the back of the building, and the hood of the car was covered with debris. The motor revved; then the car shot backwards. For a horrified moment I thought it had been aiming for us and missed, and was now making a second try, but it veered to our left, and the passenger door swung open as it turned.

"Get in!" cried the driver.

"Mother!" I exclaimed in absolute astonishment. "Where did you—"

"This is *not* the time to discuss it! Get in!" She sounded angry rather than afraid.

I glanced over the roof. The occupants of the house were beginning to pour out the front door. Peter and I fairly hurled ourselves into the front seat beside Mother, who tore away before Peter even had the door shut. The rear wheels sent a shower of dirt and gravel hurtling toward our pursuers. One flung himself on the top of the trunk and held tight, snarling at us through the back window, but we went off the curb with such a bang that he was bounced off onto the pavement.

"I've never been so glad to see you before in my life!" I exclaimed. "Now what the hell are you doing here?"

"Never mind that! What do you mean by doing something so

stupidly dangerous?" she demanded as the car barreled onto Grand Avenue.

"You mean without you?" I said wryly.

She shot me a glance that told me not to mess with her. "I mean at all! Honestly! I raised you better than this!"

"You mean you wouldn't have come here?" I couldn't hide my genuine surprise.

"As I said to Larry Nelson, I'm not completely barmy—a claim that I obviously can't make for my son! If I'd known what you found out, I would've gone to him straightaway!"

"Wait a minute, wait a minute!" said Peter, gasping for air more from excitement than from shortness of breath. "Jean, how did you know where we were?"

"Stevie told me!"

"You followed us to Stevie's?"

She looked at me again, scrunching up her face. "How many times do I have to tell you, I don't have to follow you when I know where you're going. I didn't go to Stevie's at all. He called me!"

"He what?"

"He called me and told me what you were going to do!"

"You mean he told my mother on me?" I said in disbelief.

"Yes, darling, he said you were going to a house full of terrorists. For some reason he thought you were crazy."

"I don't believe it!"

"I do," said Peter.

Mother leaned forward and looked across me at him. "And you!"

"If you act like he's my keeper again, I'm getting out of the car!" I said quickly.

She ignored me. "Did you ever think just once that if you refused to go along with him on one of his daft schemes, just maybe it would keep him from doing it?"

"No, I didn't," he said meaningfully.

She sat back and sighed. "I supposed you're right."

I looked at Peter. "I did what I thought was best." Then I

turned to Mother. "And I'll match you daft scheme for daft scheme any day!"

"Just look at the car!" she said sorrowfully. "The front end is all done in! What am I going to tell the insurance people?"

"That you bent the hood while trying to run down an Iraqi terrorist, of course," said Peter.

I slewed around and looked out the back window. "There's no one following us."

"Of course there isn't," said Mother. "I *have* seen *The Sound of Music* once or twice!"

"What?"

"While I was waiting for you I pulled the rubber hoses off the thingies on their engines."

"The rub—You mean you pulled the wires off the spark plugs?"

"I don't know the technical term for it, but I know it stops a car from going. By the time they figure out what's wrong, it'll be too late to follow us."

"When the hell did you do that?"

"Right after I got there. You were nowhere in sight, so knowing you, I figured you'd gone inside. I parked by one of the deserted houses and fixed the two cars at the curb."

"I didn't know cars even had spark plugs anymore."

"Darling, those cars were older than you! This group can't be very well funded."

"I think they've been using their money for other things," I retorted.

Peter laughed. "Jean, you really are incredible. We never thought of doing that."

"We were on foot. I hardly think it would've made any difference." I turned back to Mother. "But I don't understand why *nobody's* following us."

"I told you—"

"No, I mean *nobody*. Not even our friendly government tails. Did you do something to lose them?"

"I didn't even give them a second thought. The only thing I

210

was thinking of was getting over here. I saw our guards when I left. They were still on duty. But I didn't notice anyone following me."

"I still don't understand. They've been listening in on our calls. They must've heard Stevie."

"Maybe they haven't really been tapping our phone," said Peter. "Remember, we don't know that they were doing that. We just assumed."

I heaved a sigh. "The one time we need them following us, and they're not there!"

"Did you at least find anything out while engaging in this current bit of lunacy?" Mother asked as she steered the car onto LaSalle Street and headed north.

"A basement full of explosives. Or, at least, the makings for them."

"Oh dear," she said after a pause.

"*Big* explosives. World Trade Center–type explosives. And we found something else: James. We now know he's one of the terrorists. He told us himself."

"He didn't exactly say that," said Peter.

"You heard him!"

"I heard what he said, and he didn't come right out and say he was one of them."

"I don't believe you! What does he have to do, say, 'Hi, I'm a terrorist. Fly me'? His meaning was pretty clear."

"You actually saw James?" said Mother. "He was alive?"

"We weren't holding a seance in there."

"That just doesn't fit."

"Did you want him to be dead?"

"Alex, they sent someone to shoot him down at the bar. Why would they do that, then keep him alive? It doesn't make any sense."

In the shock of finding James there, not to mention the shock of finding the explosives, I'd completely forgotten about the attempt on his life. "Maybe . . . maybe it was a ruse."

"A ruse?" Mother said, lapsing into Lady Bracknell. "To what end?"

"To make us think he wasn't one of them. It's the oldest trick in the book. They use it in the movies all the time. You know, make an attempt on the life of someone so they don't look like a suspect."

"Clever as that may be, darling, I don't see why they'd go to the trouble. At the time we didn't think he was one of them."

"I don't get it, either," I said, getting impatient with my own lack of answers.

"Why don't you tell me exactly what he said?"

As Mother steered the car around the crazy turn that leads from LaSalle Street onto Stockton, the street that runs through Lincoln Park, I gave her as near a word-perfect rundown of the short conversation as I could. I looked to Peter to fill in any gaps, but he said he remembered it pretty much the way I did.

"A restaurant?" Mother said incredulously.

"That's what he said," I said. "I don't know anything about bombs, but it looked to me like they had enough stuff down there to take down the Hancock Building."

"The only restaurant anybody's said anything about in this case is The House of Persia. And I certainly can't imagine them wanting to blow up their own place. What would be the point of that?"

"Oh, that restaurant idea is probably just another one of James's stories. I don't know if you heard what al-Ansari said to us . . ."

Mother shook her head. "I was too far away."

"He told us Kahil—James, I mean—is a liar, and we were fools to believe him."

"To be perfectly accurate," Peter amended, "he said *anyone* would be a fool to believe him."

"I see," Mother said reflectively as we turned onto Fullerton.

"You sound doubtful," I said with disbelief. "Don't tell me you still can't decide whether or not James is part of the jihad."

"Oh, no," she replied. "I've very much made up my mind. I was just thinking it doesn't matter much what I think anymore, does it? No matter what's up with James, like as not we're going to have to call Larry the minute we're home."

"We may be too late. They had a truck out back and what sounded like an army upstairs. They'll have the place cleaned out before anyone gets there."

"I doubt that," said Peter. "There was tons of stuff to move."

"How are we going to explain that we even knew about the place?" I added.

"It's no matter now," Mother said resolutely. "We simply can't have these people mucking about with explosives!"

THIRTEEN

Nelson got to our house in less than ten minutes, which meant either he broke all speed records, or he wasn't at his hotel when Mother called his cell phone. He listened intently as I told him about the house with its cache of explosives. When I finished, he stared at me for several moments.

"How do you know about this?" he asked at last, his face as hard as granite.

"Kismet," I said.

"Let's just say we happened on it," said Peter.

"I'm not asking how you know about the house, I'm asking how you know what's in the basement."

"We looked," I said with a glance at Peter.

"You were inside the house?"

"Yes, but you're wasting time! Right now they're—"

"Were you in the house legally?"

"We weren't invited, if that's what you mean."

"I mean, did you break in?"

I glanced at Peter again, then back at Nelson. "The door was open."

"Open, or unlocked?"

"Oh, for Christ sake, don't you realize—"

He raised his palm, his expression unchanging. "Despite what you may think, we can't rush over there and arrest them because of what you saw in a basement that you weren't in legally. We can't even get a warrant to search the place based on what you saw. We would have to find some other reason to go in."

The four of us were standing in the middle of the living room. Mother, Peter, and I looked at each other, apparently all having the same unpleasant thought: If we told Nelson we had traced James to that house, he could probably go over there. But then, of course, we'd be implicating ourselves. Under the circumstances we could've just told him that we'd happened to see James there—maybe through a window—and perhaps that could've given them what they needed to get a warrant. And the situation was now dicey enough that it's probably what we should've done. But I just couldn't bring myself to do it. I couldn't bring myself to turn James in so bluntly. I left it to Mother, reasoning that with her newfound resolve to call Nelson in, she would go ahead. But she and Peter remained mute as well. Anyway, we'd told Nelson where the house was, and I figured if the feds went there, they'd find James for themselves.

"You don't need a warrant if something's out in plain view, do you?" I asked.

"That's correct."

"Well, unless they're complete idiots, right now they're loading the stuff in their truck, so they can run. There's a deserted house next door. If you go behind it you'll be able to see what they're doing. I mean, if you actually see them loading explosives, you can arrest them, right?"

"We'll still eventually have to explain how we made the connection."

"We can go into all that later," Mother said quickly. "You'd better get a move on now, or they'll be gone!"

"You're right," he said after a beat. He was pulling the cell phone out of his pocket as he headed for the door.

"Larry!" Mother stopped him. "These people know where we are now."

He hesitated for a second, looking as if he wanted to ask how that was possible. But he thought the better of it. "Don't worry, Fredrichs's men will remain on guard. I'll see to it."

"And Nelson," I added, "let us know . . . what you find there, will you?"

"Very well," he said after a long pause.

Once he'd gone, I said to Mother, " 'We'll go into all that later'? How are we going to do that? We can't tell them how we tracked James to that house without implicating ourselves—and Stevie—in his escape."

"First things first," she replied, looking more concerned than I could ever recall seeing her. "First let Nelson and Fredrichs stop them, then we can worry about explanations and the rest."

Of course, the concept of "worrying about it later" is all well and good if all you've done is killed a Yankee; it's a different matter when you've run afoul of a bunch of terrorists who are known to be vengeful, and your own government, and you don't exactly have anything more pressing to occupy your mind.

It had been after ten-thirty when Nelson left us, so we knew it would be late before we heard anything. We sat in front of the TV set not-watching the news, then not-watching reruns of sitcoms. None of us spoke or made a move to go to bed. I was surprised to find myself secretly hoping they wouldn't find James when they got to the house. At the same time a part of me wanted him to be picked up so that the whole thing would be over. At least for us.

Then again, I didn't know if it could ever be over for me. If James were to disappear into the American judicial system, which is what was sure to happen if he was caught with the terrorists and explosives, I don't think I'd ever be free of the ghost of that misty-eyed boy at the foot of our bed telling us he was homosexual. Even the memory of it right then started my heart on a swing back in his favor. But the pendulum was stopped in its course when I remembered his duplicity and what he was involved in. Fredrichs had been right: these people would use anything to win you over to their side, and in this case I'd been the chief dupe—so strongly duped that even knowing what we now knew, I still didn't really want him to be found.

I pressed my fingers to my temples as if that might stop my mind from spinning. Peter, sitting next to me, noticed this and said, "Do you have a headache?"

"Not really," I said as I rubbed the sides of my head. "I think I have a merry-go-round in there."

He smiled and stroked the back of my head with his palm, then slid his hand into mine. Mother was starting to doze in an armchair a few feet away when the three of us were jolted to our feet by the phone.

"I'll get it," Mother said, reaching for the phone on the end table by the couch. She picked up the receiver, put it to her ear, and said, "Hello? . . . Oh, hello, Larry." She listened for several seconds, her expression growing very dark. "Really? What will you do now? . . . I see . . . Yes, well, thank you very much for letting us know." She said goodbye to him, then replaced the receiver.

"Well?" I said.

"They didn't find anyone."

"What?"

"Nelson and Fredrichs and his men did just as we suggested. They went back of the empty house and looked. The truck was gone."

"That's impossible," said Peter. "They couldn't have gotten all that stuff loaded since we called Nelson. There was to much of it."

"They didn't," said Mother. "Apparently they fled very fast. Nelson found the basement door wide open—"

"Of course he did," I said sardonically.

"Their men went in: it was about a third empty. So the jihad got some of the material out, not all of it."

"And . . . the people?"

"Nowhere to be found. Larry is on his way here now. I've a feeling he'll have some rather pointed questions to ask."

"What are we going to do?"

She pursed her lips. "Discretion is no longer the better part of valor. We're going to have to tell him everything we know."

"Everything?"

"Well . . . almost everything," she said with a sly smile.

Nelson arrived alone and was with us for over an hour. I was glad Fredrichs wasn't along, because that was an ordeal that I just wasn't ready to go through. Despite the late hour and the seriousness of the situation, Nelson's equilibrium never varied, while I grew increasingly irritable. He opened by asking us how we had found the house, and we maintained steadfastly that we'd simply happened on it, an idea he received with guarded skepticism. There was nothing else we could've told him. Aside from implicating ourselves in James's escape, to have owned up to how we found the house would also have implicated Stevie and possibly Joe and Mickey as well. Having so thoughtlessly gotten them involved, I'd silently resolved I'd rather go to jail than cause my friends any more trouble. It didn't matter that they'd all agreed to become involved because they believed in what we were doing.

Nelson then asked for the details of what we'd seen in the basement so that they could have some idea of what was missing, and we filled him in as best we could. As near as he could figure, the jihad had removed two rows of the fertilizer and at least two of the metal drums—maybe not enough to topple a tower, but still enough to wreak some havoc.

Then he reverted to how we'd found the house.

"For Christ's sake! What does it matter?" I said. "You've got the explosives! It's not like the jihad is going to come back to claim it and take you to court because you found it illegally!"

"But they took *some* of it," said Nelson. "And if we catch them, when we go to court we're going to have to explain how we tracked it down. Unless, of course, they use what they've taken first."

"Larry," said Mother, "you are simply going to have to take our word for it. It was just blind luck. That's all we can say about that!"

She looked over at me and cocked her head in his direction. I realized this was my cue to tell him the rest.

"Uh, Nelson, as for them using it . . . there's a couple of things we didn't tell you about what happened when we went there. We didn't have time to tell you earlier. First of all, we saw James."

"Did you?"

I nodded. "And we talked to him. He told us . . . I know this sounds crazy, but he told us that they were planning to blow up a restaurant."

"James told you that?"

"Yes. I know it doesn't make sense."

"The only restaurant we've even heard of in this case is The House of Persia, and they wouldn't blow that up, would they?" Mother asked.

"I wouldn't think so. It's in Uptown. There's nothing of any value or real importance around it. And they had much more fuel than they needed to use on it."

"There you are," said Mother.

"But still that's what he said," I added.

"That's very interesting," said Nelson. He got up from the couch, signaling that the lengthy interview had finally come to an end.

"You think that means something?" I asked. "That they were going to hit a restaurant?"

"Yes, I do. If it's true."

If it's true, I thought. That's the problem. "Do you think it actually could have something to do with The House of Persia?"

"That's the first thing I intend to look into."

He started for the door.

"Oh. Nelson. There's one other thing. We saw someone else there: Yusuf al-Ansari. He's come to town."

"Yes," he replied. "I thought he might."

Once Nelson had gone, there was nothing left for us to do but go to bed frustrated, dog tired, and more than a little uneasy. Having a group of terrorists—a group we'd crossed—on the lam in our city wasn't exactly comforting.

* * *

I was woken by the ringing of the phone. At first I thought it was the middle of the night, but when I forced my eyes open I found the sun was out and the clock read 9:20.

I grabbed the receiver off the phone on the bedside table.

"Yeah?" I said groggily.

"Alex? Alex! It is me!"

The sound of his voice was enough to snap me fully awake.

"James? What . . . what the hell are you calling here for?"

"I need help! I need you!"

"You've got to be kidding!"

"What is it?" Peter asked, roused to full consciousness by the tone of my voice.

"James," I mouthed at him.

"No! No, I do not kid!" James said. "I get away from them! I don't know where to go! Please! I need you!"

"What do you mean you got away from them? You're one of them!"

"No! I am not one! I tell you that already, but you do not believe me. I am not one!"

"Last night you said—"

"I say what I say because I want you to leave, to be safe."

I was silent for a second. That might be all well and good, but I couldn't reconcile it with other things he'd said. "Did you really go to them, or did they kidnap you? Did they come and get you from Stevie's?"

He hesitated. "No. No, go there myself, but—"

"But nothing! That's that!" I said sharply, although I couldn't for the life of me figure out why he would tell me the truth about that if he wanted my help. Surely under the circumstances it would've been wiser to lie.

"Please! Please, Alex," he pleaded sadly. "I explain everything to you later, but I—"

"How did you get away from them?"

There was a hollow sound through the receiver, like the noise

220

you get when you hold a shell to your ear. He'd put his hand over the mouthpiece. Or someone had. It only lasted a couple of seconds.

"In the . . . in the . . . after you left . . . I don't know the word. Everybody is running around, clearing the house. I get away then."

I went silent again, my mind clouding over as it sometimes does when I've worried a problem so much my brain takes a holiday. I suppose what he was saying could be true, but I doubted it.

"Well, if you need help, all right. Just come here to our house. We'll try to sort it out."

"No, no! I cannot do this!" he said anxiously. "There are men that watch your house! They will arrest me!"

Once again, plausibility—helped by the fact that his throat sounded raw and I could tell he was crying.

"Please," he continued, "please, can you and Peter come to me? I am alone! Please, Alex!"

I shook my head, both to clear it and to mourn the death of the last vestige of my sanity.

"All right, where are you?"

"I am at bar you take me to. I am outside of it. It is only place I know."

"Charlene's? All right. Stay out of sight. I'll be there as soon as I can."

There was another hesitation on his part, then he said, "Thank you."

I hung up.

"What's going on?" Peter asked.

"Get dressed," I said, jumping out of bed. I opened the bedroom door and called out, "Mother? Are you up?"

"I'm down here, darling." Her voice floated up the stairs. "Who was that on the phone?"

"Come up here, would you?"

Peter and I threw on some clothes as Mother came up the stairs and down the hall. I was buttoning my shirt when she reached us.

"That was James," I said. "He wants our help."

I repeated what he'd said. Mother sat on the end of the bed and listened, her face a sober mask.

"That sounds really fishy," Peter said when I'd finished. "He got away from them? They don't seem that careless to me."

"How did he sound?" Mother asked.

I shrugged. "Exhausted. Frightened. He could've been putting it on, but . . ."

"But you don't think he was," said Peter.

I heaved the weariest sigh I could muster. "I've told you before, I don't know what to think of him anymore. He said he can explain everything."

"What do you want to do?"

I took a deep breath. "Go down there and get him. Talk to him."

"Alex, they lost us last night. They could be trying to get us back."

"I know that! I'm not going down there alone!"

He put his hands on his hips. "Who were you expecting to go with you?"

"Don't worry, I didn't mean I'd be all right because you'd be with me. I haven't completely lost my mind. Yet. I'm going to call Nelson." I went to the phone and started to dial the number of his cell phone.

"What if James is telling the truth?"

"If he is, he doesn't have anything to fear from Nelson." I let the phone ring several times. There was no answer. I hung up. "Damn! He's not there!"

"He's not in his coat?" said Peter.

I curled my lips. "He's not answering. Look, you stay here and keep trying to get him. Tell him what's happened and where I've gone, and ask him to meet me there."

"Why not just go out there and tell one of our guards to come with you?"

"Because they're Fredrichs's men. If James in on the level—and alone—he'll have a chance with Nelson. Nelson will at least listen to him. He doesn't have a chance in hell with Fredrichs. Anyway, if they're still listening to our calls they already know where he is and they'll probably beat me to him!"

"At least wait till I get hold of him before you leave, then I'll come with you."

I shook my head. "There's no time. I'll be careful. I'll try to scope out the situation before I do anything, and I'll try to wait for you and Nelson if I can. But if I take too long to get down there, he's going to think something's wrong. Remember, he knows how long it takes to get there from our house."

"Exactly! If it's a trap, that's probably why they chose it!"

"Either way, they're going to think there's something wrong if I don't get there fast. Once you get Nelson, follow me down. Remember, you're the only other one who can point Yusuf al-Ansari out to him."

"Not quite the only one," said Mother.

"You're not coming with me!" I announced loudly, jabbing my index finger at her.

"Of course I'm not!" she replied.

"You're not?" I couldn't have been more surprised if she'd sprouted horns. I was expecting the usual protests, or the innocent smile she gives me when she agrees to something but has no intention of following through. This sudden sincere acquiescence scared me.

"No, I'm not. I'm going to Stevie's."

"What? Why?" I asked incredulously.

"I want to have a talk with him. Now, I want you to do something for me, Alex. If you find that James is indeed alone, if it's at all possible I want you to bring him to Stevie's apartment."

"You're kidding!" I said. "I'm ready to turn him over to Nelson and you think he's entirely innocent. Why?"

"For many reasons," she said kindly. "I think I know why he's done what he's done, but there's no time to go into it now. Besides, I think it may be better if you learn it for yourself."

"Thank you, Billie Burke!" I replied. "His own people think he's a liar!"

"That in itself should be significant enough," she replied opaquely.

I sighed. There was no arguing with her when she got like this. "Have you forgotten that Stevie is still under surveillance?"

"We didn't see anybody when we were there," said Peter.

"That doesn't mean there wasn't anyone!"

"It doesn't matter now," said Mother. "It's a chance we'll have to take."

"Whatever you say!" I said as I headed for the stairs.

I had the cab driver take me to North Avenue, then head south on Wells.

"Okay, now drive slow—but not too slow, I don't want to attract any attention. Just . . . drive sort of slow."

The driver gave me a lingering glance in the rearview mirror, assessing just how much trouble he thought I might be, but he did as I asked. As always, the street was lined with cars on both sides, but given the time of day there were some gaps.

"Okay, okay, a little slower," I said as we approached Charlene's. "But not too slow!"

At first I didn't see James, but when we glided past the bar I spotted him huddled in the space between Charlene's and the building directly to the north. His head was lowered and he was resting it against the wall.

I had the driver stop at the next corner. I toyed with the idea of having him turn the cab around, pick James up, and take us back to our house, but I thought it better to wait there with James for Nelson to show up rather than walk him into a nest of Fredrichs's men. I paid the driver and got out of the cab. He peeled away as if trying to make up for the lethargic way I'd made him drive down the street.

As I walked back to the bar I kept my eyes open, scanning the nooks and crannies around the buildings and peering up toward their roofs for any sign of an ambush, but didn't see anyone. The sun was bright, and Wells is very open, practically devoid of anything that would obstruct the view. Nobody was approaching me on the sidewalk from either direction, and nobody appeared to be sitting in the parked cars. The whole area seemed deserted.

I came to a stop at the opening next to the bar. "James."

He raised his head slowly. His face was badly bruised, and there was was dried blood on the rim of his left nostril and the right corner of his mouth.

"Alex . . ." he said haltingly, his eyes filling with tears. "I am sorry . . . I am sorry!"

"There's no need to—"

I was cut off by a voice from behind me.

"Get in!"

I turned around very slowly, and swallowed hard at what I saw. Yusuf al-Ansari was seated in a car at the curb. He and the driver had apparently secreted themselves on the floor out of sight while I approached. The window was open and the nuzzle of the same automatic weapon he'd sported the night before was pointed at my heart.

"I'm sorry," James said. "They tell me what to say. They make me do it."

"Get in!" he ordered again. "Or I will kill you where you stand."

He reached back and flung open the rear passenger door. I glanced over my shoulder at James, hoping to convey that I understood the full weight of his betrayal, then slowly walked to the car. Once I was inside, al-Ansari ordered me to slide over to the other side. He then leapt out and climbed in beside me, while James got in the front seat.

"Go, go, go!" al-Ansari shouted at the driver, who complied immediately, hanging a quick U-turn and heading for the Loop.

Al-Ansari shoved the gun painfully into my chest with his left hand, then drew back his right and backhanded me several times across the face. The bones inside my head seemed to rattle as my face was thrown one way, then the other.

"Where is your friend?" he said. "You were both supposed to come!"

"He's busy."

He delivered several more slaps. I felt like my thoughts were being dislodged: as if my head were swinging back and forth, but my brain was staying in place.

He stopped hitting me but kept the gun jammed into my chest. "It does not matter. We will attend to him later. First we take care of you. Because of you, our plans have to change! We were almost ready to begin, but you make us lose our materials. Now it will take time to stockpile again! Precious lost time while people die!"

"While people die? What are you talking about?" I asked, knowing it was inadvisable for me to speak.

He leaned into me harder, making the gun bite into my flesh. "You starve my people to death with your sanctions! You rape the resources of the world, living like kings while the rest of the world starves!"

I don't believe this, I thought. *I'm going to be killed over foreign policy!* "I don't have anything to do with any sanctions! Hell, hardly anybody in this country has anything to do with what the government does!"

"That is the point," he said, his nose so close to mine I could feel the hot puffs of air coming from it. "We are going to wake your people up to what you are doing! To the way your government is killing the rest of the world! What are a few American lives compared to an entire population that starves in the streets!"

"So that's what the Red Jihad is all about? Food?"

He reared back and struck me several times with the back of his fist. A warm trickle of blood ran from my nose to my lips.

"And you cause us a delay! We were almost ready to strike, here and in other cities, but you cause us a delay! Now it will take more time to gather more materials!"

I didn't suppose it would have been any good to say I was just trying to help a little homo find happiness. Besides, I didn't know if he knew about James, and betrayed or not I still wasn't about to cause his death by revealing his sexuality.

"All delays cost more of the lives of my people, and for that you are going to die!"

He sat back, shoved the weapon into some sort of holster under his long coat, and sat back, glaring out of the window with undisguised contempt for the riches evident in the passing cityscape. James sat motionless in the front passenger seat, staring out through the windshield. Tears stained his left cheek, but I didn't know if they were for my fate or if he was moved by the impassioned speech about his people.

God, he's been clever, I thought. *And I've been a complete and total idiot!*

When we reached Wacker, the driver turned west and followed the street as it curved south. I hazily wondered if just maybe Peter had managed to get hold of Nelson and get down to Charlene's in time to see me being taken away, but I was too slaphappy to give the idea much consideration, let alone attempt to see if we were being followed. I was sure that any move on my part would be met with a renewed assault. Instead I wondered where they were taking me: if they were just planning to do away with me for the sake of pure vengeance, or if I was to be the center of their first blow against the Evil Empire. I had a feeling that the latter was true, since they'd headed into the center of the city.

When we came to a stop at a red light at Madison, beside the Civic Opera House, al-Ansari said, "Turn here," to the driver.

I looked up and saw that directly across the street was the Mercantile Exchange, a building made up of twin towers whose corners are shaped into accordion pleats. I had a sudden sinking feeling in the pit of my stomach. This is where they trade in agricultural futures. It would make sense, if the Red Jihad was enraged over the lack of food in Iraq because of American sanctions, that they would try to hit us where we live—or trade. The light changed and the driver steered the car around the corner, swinging to the far left side of the street and coming to a stop at the back end of the building, which is bordered by a plaza overlooking the Chicago River.

Al-Ansari flashed a malicious smile at me. "You will not give any sign that anything is wrong!" He pulled a soiled handkerchief from his pocket and tossed it at me to wipe the blood from my nose. "If you do this, or you try to run, I will shoot you dead. Now get out."

I opened the door and as I climbed out al-Ansari jumped out from his side. I was surprised to see James get out of the car as well, although I don't know why. Since he was one of them, it was perfectly logical that he should see it through to the end—or, I should say, *my* end.

They came around the car. Al-Ansari paused and said to the driver, "Go join the others."

The driver said something in Arabic and sped away.

"That way," said al-Ansari, motioning us toward the plaza.

I obeyed and headed into it. James stayed to my side and slightly behind me, and al-Ansari followed us both.

I estimated it to be a little after ten-thirty, which accounted for the small number of people on the plaza. On the right were racks so loaded with bikes they looked like an ugly modern sculpture. To the left was the glass wall of the first floor of the building. I caught my breath when I realized that behind the shaded glass of the first half of the wall was a restaurant of some sort. I wondered if this could be the restaurant that James had said they intended to blow up. It would make sense, since until Peter and I had blundered into their hideout they probably had enough explosives to take down the entire Mercantile Exchange, including both towers. When al-Ansari instructed us to keep going, I breathed a sigh a relief.

But it was short-lived. The second half of the back of the building had its outer glass wall completely covered with brown paper, hiding the interior from view. Al-Ansari brought us to the door of this and handed the key to James.

"Open it," he ordered.

James stepped up to the door, twisted the key in the lock, and pulled it open.

"Go in!"

I crossed the threshold into a vast, open, empty room. Along with the west wall, the glass walls on the north and east sides—

which bordered the lobby of the building—were covered with brown paper. In the center of the east wall was a pair of doors whose handles were bound with a heavy chain and padlocked. The south end of the room was a solid wall with two swinging metal doors in the interior corner. To the right of these doors hung a schoolroom-type clock that read ten forty.

The room was divided by four square cement support posts, and dead center were two of the barrels that had been in the cellar. On top of them was some sort of mechanism with wires leading out to a pack of sticks that looked like flares banded together. It didn't take a great leap to guess that they were dynamite.

"What is this place?" I asked as al-Ansari locked the outer door.

"This was to be the future location of the second House of Persia restaurant."

Their plan suddenly came clear to me. Using the cover of a restaurant they had already established to the point of respectability, they would spread into important buildings such as this one. They could then slowly—or even quickly, for all I knew—fill them with enough explosives to level the buildings.

"I take it you're planning a national chain?" I said.

He merely laughed as he pulled out his automatic weapon. He crossed behind the barrels and retrieved a length of rope, then came over to me.

"Hug the post," he said, motioning to the one closest to me.

"But I hardly know it," I retorted.

In a flash he whipped the butt of the gun against my temple, sending me sprawling to the floor. Pain shot through my head, echoing back and forth until centering on the spot where the gun had made contact.

"Get up and do as I say!"

With some difficulty I got back to my feet, then staggered over to the post and put my arms around it. My wrists just barely cleared the opposite side. He extracted a knife from his pocket, cut a length of rope, then roughly bound my left wrist and knotted it off so tightly I was sure it cut off the circulation. He then did the same to my right wrist with the other end of the rope. My wrists extended slightly past the end of the post with about a foot of extremely taut rope binding them together.

"You don't have to do this!" I said. "Not here! Think of all the innocent people who'll die!"

"Think of all the innocent people you have killed in my country!"

"Murdering people here won't end hunger in Iraq! It'll just make matters worse, don't you see that?"

"Don't worry yourself," he said, bringing himself into view so that I could see his flat smile. "Not so many will die this time. You saw to it that I do not have enough explosives to destroy this building. But there is enough to blow a hole in it. A big hole, and you will be in the middle of it!"

Al-Ansari went to over to the barrels and grabbed a rag from a pile lying beside them. He came back behind me, held the rag by the corners, and slipped it over my head and down to my mouth.

"Open!" he said, dropping one corner just long enough to slap the side of my head.

I opened my mouth and he slid the rag in, tying the ends at the back of my head.

I fully expected them to leave then, and was completely shocked when al-Ansari marched purposefully to James and hit him hard across the face with the back of his hand. James didn't cry out, as if he knew that would only make it worse. Al-Ansari then grabbed him by the neck, forced him over to another post, and slammed him against it.

Although it would've been impossible to yell for help, I found that with effort I could just barely speak well enough to be understood.

"What are you doing?" I can't even attempt to approximate what this sounded like.

"We are done with him. It is time for him to die!" Al-Ansari replied as he trussed James up exactly as he had done to me.

"Why? Why would you kill one of your own?"

"Because he betrayed us!"

"No he didn't," I said. "We found your hideout on our own. He didn't lead us there! Not directly."

Al-Ansari paused in his work and looked over at me. "You know I do not talk of that! He made the call that betrayed me!"

The rag was cutting into the corners of my mouth, and I was getting lightheaded from the amount of oxygen it was costing me to try to talk, but I didn't understand.

"What are you talking about? How?"

"He made the call!" he said angrily. "The call that brought the authorities to me! Did you think I am so stupid I did not see that I was being watched! The instant he called me! I know that was how they found us! And now it will be a long, long time before we are able to recoil and make our strike against your country! For now I will have to settle for a smaller strike, and getting rid of the two of you!"

He went back to tying James to the post. I closed my eyes and hit my forehead against the post. That fucking stupid dumbass Fredrichs! In his eagerness to find the jihad, using James and even putting us at risk, he had rushed surveillance onto al-Ansari, and they'd been sloppy and were seen. And as a result, al-Ansari had taken James's call as a Judas kiss. Of course, it was, but James hadn't known he was doing it.

But that didn't explain everything: James's going to them and telling us he was with them. Unfortunately, I didn't think I was going to have time to get the rest sorted out, and it didn't give me any comfort to think it might all be made clear in the next life.

Al-Ansari gagged James, then went over to the barrels and fiddled with the mechanism on top. I don't know exactly what he did, but when he was finished, he came over to me and stood with his face close to mine.

"Do not worry, Mr. Reynolds, about your friend. He will be joining you very soon. We know where you live. I have set the timer for five minutes."

I glanced at the clock. It read 10:55.

"I am now going across the river to watch the fun from a safe distance." As he went to the door, he added, "You can be happy in knowing that you will be part of the first strike to make this a better world!"

He tucked the automatic under his coat and went through the door to the plaza, quickly turning the key in the lock.

"But I don't want to change the world," I muttered to myself.

The minute he'd passed through the door, I started to struggle to pull myself around the post, something I was almost startled out of doing when I heard a voice outside call out, "Yusuf al-Ansari!"

Several other voices cried out as he answered, "Stop or everyone will die!" I knew he'd managed to pull out that damned automatic before being shot.

I continued to try to move myself to the right, trying to position the rope on one of the corners of the post. I was tied so tightly that I could barely move, but knowing that you're going to get blown to bits tends to make you care a lot less about scraping your skin or pulling your wrists and arms out of their sockets.

"What do you do? They will save us, won't they?" James managed to say around his gag.

"They won't have time!" I said. "He's stalling!"

With great effort and a lot of pain, I managed to pull my right wrist past the corner so that the rope was just slightly over the rough cement edge. I started to move the rope up and down as quickly as I could, scraping the skin off my wrists in the process, trying desperately to cut the rope. I glanced at the clock. A minute and a half had gone by.

Outside, al-Ansari and whoever was in authority were shouting warnings back and forth at each other. Apparently, they were afraid to shoot, not knowing the situation inside. For all they knew he could be holding the button that would trip the bomb. They didn't know the bomb was already set, and I couldn't cry out loud enough to tell them. They also didn't know that al-Ansari was willing to stand there and die for his cause. I glanced over at James, who was attempting to do the same thing I was, only without much success.

As I frantically rubbed the rope, I said, "I want to know something! Why did you go to them? Why did you go to their house?"

"Because . . . because . . ." He went limp and started to weep.

"Don't stop!" I said. "Try to do this!"

He straightened up and renewed his effort to pull himself around.

"I do it because . . . nobody ever do anything for me before. You and your friends, you show me what it can be like." He was hard enough to understand under normal circumstances—it was even harder now.

"So?" I said, sawing madly.

He finally got his rope around a corner. "I know these people. I don't know why they try to kill me, but I know it means they think I betray them, and they will try again, and try to kill you because of me. So I call Yusuf again, and tell him that I do nothing to them, and I do not understand why they try to kill me. He says he know I do it, and that I do nothing and that you do nothing also. I say over and over, and he tells me I must prove this."

"Keep sawing your rope!" I said as he flagged.

"He give me the number of his people here. I call them and they tell me to come. I do not want to go, but you have been so good to me, and so has Stevie, and I do not want anything to happen to you, so I go to them. But they do not believe me. They never did. They keep me there. And then Yusuf came."

It was then that my rope, frayed from the friction, suddenly snapped and I went flying to the floor. The standoff outside was continuing. I scrambled to my feet and ran to James, with another quick glance at the clock. There were two and a half minutes left.

I pulled the gag from my mouth and yanked James's from his head, then went to work trying to untie his hands.

Suddenly Peter's voice called from the distance outside.

"Alex? Alex, are you in there?"

"Yes!" I yelled. "And there's a bomb!"

The debate outside grew more heated, with someone ordering al-Ansari to drop his weapon. Of course he refused.

"Why did you tell us you were with them, then?" I said, furiously trying to untangle the maze of knots al-Ansari had used.

"I try to convince them that I am one of them, so that they will believe me and that you have nothing to do with it."

"To do with what?" I snapped, more out of frustration over the damned knots than at what he was saying.

"To do with whatever make them think I betray them! I know if they believe you did this, they will try to find you and kill you. But last night, when they find you at the house, they think I lie to them—they think I lead you to them."

At last I managed to pull the end of the rope through the last loop in the knot, releasing him. Just at that moment, shots rang out. We both looked to the outer wall. A body fell hard against the glass, then slid down to the ground. Al-Ansari had been killed.

"Alex!" Peter called out from the same distance.

"Reynolds?" called another voice that I thought belonged to Agent Fredrichs.

"Why would you do something so ungodly stupid as to go to them? We were trying to keep you safe from them, and from our government!"

"Because you risk your life for me. I know you are not safe from the jihad! And . . . nobody has ever done for me what you do, and I want to give back to you. I want to protect you! You must believe me!"

I had another one of those moments one experiences during desperate situations where time seems to stand still. It was a moment of truth. All through this case I'd wavered back and forth about James, what he was and what he was trying to do. Even now, after al-Ansari had tried to kill him, I wasn't sure that this wasn't just another story. Perhaps now that his group had turned on him, he was trying to win me over again. I had to decide—and fast.

Peter had said this was all about trust, and he was right, but he hadn't touched on the trickiest part: there comes a time when, for better or for worse, you simply have to decide whether or not you're going to trust someone. And in the most difficult moments, you can't act out of knowledge, you have to act out of faith. It was the moment for me to decide, and I did.

The outer door would lead us into their hands, and the inner door was chained and locked. I glanced at the clock. Seventy-five seconds.

"Reynolds!" Fredrichs called.

"Don't come in!" I yelled. "We're tied up! There's a bomb in here! There's no time!"

"Come on," I said to James. I grabbed his wrist and ran for the swinging doors. If this building was like every other one on Wacker, it was supplied through a dock on Lower Wacker Drive, the underground street used for deliveries, so there would have to be another exit leading down to it. And that had to be through the kitchen, since there were no other doors visible in the main room. I prayed that I was right and that it wasn't chained.

We went through the doors and I almost cried out with joy when I saw the door across the kitchen that was never to be. Standing next to the double verticals of a freight elevator, it was one of those doors that opens with a lever from the inside but must be opened with a key from the outside. We raced to it and I pushed the lever, but it didn't move. For one split-second, I almost screamed. Then I jabbed at it again, and this time the door popped open. We went through it and down the stairs, taking them two at a time. Then it happened: the blast we'd been expecting roared like nothing I'd ever heard, shaking the entire building, including the staircase we were on. The heavy metal door we'd just come through was thrown off its hinges and flung down the staircase, narrowly missing James's back as he rounded the landing. The door crashed into the railing on the landing with a loud clang. We kept going, still taking two steps at a time, and went through the door at the bottom of the stairs and out into the grimy darkness of Lower Wacker.

We stopped in the loading lane while I tried to decide which way to go. Traffic was whizzing by in both directions. Directly in front of us in the center of the street was a ramp leading above ground. We couldn't use that one because it would bring us up directly in front of the Merc.

"Come on. This way." I led him north. The next-closest ramp was two blocks away. Once we were moving, I realized that the ropes were still tied around my wrists, their ends dangling. "Get these things off me!"

James untied them as we hurried up the street. We didn't run for fear of attracting attention. Fortunately there is very little foot traffic on that stretch of Lower Wacker, and the explosion had drawn most people topside.

When we got to the next ramp we waited for a break in the rushing traffic, then ran to the center of the street and went up the ramp. Once we were back on upper Wacker, I looked down the street toward the Merc. There was no sign of damage to the front of the building. People were pouring out of the front entrance and fleeing in all directions. Traffic, both cars and pedestrians, had come to a halt.

"We need to get off this street," I said, guiding James down Randolph.

I stopped at Wells and pulled out my wallet, extracting some money and one of my business cards. Then I stuck the wallet in my back pocket, took out a pen, and scribbled an address on the back of the card.

"Listen, you know Stevie's building by sight, right?"

"Yes."

I turned the back of the card to him. "This is his address. Can you read it?"

He stared at it with wide eyes. "Yes."

"Okay. Here's some money and the address. You know how to take a cab. I want you to go there. Mother's waiting for you."

He looked up at me quizzically as he took the offered items. "Your mother, she waits? How does she know I come?"

"My mother knows everything." I waved for a cab. "Do you think you can do this?"

"You not go with me?"

"Good heavens, no! I have to go back! Peter thinks I've been blown up. Can you get to Stevie's on your own?"

A curious smile appeared. "To Stevie? He will be there?"

"I'm sure he will."

"Yes, I go."

A cab came to a screeching halt at the curb. I opened the back door and James climbed in. The cab was speeding away almost before I'd let go of the door handle.

I watched the retreating cab for a moment, silently muttering, "I trust you . . . I trust you . . . I trust you . . ." Then I took off for the Merc.

Chaos was still reigning when I got there. It had been less than fifteen minutes since the explosion, and whatever government agents had been there before it happened had been joined by a handful of uniformed police officers. The higher-ups would be on their way. A couple of ambulance crews were already on the scene, rushing in and out of the restaurant—the one that had been open—carrying people out on stretchers. Screams of pain and terror were coming from inside.

Yusuf al-Ansari had been right: he didn't have enough materials to level the building, but he did have enough to blow a hole in it. There was a very large opening where the empty restaurant had been. It appeared to have blown in every direction with varying degrees of effectiveness, taking out part of the first two floors and half of the restaurant next door. Perhaps because the room had been so hollow, it seemed that much of the blast had traveled outward toward the river, taking the line of least resistance.

The uniforms were busy keeping the crowd back to the sidewalks. I scanned the debris-strewn plaza until I found him. Standing in the midst of the mess like a fixed point in the center of a whirlwind was Peter. He was stock-still and staring toward the point of the blast.

I waited until the cop closest to me was distracted by a question from a woman in the crowd, then slipped past their line. I carefully stepped through the debris—there was a lot of glass—and came up behind my beloved husband.

"Waiting for a bus?" I said in his ear.

He spun around, stared at me goggle-eyed for a split-second, then yelled, "Jesus!" and threw his arms around me, hugging me with all his might.

"Don't go all to pieces. I didn't," I said.

His embrace tightened.

"Careful. I've been abused."

He pushed me back to arm's length, keeping hold of my shoulders, and glared at me. "Don't you ever do that again!"

"Do what? Escape from an exploding building?"

He broke into a smile, then threw his arms around me again. "Christ, I love you! I thought you were gone!"

"I know. So did I!"

Over his shoulder I saw Nelson approaching.

"Alex," he said. "I'm glad to see you're alive."

Peter released me but kept an arm around my waist.

"You know, Nelson, I wish just once you could actually *sound* like you were glad I'm alive."

To my great astonishment, he smiled. "I've had superior training. It gets in the way of things like that. But I am glad. Now would you like to tell me how it's possible?"

My face went blank. "Oh. Yeah. I got free. I went out the service entrance. Down to Lower Wacker. I thought I'd be safer there. I barely made it."

"I see."

"How did you find me?" I asked quickly, wanting to change the subject. "Did you see them take me?"

"No. As a matter of fact, it was through quite another means."

"I got hold of him right after you left," Peter interjected. He was beginning to regain his composure.

"I was at your city's Department of Revenue."

"For what?" I asked.

"I was checking to see if the owner of The House of Persia had applied for a license to open another restaurant. They came up with this place."

I broke into an admiring smile. "You are one smart man."

He shrugged rather humbly. "Much as I'd like to agree, the fact is that it was the only tangible thing to do, other than just interrogate the owner again. I had my phone off while I was talking to the clerk there. Peter's call came when I was leaving. I had him meet me at the spot you were supposed to be, and when we didn't find you there I took a chance and we came down here. I called Fredrichs on the way and alerted him, and he and some of his men joined us. Peter identified al-Ansari when he came out the door. He paused and looked over at the wreckage. "We should've been able to prevent this."

"You couldn't," I said. "The bomb was on a timer. Al-Ansari was just stalling you guys until it went off. When he was shot, there was less than two minutes left. Nobody could've defused it."

"Reynolds!" A shocked voice called from inside the bombed-out side of the building. The three of us turned to see Fredrichs heading our way. "I thought you were in there! What happened?"

"Obviously, I got out."

"We understood that you were with James. Where is he?"

I looked at the gaping hole, then back at Fredrichs. "He didn't get out."

"You left him in there?"

I shrugged. "I had no choice. I got loose but he was tied up too tight. I couldn't get him free."

Fredrichs emitted a derisive "Huh!"

Peter tightened the arm around my waist, offering me moral support. I glanced at Nelson. He face was turned away from us, but I could see the corner of his mouth. It was just slightly curved upward.

FOURTEEN

Fredrichs insisted on debriefing us, but he didn't get to it until the next day because he and his men were busy rounding up everyone even remotely connected with The House of Persia. The delay was a good thing, because Mother didn't get home until very late that night and, knowing Fredrichs, her absence would've been suspect.

True to his word, James had gone straight to Stevie's apartment.

"Honestly, Alex! Every time he goes out with you, he comes back alone!" Mother said as she collapsed onto the couch. "When I saw you weren't there I thought there'd been another shootout. Imagine my surprise when he told me what actually happened!"

"He did tell you I was all right, didn't he?"

"Yes, but I fancy I would've known if you weren't, anyway. You should've seen the reunion between those two!"

"Stevie and James?"

"Yes! You would've thought they were long-lost loves!" She sniffed wearily. "Maybe they are."

"He was trying to protect us," I said. "James, I mean. He was afraid the Red Jihad would somehow track us down and kill us.

And Stevie. He didn't want that to happen. But you knew that, didn't you?"

She nodded. "I thought that might be the case. You told me after he disappeared that Stevie said he'd talked about how much we'd done for him."

"I should've seen it myself. When we were dressing him up he kept telling me how dangerous it was to help him, and what a risk we were taking. I still don't know how the Red Jihad could've found out about us if he'd just stayed put."

"Yeah, but he knew them," said Peter. "And he was terrified of them. He probably really believed they would find us somehow."

"Instead of that, he led them right to us."

Peter smiled at me indulgently. "Uh, excuse me honey, but we were the ones that went to them."

I laughed lightly. "For all the best reasons!"

"Where is he now?" Peter asked Mother.

"Stevie has agreed to take him out of town." She turned to me. "By the way, darling, you'll be glad to know that Janet Leigh still could do it today."

"You bought them a car?" I said.

"A used one. It wasn't very expensive, but it should get them where they're going."

"And where's that?"

She smiled.

"They're still going through the wreckage," said Fredrichs, slewing his narrowed eyes back and forth between us with all the subtlety of Jennifer Jones in *Duel in the Sun*. "They still haven't found any remnants of your friend James."

"Would they?" I asked innocently. "He was tied up awfully close to the bomb."

"They should find something. Are you sure he didn't get out?"

I affected an impatient huff. "I barely got out myself! He didn't come out the way I did, the lobby doors were locked with a chain, and you were watching the front door. I'd say it's pretty clear he went over the rainbow!"

"Move on," said Nelson.

The five of us—Mother, Peter, Nelson, Fredrichs, and I—were gathered around our dining table. My family members sat with hands neatly folded on the table like angelic schoolchildren. Nelson leaned rather casually against the back of his chair with pen and notebook propped on his knee. Occasionally he jotted something down, but at such irregular intervals that I could've sworn he was making a grocery list. Fredrichs sat at the head of the table, his shoulders tensed, leaning forward with an expression that was both grim and helpless, as if he knew he'd lost control but still wanted us to know he was in charge.

I gave him a fairly detailed account of the call from James and how I'd ended up with the bomb at the Merc, stressing, of course, James's innocence. But he wasn't as interested in that as he was in trying to get us to explain how we'd found the house full of explosives on Kestler. We still couldn't own up to that one for fear of prosecution, so we held to our story that we'd just happened on it.

"You expect me to believe that?" Fredrichs said when we refused to budge. "What the hell would you two be doing in that deserted area?"

"Cruising," I said. "You know how it is when you cruise, don't you, Bob?"

His face flushed. "Keep making jokes, buddy! Do you have any idea the damage you've done?"

"*We've* done?" I said angrily, rising from my chair. "This whole mess was caused by your people! The reason the Red Jihad tried to kill James was because the agent you sent to tail Yusuf al-Ansari was so goddamn inept he was spotted the very first night! If you'd been up front with James in the first place about what you wanted from him, none of this would've happened!"

"He wouldn't have told us!" Fredrichs insisted.

I sat down slowly, never taking my eyes off his. "I think he would have."

Mother and Peter looked at me. They looked proud.

"And if he would have," I continued, "maybe you could've protected him properly. For Christ's sake, Fredrichs! If he'd known what you wanted, he could've just given you his cousin's phone number! He wouldn't have had to call it and put himself in jeopardy! But you people have to do everything in your goddamn underhanded convoluted way!"

"We didn't even know he had a phone number for him!"

"Did you ever think of asking him?" said Peter.

"And we weren't just after his cousin, we wanted to know everyone he contacted! And we didn't know whether or not he was a member of the jihad himself!"

We fell into a silent stalemate that wasn't ended until Nelson said diplomatically, "Well, at least we have al-Ansari's phone records and know everyone he has been in contact with. We should be able to track down the rest of the jihad."

"That's good," said Mother.

It was not long after that that Nelson called an end to the questioning, leaving Fredrichs dissatisfied, but apparently resigned to the fact that he wasn't going to get any more from us.

As we walked the agents to the door, I said, "Hey, Fredrichs, I have a question for you."

He stopped. "What?"

"You had someone tailing us, and then you stopped. I mean, we were being followed when we didn't need you, and then when we actually needed you guys, you weren't there! What happened?"

He flashed a superior smile. "We were following you to find where you stashed James. As soon as we knew that, we didn't have any reason to keep a tail on you. I don't have unlimited manpower, you know!"

"What do you mean, as soon as you knew that?" I asked incredulously.

"We've been following your friend Stevie ever since he left that store your friend here works at."

"You *were* tapping our phone!" I was not only indignant, I was thoroughly confused: Mother had assured us that Stevie had gotten James out of town. I had a horrible feeling that the whole debriefing we'd just undergone had been a sham, much like the one they'd performed with James. "If you thought Stevie had James, why didn't you pick him up?"

"We couldn't just storm into his apartment. We were keeping him under surveillance, waiting for him to make his move. Since we knew your friend had him, we put most of our resources there, to make sure he didn't get away."

"You did?" I said, more perplexed than ever.

"And until we're absolutely positive that James died in that explosion, we're going to keep 'Stevie' under surveillance."

"You are?" I said after a beat.

"That's right!" He smiled smugly. "You thought you were pretty smart, using a code name."

"We did?" I looked at Mother and Peter, who appeared to be as lost as I was.

"But within thirty minutes of his leaving the clothing store, we had his real name."

"You did?"

"Yes," he said triumphantly. "Tony Davis!"

"Oh." I suddenly felt so giddy my legs went rubbery. "Oh, well, you really are too quick for us!"

"We're not total fools, you know," he said as he went out the door.

Nelson paused in the doorway and faced us. "Jean, Peter, Alex . . . good work."

"Nelson, would you tell me something, straight out, without any of your . . . your . . . the way you are?"

"What is it?"

"Do you really think that James is a member of the Red Jihad?"

There was a slight pause. "You mean *did* I."

My cheeks grew hot. "Yes, that's what I mean."

He looked me in the eye. "No, I didn't. In fact, if he were still alive, I would do everything in my power to help him."

"But . . . would it be wise for him to seek that help?" I asked hesitantly.

"Who can say?"

With this he left.

I closed the door after him, then leaned my back against it, put my hand to my chest, and started to laugh with relief.

"Who the bloody hell is Tony Davis?" Mother asked.

"The guy that tried to pick me up at Farrahut's!" I said breathlessly. "They must've seen him talking to me and thought he was our contact!"

Peter gathered me up in his arms. "Thank God you're irresistible."

"Oh . . . shut up!" I said as we kissed.

I wasn't surprised that Mother had been able to talk Stevie into taking James out of town, but I was surprised that he didn't come back. Peter said I shouldn't have been, because we'd experienced love at first sight ourselves. Then again, Stevie and James had a long drive, during which I'm sure they got to know each other better. The minute they reached their destination, they found an apartment and settled in together, where they've been living ever since. And we're the only ones who know where they went.

With the possible exception of Oscar Wilde.

1/02

SILVER FALLS LIBRARY
410 South Water St.
Silverton, OR 97381
(503) 873-5173